# TO THE STARS FOREVER

GLENN ERIC

**BEACHFRONT PUBLISHING**

# To The Stars Forever

# 1

Pulling them forward like wraiths. That's what Kevin was thinking. Maybe it was the hunger. Growing like a disease in his stomach. But that's what he was thinking. Death was pulling him forward like an insubstantial wraith. It was pulling all of them. And there was nothing Kevin Kent or anyone else could do about it.

It was noisy. The city always was. Cars. HVAC units. Warm wind whistling through the concrete corridors. The homeless mumbling, and there were more homeless and more mumbling every day, sprouting up like weeds between the cracks in the sidewalk, like spirits squeezed out between the chinks in the mortar.

Eyes averted, hands outstretched, the homeless mumbled for handouts. He couldn't blame them, only feel sorry for them. For all intents and purposes, he was one of them.

The American dream had become the American pipedream. Loud voices from the rushing three-piece suits who yammered to be heard over the noisy background as they screamed into their cellphones. Only the most avaricious and selfish people seemed to find success—he was living in a world that only seemed to reward the monsters. Everyone else struggled.

The streets smelled rank and moist. Car exhaust, trash, human sweat, pigeon droppings. The smell was inescapable. Pungent in the worst way.

It was hot too, though it was yet early spring. While everybody was still arguing over its causes, global warming had come spreading doom and gloom. The glaciers had melted, the oceans had spread over the land and average temperatures soared into the upper nineties and continued rising with no end in sight.

Morning rush hour on a Monday was one of the worst times ever to be on the streets of New York City. But what choice did he have? Why did they call it rush hour anyway? Was that somebody's idea of a joke? Why not call it bumper to bumper hour—call a bee a bee?

Right now, all the little worker bees were heading out from their little hives in search of greenback pollen. People might have stopped to smell the flowers, if their petals had carried the scent of money. *Breathe deep, my friends. Success is just around the corner*, Kevin chuckled to himself.

Not for B-Class Citizens, of course. Most of what Kevin had heard they used to call the middle class was now categorized legally as B-Class Citizens. They had few rights and little property. The debt-owed nations of the world, under the tight-fisted control of an economic oligarchy, had long ago pulled the plug on the US economy. A nation founded on so-called democracy had perverted itself into a country running on the fuel of consumerism. Gross, excess consumerism.

Had anyone really thought it would last?

The Americans worked for the Chinese, Indians, Malaysians, Venezuelans, you name it—everyone but themselves. The people of the US had been reduced to the New World serf class. A class of toilers of the corporate landscape and service industry.

Superpower has-beens.

Foreigners held title to the city's proud buildings. Few Americans could afford to buy a home, most rented, working for wages that were laughable already a generation ago. Kevin had even read somewhere that the White House was owned by the government of Qatar and leased back to the US government on four-year renewable terms. The president was said to wear a suit bearing a "Made In China" label right on its lapel. And that wasn't the only logo the president was required to wear. Like PGA golfers, politicians, judges and every GI in a uniform was plastered with sponsors' names and logos. The price to pay for being well-clothed.

The presidency itself had become a reality TV show with the last man or woman standing becoming the next president of the US.

The US military had been forced to lease out its nuclear class submarines and warships to the highest bidders. The EU had sold off the formerly sovereign nation of Greece to the Chinese in a desperate attempt to reduce its debt.

Welcome, progress!

No, this was no place to be. But, again, what choice did he have? A penthouse apartment overlooking Central Park? A brownstone in the Bronx? A third floor walk-up in East Harlem with cold yellow water dripping from the faucets?

None of the above.

The streets were Kevin's home. And these people were invading his home. Jostling him, taunting him with their healthy, glowing cheeks and fat bellies. He despised them all. He loathed them. They'd taken his job, his life. Given it to the Indians and the Chinese and the fat cats with their bloated bellies living in their bloated mansions.

Fat cats who treated their workers like chattel, then gave a few bucks, that they'd slowly squeezed, stolen from their underpaid employees, to some charity or another. Saying: Hey, look at me! What a nice person I am! And the papers printed their pictures, and the masses bought the lie and the papers that the stink came wrapped in.

To be honest, Kevin envied them. He envied the fat cats and he envied the idiots who bought into the dream. He'd had dreams once. They'd disappeared with his family and his humanity. Only thirty-three years old, facing a long life and a dubious future.

So he didn't mind at all when the ships came. Big black clouds rolling silently overhead. Blocking the sunlight, threatening to topple Manhattan like a collection of children's toy wooden blocks. He didn't mind it at all.

Then again, a part of him, a not insignificant part, thought he might be hallucinating again. He did a lot of that. Sometimes it was with purpose. An escape from reality, both the OR and the NR—the so-called Original Reality that had been man's lot for as long as the species had up till now existed, and the New Reality—the NR now being touted as the latest greatest thing.

The masses had 3V and the NR, both subtle drugs that not so subtly stole minds. This 3V was the newest version of NR being marketed as a major breakthrough in all the ads.

His mind, he realized, had been stolen long before and when he wasn't purposefully technologically flipping out he was flipping out naturally. Unavoidably.

It was the hunger that did it, he supposed. The constant hunger that clung to him like a cloying shadow, and his own tenuous grip on reality. Reality for Kevin was a murky construct even on the best of days. At least that's what his ex-wife, Linda, had told him. Time after time after time…

The NR, enner, as everybody called it, wasn't an option. He couldn't have afforded it if he'd wanted to. You needed a mind-material connection for that. And connections were expensive. They required brain implants, and that meant surgery, the kind that only the highly skilled Indonesians could perform.

But the enner had become the place to be, the place where virtual selves lived the lives that their fleshy counterparts could only imagine and dream of leading.

People said if you weren't living in the enner, you weren't alive at all. In fact, he'd heard people say that they felt more alive in their enner bodies than they did in their earthly ones. It was even said that it was a common phenomenon that when a person's virtual self was murdered or died in an accident in the enner, the flesh and blood person nine times out of ten became a vegetable, nothing but a catatonic mass of flesh. Devoid of any reality at all. In the tenth case, they went crazy and had to be institutionalized. Unable to cope with being among the unliving.

Kevin looked up at the strip of sky visible between skyscrapers.

The big silvery ships blotted out the sun. People were screaming now. Kevin could have screamed, too. But why bother? One more voice wasn't going to make much of a difference, was it? So why bother?

He knew what everybody was thinking. Everybody was thinking that they were being attacked, invaded by terrorists. Come to wreak their indiscriminate mayhem on an unsuspecting and, mostly, undeserving public. Then, he supposed, that's the point of terrorism, isn't it? To hurt the innocent and undeserving?

And hadn't the Founding Fathers been something like terrorists themselves as they fought the British system? It all depended on one's point of view, didn't it?

Of course, it was just this sort of thinking, this sort of blasphemy, that had often spelled trouble for Kevin Kent. Trouble was his other constant companion. Trouble, say hello to Hunger. Hunger, say hello to Trouble.

The two chatted it up, ignoring their host and his running thoughts.

Were they being invaded by terrorists?

If so, they'd come a long way and he didn't mean in distance. He meant technologically, because these ships were huge. Big as the biggest thunderclouds he'd ever laid eyes on.

A pair of US Navy jet fighters, bearing ads for a popular soft drink, flew towards the mysterious objects but never got very close. The jets hit some invisible barrier and fell from the sky like a child's windup toys that had run out of kinetic energy.

The jet fighters fell far away. Kevin didn't hear the crash but he could imagine it. He didn't see the cloud of dust and debris their impact must have raised, but he could imagine that too. The crash had to have been many blocks from where he now stood.

Someone grabbed him and started shouting at him. It was a woman, her face contorted and purple, almost inhuman in its torment. She was screaming words he couldn't understand. But her fear was palpable and washed over him in its ugliness and frailty.

Funny, because she was wearing a pair of RCGs. Roses were the latest thing for those who had the money. Rose Colored Glasses—invented by a clever Paraguayan. Put them on and they filtered out all the ugliness in the world. Filtered out all the shabbiness, all the advertising, sloganism, graffiti, your wife, whatever it was you didn't want to see. Program the glasses and they'd remove that unsightly billboard blocking out your view of Sag Harbor if you wanted. Replace your wife with a vision of some Bali goddess. Got a thing against black people or white people or bluebirds? RCGs would let you see nothing but Muldovans or sparrows, if you so chose.

But the glasses weren't helping this woman now. They hadn't been preprogrammed for what was now happening around them, for what she was now seeing. How could they? Nothing like this had ever been seen before. She was having to face her fear straight on. Look ugliness in the eye. And she was not up to the immense task. Her words were incomprehensible. Gibberish pushed out her lips by a panicked mind.

He tried to calm her down, ease her death grip on his arms, her sharp nails biting into his flesh. Spittle hit his face as her mouth contorted in a large O and she howled. He freed one arm and reached for the bridge of her nose, thinking that if only she removed her Roses, maybe that would help. Maybe they were short-circuiting, making her see monsters where there were ships, making her anguish worse.

The woman seemed to sense what he was up to. She threw him off and raced awkwardly and madly down the street. He never saw her again.

He wondered if she had been real. The pair of Roses lay on the pavement. They must have fallen off after all. For a moment, Kevin considered popping them on his nose. But what would he see if he looked in the mirror? Just some pasty, doughy, overweight man in his early thirties with a head of short brown hair that looked like it had been more attacked than trimmed, and lusterless brown eyes that had seen too much.

He crushed the glasses underfoot. The sound of snapping plastic gave him a sense of satisfaction. The glasses at least had been real. They were real still, but they were no longer Rose Colored Glasses.

Wisps of white floated everywhere, covering everything in sight. It was as if a giant spider or a huge colony of spiders had come silently in the night and laid bits of web across the world. The stuff broke easily as he passed through it, but was sticky like spider web and, where it touched his bare skin through the gaping holes in his ratty-sleeved shirt, the skin tingled and itched. He wondered what it was but didn't really have much time to think about it.

Kevin turned towards Greenwich Village. He used to live in the Village. Maybe that was why he was heading that way now. It sounded like every siren in the city was singing and his head ached all the way to his vibrating jawbone. His eyes teared up with pain.

Hologram emergency cams hovered on every street corner. The HECs had been installed citywide several years prior and hardly anyone had objected. They were there to protect the good citizenry, after all. Weren't they? Or were they really spies? Could they receive his thoughts as easily as they sent his image? Kevin had his suspicions but wasn't sure. How could he know?

What he did know was that there was a time when at least some people would rail against such things. Nowadays, nobody remembered the fear of an unseen Big Brother, the novel 1984, and what it portended. Nobody remembered George Orwell.

Nineteen-eighty-four was the year the Tigers won the World Series, trouncing the old San Diego Padres. That was in the days before the Pacific Ocean had gotten larger and California had grown smaller by an equal degree. Lost to the Great Quake that many as far away as the Rockies claimed to have felt. The Apple Macintosh had hit the streets in 1984 and been part of a revolution. And wasn't that the year someone assassinated Gandhi?

Kevin couldn't be sure of anything anymore. And there was

no way to check the veracity of anything. At least, not with any certainty. Information was pliable as clay. Information was to be accepted, had to be. What choice was there? None. But information, Kevin knew, could never be trusted.

What would George Orwell think? Kevin wondered. Or HG Wells for that matter?

There was a line that he'd read years before. Wells said: *Human history becomes more and more a race between education and catastrophe.*

Nobody remembered HG Wells either. And while nobody remembered Big Brother, Big Brother had stealthily and relentlessly engulfed them all. How can you see what's all around you? And we didn't need any Thought Police because we all knew what we were all thinking. And we were all thinking Nothing.

Besides, nobody really read books anymore. Maybe the words and warnings of writers like George Orwell and HG Wells were coming to fruition. Yes, this could be the day...

Maybe there really were Martians after all—like that old film director Orson Wells had once tricked the public into believing—and just maybe they really were invading today.

Kevin wished he had a copy of one particular HG Wells book now. It was called *Mind At The End Of Its Tether*. He felt like that himself, his mind at the end of its tether, floating like a small gray balloon at the end of a long white cotton string running from his head to the clouds.

If he had a copy in his hands now, he'd carry it to the park and read it slowly, savoring every word while the world ran madly by.

But there wasn't much chance of that, was there?

He scratched his head, wondering when he'd last seen a book. Hadn't there been a yellowed copy of a King James Bible in that antique shop on Washington?

The HEC was rotating slowly, defying gravity. Ridiculously calm looking newsmen and women spoke slowly and evenly, trying to make sense out of something they didn't understand.

A man caught Kevin's shoulder. He spoke brusquely in a thick accent. Spanish maybe. Kevin knew a Spanish consortium had foreclosed on the Statue of Liberty six months ago. It was being disassembled and shipped to its new location on the Rock of Gibraltar where it would stand as a potent symbol of Iberian resurgence and American decline.

"What is going?" shouted the man. He wore a brown trench coat and an expensive pair of shoes with old-fashioned laces. Kevin noticed such things. "Please, señor. What is going?" He jabbed at the HEC on the screen.

Kevin smiled wanly, showing teeth that were regular but in need of a good brushing, as he watched the woman's painted red lips move across the screen. She spoke mechanically like a SCUID. One of those Scientifically Created Uber Individuals that everybody was talking about. They'd been developed by BioBerm, the Swiss-Austrian biotech giant.

Supposedly, they were biologically superior to humans, yet intellectually fragile and pregnant with subtle frailties and mental quirks which were difficult to diagnose and unpredictable in their appearance.

Maybe she was one, though he didn't know they were being used as on-air personalities. Of course, this woman had no personality whatsoever. No REAL personality, anyway. Only a painstakingly manufactured one.

But that was the norm, even for non-SCUIDs; especially for non-SCUIDs.

Kevin could barely hear her over the relentlessly screaming sirens. He ran a hand through short-cropped, bristly brown hair. More human stupidity. He turned to the man beside him. "It's simple," Kevin said, flatly. "They're coming for us."

"Please?" The poor fellow looked utterly confused, drowned in confusion, if that was possible.

Kevin had no life preserver to toss him. He pointed to the sky. "They're coming for us."

The man's eyes followed Kevin's finger out into space but Kevin could tell that this man could not see what he could see.

They were coming for them. He had not been certain of

anything for a number of years now. But, of this, Kevin was absolutely certain. He couldn't explain how he knew this with such immovable certainty any more than he could explain all those other vague and impossible things going on inside his head. But of this he was certain.

More spidery web fell from the sky, burning his cheeks like bitter tears. He didn't bother to brush it aside. He was certain there would just be more.

The maybe Spaniard hurried off just as quickly as his expensive laced shoes with those pricey yet terribly inadequate rubber soles could carry him. Kevin passed straight through the talking hologram. A minor but satisfactory act of defiance, he knew, but he enjoyed the act nonetheless.

# 2

He stepped into a store on Bleecker. The boxish place was small, low-ceilinged and crammed with cases of cut-rate beer and cigarettes. Two rows of unsteady-looking shelves cut the place in fourths, and held all the useless little sundries that make up peoples' lives. A couple more grams of gravity and Kevin calculated the whole place would fall in on itself.

The smell of decay rose above all else.

A clerk with greasy black hair, hanging down from his forehead all the way to a pair of pudgy black eyebrows, put down his phone as he came in. "Do you have any chocolate bars?" Kevin asked.

The clerk laid his fleshy hands on the chipped and buckling counter and eyed him with open suspicion. His paunch spilled over the edge. "You have any money?"

Kevin frowned. Did he have any money? It had been so long. He had no idea and dug around in his pockets. Hoping for a miracle.

He found one. Or rather two. Two scruffy tea-colored quarters. Now he remembered. He'd found them near the hydrobus stop on Malcolm X the day before last. He held the two quarters aloft between his thumb and forefinger, gazing hungrily at the candy display. "I'd like a chocolate bar." It cost a dollar, but maybe..."Please?"

The clerk squinted. "You're not wearing an ID. How come, buddy?"

Kevin's hands went involuntarily to his chest. Everyone was supposed to wear their laminated US National MagnetIdent on a lanyard around the neck. "I lost it," he stuttered.

The clerk's own MagnetIdent dangled over his weighty chest like a rebuke. Gig Shephard, age 37.

Kevin's hands fiddled with a non-existent ID card. Truth was, he hadn't lost it. He had sold it on the black market for fifteen yuan. Kevin didn't know why the buyer had wanted it, or what it was being used for now, and he didn't care. Only the money had mattered at the time. He hadn't eaten in days. Parting with the MagnetIdent was easy. He'd have sold his right hand for fifteen yuan that day.

The clerk looked at him some more, apparently chewing Kevin's words over, then opened his palm with a sigh and Kevin dropped the two quarters into it. His hand reached for the bar.

The clerk shook his head. "Not that one," he said. "Take the other. One shelf over and down near the bottom."

Kevin bent and scanned the metal shelving. A row of cheap American knock-off confections. No matter. He took a chocolate bar in a dull, waxy blue-and-white plastic wrapper and held it up for the clerk to see. The clerk nodded his approval and Kevin started peeling back the wrapper.

"Not in here," complained the clerk. "Take it outside, buddy."

Kevin wondered why it was that every time someone does not like you they call you buddy. Why not just call you a jerk and be done with it? "Take it outside, jerk." Simple, to the point. Honest.

Kevin looked out the door. People rushed by. The panic hadn't subsided. "Do you know what's happening out there?" he said to the clerk.

"Don't tell me—the sky is falling," cracked the clerk, obviously bored and out of patience with him and his presence reeking up his crummy little shop.

"That's right," said Kevin. "It very nearly is."

"Beat it, buddy." The clerk made a skit of looking at his cheap watch. Probably made in America. "I've got a business to run."

Kevin left.

Around the corner in the alley, he leaned against the bricks, studied the partially unwrapped bar as if the thing were his prey.

He tore back the paper and then bit the bar neatly in two.

He began to salivate, swirling his chocolate prize around and around in his mouth. Making certain each and every taste bud got its share, its fill of wonder.

Kevin ate the remainder of the bar more slowly, deliberately. His tongue moved like a slippery fish swimming round his mouth, scavenging chocolate the way a discfish—one of those cleaner fishes—swims unafraid into the gaping mouths of sharks and cleans the debris from their naturally deadly teeth.

Maybe that was how the tongue had gotten its start—as a slippery slug in Man's throat that had evolved into a symbiotic relationship that had eventually married the two together: Man and Slug.

Kevin didn't understand what impulse had driven him to spend his only coins on that bar of chocolate but was glad he had. He held no regrets. Maybe somewhere deep down in his core he knew he wasn't going to need those two old coins—he wasn't going to need any money any longer.

A mound of litter had piled up around the outside of the trash bin. Still, he carefully dropped the wrapper into the steel bin and shambled over to the East Village, passing through Little Bombay—pinching his nose because he didn't like the smell of Indian food—and gazed thoughtfully at an ordinary looking apartment building, one of thousands in the city, he supposed. But this one was special to him.

He mentally counted four floors up and three windows over from the lefthand corner. His old apartment. Their last apartment as a family. Sarah and Quinn, his ex-wife and daughter, lived alone there now. Only the two of them. No more Kevin.

At least, he thought it was only the two of them. Maybe Sarah had found someone new. Someone more whole.

He spotted Sarah gazing out the window, worriedly wringing her hands. A warm breeze blew her long blonde hair, momentarily obscuring her face.

So she hadn't gone to work today. She held a job twenty hours a week at the Prince So Hotel, working in the basement laundry. It wasn't much but it was all the work she could get in these hard times. And she felt lucky to have it. What else was she supposed to do with a degree in Comparative Lit?

Kevin figured she'd probably stayed home because she was scared. Not for herself. For Quinn's sake. She would never have risked losing her job otherwise. Jobs were too hard to come by. Her fear was so palpable he could feel it even at this great distance.

It didn't take much to make people afraid these days. There was so much to be afraid of in life and so little to take comfort in, to gather courage from.

Kevin waved up to Sarah.

As he did, a dark cloud passed overhead. Only it wasn't a cloud. It was a shape. A long, tall, vaporous looking thing floating soundlessly in the sky. The thing crawled silently, slowly above the helpless city and the morning turned to twilight. The air went chill.

Sarah pushed open the window and leaned out. "What are you doing, Kevin? Get away. They'll see us!" Fear shone in her eyes.

Kevin looked from his wife, his ex-wife, to the dark shape above. It seemed to be heading towards the harbor. He didn't really think there was any hiding from the thing, whatever it was, and said so.

"The radio said to stay indoors!" Sarah shouted.

"So do the HECs." But he didn't have an indoors to stay in, so what was the point? Would she invite him up? "Is Quinn with you?"

"Yes. Now go away. I'm closing the window. And the curtains."

"Can I see her? For a minute?" It had been so long since he'd seen his daughter. A marvelously bright and vivacious seven year old who always beamed when Kevin came around, which wasn't often. For more reasons than he knew or could ever explain, even to himself.

Sarah froze in the window, her hands on the window frame. She sighed. "Fine. For a minute."

Kevin quickly climbed the narrow cement steps, waited at the gate for Sarah to buzz him up and then clumsily mounted the stairs. He had managed to make it to the third floor landing, huffing like an old steam engine, when the rumbling began. The sound was unlike anything he'd ever heard. And it frightened him.

He raced up the last flight of stairs as the noise reached its crescendo. He pounded on the flimsy door and didn't let up until Sarah answered. "What the hell was that?"

Sarah looked bewildered, shocked. "The streets are full of water...maybe ten feet deep." She wrung her hands. "Like a roiling river of water...everywhere." Her voice was low and tremulous. She pulled Kevin to the window and threw it open. "Look."

Kevin stuck his head outside. Jesus. She wasn't exaggerating. The street, every street as far as he could see, had become a brown, debris-filled river. And not merely debris. He could see people, some thrashing still full of life, others looking lifeless, all being swept away in the rapids, bouncing off buildings like hapless billiard balls.

The sight rattled his brain. The sound rattled his ears.

"What is it, Kevin?"

Her voice carried an accusation. Was she blaming him for the mayhem below? Could he be responsible? Could his sick mind have created all this?

He couldn't stop looking. "I don't know. A rogue tidal wave maybe?" But he sensed it wasn't.

He stuck his head back inside the apartment. It was eerily quiet. The electricity had gone out. The whole city had fallen powerless, both literally and figuratively. Quinn, his young daughter, was seated in her favorite stuffed blue chair in the corner. She hadn't said a word since he'd arrived. That wasn't like her. Whatever was going on was spooking her. She ran her index finger over and over through a curl of brown hair.

He could see she'd been crying. "Whatever caused it, it's over now," he said for the benefit of both mother and daughter. "The water is receding." That much was true. The flood was leaving as quickly as it had come.

Quinn's lower lip quivered. He could see it was all too much for her.

Sarah returned to the window and peeked out. After a moment, she said that, yes, she could see that, too.

Kevin gently stroked Quinn's hair. She was nearly eight now. He hadn't seen her since her last birthday. She looked so changed. Almost a year ago. He fought back a sadness that had welled up within him.

With his coaxing, Quinn spoke now, her voice a mucousy whisper. She asked him where he'd been and he told her. "Around. I've been around."

When she asked him what was happening, he told her not to worry. "Nothing to worry about." He knew that was a lie. She had every reason to worry. They all did.

He crossed back to the open window and rubbed against his ex's shoulder. The water was receding faster and faster. Incongruously, the sky was filled with acrid smoke and fire. Funny, despite the flood, half of the City of New York seemed to be ablaze. "I'll go see what I can find out."

"Are you sure that's safe?" Sarah asked, now cowering beside their daughter.

He shrugged. "No." He paused at the door. "Better lock this behind me." He jiggled the door knob. Kevin stood in the hall waiting for the rattle of the locks clicking into place then headed down the dark stairwell.

The street smelled funny. Like the ocean. Not the normal smell of humanity and garbage. That was almost pleasant, homey. He'd always loved the salty scent of the sea.

Plenty of people gazed out their windows, their expressions troubled, yelling at each other. Wondering what was going on. Wondering what was going to happen next.

Of course, no one knew.

He descended the building's worn steps until his feet were an inch deep in water. Though the water was definitely going down —he'd been right about that— it was still a good five or six feet deep, by his estimate. And full of the dead: people, pets, cars, bicycles...bits of the city being inexorably swept out and away.

A muffled scream startled him. It sounded close. Kevin's eyes darted left, then right. A woman was thrashing in the brown water, clinging to a piece of a plastic sign about forty feet up the street, coming fast.

Her head went under. She came up again coughing. Their eyes met and her frightened eyes cried out to him. She waved. She shouted. He couldn't make out the words. She was choking on foul water. But he understood what she wanted.

She wanted him to help her.

He took a cautious step into the water. It was frigid and fast.

"No, Kevin!" shouted Sarah from the window above. "Are you crazy?"

Kevin didn't even look back. He had to smile. Sarah always asked him that. If he was crazy. Maybe she'd said it so often that she had created a reality in which that had become so.

No, he supposed it wasn't fair to blame Sarah for his flaws.

The helpless woman came hurtling his way. As she came perpendicular to him, he stretched out his arms and hit the icy water with a graceless belly flop. His stomach stung like he'd taken ten thousand volts from a giant blue jellyfish but he had no time to worry about the pain.

Thrashing wildly, he reached for the woman. Their hands met but couldn't hold. His chest hit something hard under the surface of the murky water. He thought it might have been a car. In fact, he thought it must have been a Ford Freedom—one of those cheap hydrogen jobs. But that was nonsense. Even he knew that. Nobody could judge the make and model of an auto from being thunked in the head with it. Or could they?

Maybe if its hood ornament left a dent in his forehead. It quite possibly might have, though this was no time to check.

The water was rising above him. He was going under.

Something strong grabbed his ankle and jerked. He managed to push his head above the waterline and gulped for air. The woman was shouting but his ears were full of cold brackish water and all he heard was a meaningless roar.

She pulled him up and he was able to get a grip on the debris she was clinging desperately to. It was a busted bus stop bench, hollow, recycled plastic. But hard enough. He ran his tongue around the edges of his mouth. His lower lip was cut and bleeding.

She spluttered something that sounded alien to him. He shook his head and she gave up. They didn't speak after that. They just hung on.

They were moving swiftly towards the sea.

Perhaps, thought Kevin, this wasn't a good idea. He never had learned to swim.

# 3

The last thing Kevin remembered seeing before he woke was a wall of glass coming fast. A steel and glass skyscraper —the Yamaguchi Towers—and his reflection and the equally frightened looking image of the strange woman beside him staring back.

The woman clawed at his back, screaming. But there was nothing to be done. He turned his head at the last second, taking the brunt of the blow on his shoulder.

There was a moment of pain and light. Then peace.

When he regained consciousness, he was lying in a puddle of a bombed out lobby. Shattered glass and busted furniture. He struggled to his knees, wincing in pain with every move. The nauseating smell of New York's polluted waters soaked through the walls, the furniture, the carpets, his skin.

The woman lay a few yards away. She didn't need his help now. Her MagnetIdent twisted itself savagely around her neck. Ilene Viets—a name she wasn't going to be needing any longer. Her skull was surrounded by a halo of blood. She must have hit the glass head on.

Kevin picked himself up, swaying dizzily. Maybe she'd been the luckier of the two of them.

He fumbled out-of-doors to get his bearings.

A good-sized crowd marched up the street. Some were obviously businessmen and women, in proper business attire; others laborers, professionals like police and fire personnel. Still others looked like they'd just awakened and wandered around in their slippers, pajamas and robes.

There were men, women and children. There were the young,

the old, the blind and the otherwise handicapped—soaked through and disheveled. They didn't look any better to Kevin than he himself did—a sodden wreck of a man. Lacerated and bruised.

They all had one thing in common. They appeared to be shell-shocked. Each and every one of them. Like somebody had pulled the Reality Rug out from under them.

Whoosh!

And they were all, to a man, woman and child, heading in one direction—to the harbor.

What was going on? Was it all related to the dark shapes in the sky? The ships? It had to be. Too much of a coincidence otherwise. Kevin didn't like coincidences. The ships, the flood of near biblical proportions, the commotion and then the dead silence after the blackout. The people surrounding him on the street, marching like zombies to their collective doom.

Kevin stepped in front of a man in a three-piece brown corduroy suit and fedora. "Where are you going?"

"It's time." The man said, his voice flat and emotionless. His eyes were glazed over, reminding Kevin of a couple shiny glazed donuts, dead to the world as a fried donut. Kevin's stomach grumbled hungrily with the thought.

"It's time to go." The man in the brown suit sidestepped around Kevin.

Kevin let him go. He wanted to learn more, but knew this man wasn't going to be the one to tell him. Probably couldn't. He didn't seem all there. Didn't appear right in the head. Kevin probably couldn't have stopped him if he tried. So why try?

Besides, Kevin had something more pressing to attend to. He watched the voiceless marchers splashing their way down the street toward the sea for a moment—how strange to see such a large group of people in the street, yet not a peep out of them, no crying, no laughing, no shooting the breeze conversations and, more significantly, no theorizing about what madness had so swiftly taken over, come into their lives like a black plague.

He hurried back toward his old apartment, Sarah and Quinn's

apartment.

It wasn't easy. He fought against the stream of humanity intent on going in the opposite direction. Something inside him made him want to go along. Surrender. Become one of them.

He fought this, too.

The entrance to the apartment building gaped open, held in place by a single chipped gray cinderblock. An eerie quite settled over the building. Like in the movies. Before the Bad Guy turns the corner with a bloody hatchet in his grip. Before the Monster shows up.

He pushed up the stairs, on the brink of exhaustion, amazed that his sadly maintained body—wracked with perpetual hunger and pain—hadn't given up the ghost. The door to the apartment stood wide open as well.

"Sarah?" He looked toward the dim bedroom. "Quinn, are you in here?"

A shadow darkened the apartment. Kevin ran to the window. Another one of those ships came sailing lugubriously overhead. Like the benumbed people on the streets, it also appeared to be heading toward the harbor.

Kevin made up his mind.

That was where he was going, too.

# 4

Kevin fought his way to Battery Park, Manhattan's aptly named Green Toe. Of course, these days it was more a gangrene than the natural green that its founders had intended when they'd filled in the land surrounding Castle Clinton.

The trees had long ago died and the grass turned to a septic brown. The whole lot of it had been scooped up and replaced with fade-resistant plastic plants and grasses exuding time-released scents of the man-engineered variety. Progress, thy name is plastic.

Kevin had to admit the engineering and manufacturing had been so exquisite. The Malaysians had become masters of the so-called "New Nature," with such attention to the smallest detail that every stamen bristled with false life. Each rose petal smelled like the finest rose. He knew, because he'd smelled an actual rose in a living museum once. Each and every blade of grass felt soft to the touch and gave off a freshly mown perfume.

Even the birds and the bees had been tricked at first, but eventually, in obvious frustration at the havoc being wreaked on their habits and instincts, they had long abandoned the area; except for the New York pigeons. They actually seemed to be thriving here. NYC pigeons are tough as the toughest New Yorkers.

The castle had once been an island. Later, it had been renamed Castle Garden, the world's first immigration depot. In the mid-1800s, millions had come through here seeking a new world, a better future.

Ironically, thought Kevin, it looked to be serving that function once more. Only this time, people were heading in a different direction.

But were these people all seeking a new world or were they being compelled on the journey? Would it be a better future or a bigger nightmare?

If only he could find Sarah and Quinn, he'd feel better. There had to be millions of people all crushing together as one into the twenty-one acre park. Where had they disappeared to? How was he going to find them?

Over the heads of the pushing masses, two impossibly large spaceships, the same that he'd seen overhead, floated offshore. Between the two, he could make out the Statue of Liberty, headless and torchless now, in a state of disassembly. The Spaniards were fast workers.

So were the invaders, decided Kevin. He called them invaders because that's what they were. What else could they be?

Gods come down from the lofty heavens? Come to take all of Humanity away?

It wasn't until much later that he realized just how closely his thoughts had been to the truth...

Kevin cupped his hands together and shouted. "Sarah! Quinn!" Not a single head turned his way. "Hey, anybody, can you hear me?!" No one paid him any attention.

He clambered up the Immigrants statue, standing on the backs of the bent and struggling new Americans, scanning the helplessly moving crowd.

The entire city was being drained of its population just as only a little while ago the waters had rushed in, then drained away. The dead littered the streets in numbers too great to count.

Had it been the massive ships that had caused this unheard of catastrophe, displacing untold billions of gallons of water? What else could have caused all this mayhem?

Kevin had long endured all the monsters in his head. He wondered now what sort of monsters had landed amongst them all.

Had the monsters left his head and come to life?

Kevin shivered, damp and cold despite the glaring heat.

The mouths of the vessels the monsters from the sky had arrived in gaped open, facing the shoreline. Long ramps extended outward. Vague alien shapes flanked the entryways. One minute they appeared solid, the next nearly transparent.

Lines of victims dozens wide inched their way forward, swallowed up by the behemoths whose appetites seemed endless. Thousands upon thousands had in all likelihood trod to their doom—for doom Kevin had no doubt it was—and there was no end in sight.

If he ever wanted to see Sarah and Quinn again, especially Quinn, he had no choice.

He had to join them.

Kevin merged into the long line in the middle. Nobody appeared to mind his cutting in. In fact, they didn't seem to notice him at all. Not for the first time, he couldn't help noting how spookily silent they remained.

Kevin waited impatiently as the hours ticked by and he inched towards the entrance. He'd have tried to bully his way through if he'd thought it would have done any good. But there were just too many drone-like bodies in front of him. They clogged the opening like a million army ants all heading home at once after a long day's march.

Finally, he stood within spitting distance of the entrance. A row of not-of-this-world creatures stood along the edge of the steep black ramp, chittering in some alien tongue he couldn't begin to fathom. All whistles and static. The humans remained oddly mute. The huge ship itself was soundless as a crypt, he thought, aptly.

Stepping onto the ramp, an alien mechanical voice rattled in his ear. "Welcome, Beings Led Into Service. Welcome. Welcome, Beings Led Into Service. Welcome." The line played over and over in his ear.

He supposed everyone boarding was hearing the same strange message. Beings Led Into Service? BLIS? What on earth was that supposed to mean?

He chuckled miserably. War is bliss! How very, very sick. Yet wasn't that practically what every politician on the planet would have every young person believe if they could? War is bliss! Come join us! Fun! Adventure! Oh, and a little killing or be killed on the side! But hey, can't make an omelet without cracking a few eggs, right? Equally, can't win a war without cracking open a few skulls.

Yes, war is bliss!

Kevin sucked in a breath. Eyes forward, he marched ahead, a crush of New Yorkers surrounding him, doing the same. Approaching the maw of the ship, he could see nothing within. A shimmering plasma-like cerulean blue wall blocked all vision. Following the cue of the others who'd gone ahead, he walked unwaveringly through this blue wall.

A wave of icy cold, as cold as he imaged deepest space must be, came crushing down upon him. He staggered. His breath practically froze in his throat.

Kevin looked quickly around in every direction. He was in a huge black cavern, a cavern that seemed improbably bigger on the inside that it had from the outside—and it had seemed gigantic, impossibly large, from the outside.

Something handlike, but not unfriendly, grabbed his shoulder and stopped him. Two eyes, reasonably symmetrical, with blood-red irises and the left planted higher on its elongated face than the right, studied him. The creature stood barely taller than Kevin, who just brushed past the six-foot mark himself, and had a seemingly mournful bearing.

"You are incorrect."

Kevin stuttered. "What?"

The creature leaned forward. He was deathly white, with skin like white asparagus that never sees the sun. "You are wrong." A shallow, toothless mouth with a reedy bassoon of a voice scolded him.

The creature gave Kevin a gentle push back the way he'd come, thrusting him out the blue curtain and into the smoky sunlight. "No," protested Kevin. "Wait!"

The creature disappeared. Kevin ran after him and tapped

on his bulbous back. The creature turned silently, its snaky lips turning up at the corners.

For a moment, Kevin wondered if the thing was going to make a meal of him. He took a strategic step backward.

"Please," said Kevin, "my wife and daughter are in there." He frowned, the wrinkles in his forehead forming a V. "I think. I've got to stay," he pleaded.

The pale creature leaned forward, placing his forehead against Kevin's. The creature's skin felt like soft, warm clay. Kevin had the uncomfortable feeling that the thing was trying to make a casting of his skull, but he couldn't make himself pull away.

They stayed joined that way for several moments while an unsettling tingle played across Kevin's forehead, then the alien leaned back and sighed. "Mind not right. Defective."

Kevin felt his bile rising. It was one thing to know he was ill, not right, but it was a damned other thing altogether to be told so by some anemic wad of snot from another planet.

"Listen, you snot-faced Martian stooge. You're taking everybody else in the city and you'll damn well take me, too!" Kevin planted his feet defiantly.

Several hands with too many fingers to be human grabbed him from behind. His feet left the ground. Moments later, he was dropped ignominiously into the harbor, floundering for his life in the frigid water.

Cursing everyone and everything earthly and alien alike, he dog-paddled back to shore. The line of people getting into the ships hadn't eased up a bit. This time, he wasn't waiting. He fought his way back to the front of the line. Once again, nobody seemed to notice—or, if they did, they didn't mind. Nobody spoke up.

He crossed the blue threshold with a group of lemming-like businessmen and women while trying to clear his mind of all thoughts. He grabbed the arm of one of the men on his left and that of another on his right and held onto them tightly, keeping as close to them as possible. Blending in, or so he hoped.

As a group, they were marched silently into a holding room where several thousand other men, women and children were standing shoulder to shoulder or sitting where they could find the space. Nobody said a word.

"This is too damn spooky," muttered Kevin.

A tall sentinel in some sort of suit fluid as liquid mercury swiveled its head in Kevin's direction. He quickly shut his mouth and dropped his head, fearful of making eye contact. Fearful of getting tossed out again into the harbor.

# 5

The shiny sentinel moved on and Kevin heaved a sigh of relief. But his relief was short-lived. A warm hand grabbed his arm, locking around his spongy bicep.

"What's going on?" a wild-eyed man with tousled, shoulder length brown hair demanded. He was all bug-eyed, with a scrawny body, and seemed somewhat crooked, as if he'd been pushed clumsily through an old-fashioned wringer.

Kevin pulled his arm free. The man scared him. On the other hand, the man also provided a bit of solace. This was the first person to speak with him since this whole crazy ET shipboard adventure started.

"Come on, mister." He tugged on Kevin's arm again. Kevin felt the man's fingernails digging into his skin. "Tell me what's going on!"

"I don't know what's going on," insisted Kevin. From the corner of his eye, he saw the sentinel swiveling his head back in their direction. Kevin pulled the stranger to the floor and whispered in his ear. "But if I were you, I'd keep my voice down."

The man took a gander at the nasty looking guard or whatever the creature was and nodded. "What are those things?" he asked tremulously.

"Look," said Kevin, struggling to summon up more patience than he was feeling, "I don't know any more about all this than you do. But what I do know is that we're in trouble. The whole city is in trouble, maybe the whole world, for all you or I know."

The man's Adam's apple bobbed up and down and he nodded some more. "You can say that again." He held out his hand. Pale with long fingers. "Name's Lance."

"Kevin." He made a note of the man's MagnetIdent. Lance Wong, 42 y.o., resident of Brooklyn. He looked American but could have been a half-breed. That would explain the name.

"So, what do you suppose—"

The cavernous room suddenly went dark as pitch. Yellow alien eyes, or sensors or cameras or whatever the hell they were, provided the only light and glared at them coldly in the gloaming. The floor shook, like a shuddering leviathan rolling over in the middle of a bad dream. Kevin sprawled out on the ground spreadeagled. Lance curled up in a ball.

The horrible vibration lasted only a moment or two, then came to an abrupt stop.

"Crimminy, Christ, cricket shit," said Lance, pulling himself together. "What was that?"

Kevin whispered. "I'd say we're leaving."

"Man, it's about time. Personally, I can't wait to bug out of this crypt."

Kevin shook his head, a bitter smile on his face. "I don't mean you and I will be leaving this vessel. I mean that all of us are leaving."

Lance struggled to understand. "Sounds good to me. Anything that gets me out of here is okay in my book."

Kevin ignored the stranger's remark. "Yes, this ship is leaving. Leaving Earth," he said pointedly.

Leaving—" Lance gaped and his red-laced eyes bulged. "You're crazy, man!" He laughed but it sounded forced. "Leaving Earth! Leaving for where? A ride on the Cosmic Ferris Wheel?"

It was Kevin's turn to shrug. "Maybe. Who knows? Maybe we're heading for Mars. Maybe we're diving straight into the Sun." Maybe a solar barbecue was on the ETs' menu and they were to be the main course.

Lance's eyes grew wide, picturing the end of existence as a fiery hot plunge into the liquid heat of the Sun.

Kevin bobbed his chin towards the sharp line of aliens or robots or whatever they were that had formed high above on a narrow ledge. "We'd have to ask them." He thought a moment, rubbed his temples. "Maybe we're leaving the solar system altogether. The galaxy even."

"You're freaking me out, man."

"Sorry. I'm crazy, you know," he said by way of apology.

Lance looked at him oddly. "I'll say."

The walls began to glow a sickly green, casting an equally sickly aspect onto their flesh. In every direction, Kevin could see people, people just like him, from all walks of life. They began to shuffle about, looking around at their alien surroundings with puzzled and terrified expressions pinned to their faces.

Like they were waking up from a dream...only to find themselves in the middle of a nightmare. Whatever spell they had been under had now been broken and they were awakening to a nightmare far more frightening than any they had faced in their worst dreams.

Imprisoned in the blistering, bulging bowels of some alien spaceship, awash in a sea of people. Millions of them, Kevin guessed. And he was awed to even imagine a ship that could hold so many, many people—though they were squeezed together like sheep waiting the hand of their slaughterer. Couldn't they turn up the AC? Didn't this absurd contraption have central air?

His ears were overwhelmed by the cries and shouting from the frightened and confused mass packed around him. Others stared stonily, appearing oblivious to their surroundings, some seemed nearly catatonic. Groups began to form, both large and small. The human need to cling to one another in times of danger was showing itself.

A rising, high-pitched communal scream arose from the left and Kevin and Lance turned as one.

"Now what?" Lance asked, worriedly biting his lower lip. The mass of people began scattering, clearing a path through their center.

Kevin shrugged. "We'll know soon enough, I expect."

"Could be trouble," Lance said, a nervous edge to his voice. "I say we stand our ground."

"Monsters! Monsters!" shouted many voices in unison like

some dissilient beast with a life all its own. As the voices grew nearer, others took up the cry. Everyone was running in all directions, as if a live hand grenade had been dropped in their midst.

Lance took off with them. Kevin held his ground. Why bother running? There was no place to run away to. Why didn't everybody understand that? Was it also human nature to run even if there was no place to go?

Two creatures appeared from the opening left by the fleeing humans. They seemed to be heading straight for him. One was the creature who'd thrown him overboard earlier. Beside him scurried a rail-thin creature a head shorter than the first who seemed to be nothing more than a somewhat human looking skeleton with tissue thin, translucent skin. Its insides were bubble-gum pink.

The bigger one with the uneven red eyes stopped inches from Kevin, sniffed a moment then shook its head. The smaller one was scratching his own head as if perplexed by the Earthling in front of him.

Unless those bulbs were their butts, thought Kevin. He knew so little of alien biology. But then, these were the first aliens he or anyone else had ever seen. Unless the gov was hiding something —and they always were. That's what governments do, after all.

The bigger one reached out a glove-like hand whose mitt suddenly morphed into three thick fingers.

Kevin remained still. Was the thing trying to shake hands with him? Or was he about to be thrown overboard a second time? He shivered. The icy Atlantic was one thing. He could survive that. The icy emptiness of space was another. He wouldn't last a millisec.

A hoarse sound sort of crawled from the thing's mouth. At least Kevin hoped it was its mouth. Because if that lump was the thing's butt, the sound was far more vulgar than it already sounded.

Still, it did stink a bit...

Kevin shook his head. Partly from the smell, partly to show

that he didn't understand. The skeleton critter twittered away at the big one a minute and the big one tried again.

"Sigma Six I am."

The little one chittered.

"I am Sigma Six." He/she/it—Kevin settled for he— tilted toward his little companion. "This is my Other." He dangled three fingers at Kevin.

Kevin hesitantly extended his hand. It was like shaking hands with cold goo. Another hand clamped down on his right shoulder and he jumped. "What the—"

"Holy mother of all freak shows!" said Lance. "What ARE these things?"

"It's a Sigma Six, whatever that is. An improvement on the Sigma Five model, I suppose."

"Mmmm," said Lance, stroking his chin. "Could be, could be."

Kevin pointed at the little one. "And *that* is his Other."

"His Other, eh?" Lance scratched the top of his head. "What the hell does that mean? His other what?"

Kevin rolled his eyes. "Why don't you ask him, Lance. Nice job standing your ground, by the way."

Lance shrugged. "You know what they say. Live to fight another day."

Kevin doubted Lance had ever fought anything in his life, excepting maybe his own demons. Kevin suspected that Lance had as many demons as he did himself.

"Coming," said Sigma Six. He turned and he and his companion turned back the way they'd come.

Kevin followed. Why not?

He turned and saw that Lance stood locked in place. He yanked Lance's arm and forced him along. "Come on," he said over Lance's protests. "The walk will do you good."

Lance frowned. "Yeah? Let's hope these two goobers aren't working up an appetite for breakfast with us as the main course."

"If they are," said Kevin, with no aim toward calming the man, "there's nothing you or I or anyone else on this ship can do about it."

Lance's frown cut deeper. But he followed Kevin, keeping one step behind, just in case either of those aliens got a sudden craving for human flesh, Kevin suspected.

Few of their shipmates braved making eye contact with them as they passed. Kevin couldn't blame them. Again, it was only human nature in the face of such unknowable and unpredictable danger to make one's self invisible, as best one could.

What on earth had possessed them all to so docilely and without coercion enter the alien ship in the first place? Mindboggling to imagine how millions of disparate people had as one marched like lemmings into the belly of this beast and off the proverbial cliff into outer space.

*Welcome, beings led into service…*

Welcome, bliss!

It wasn't as if they'd been threatened in any way. Aliens hadn't hit the city streets waving around explosive and deadly laser guns, pulsar pistols, radiation rockets or any other sci-fi gizmos and weaponry that Kevin had noticed—a real blow to Hollywood film makers' conventions. Even the sentinels, if that's what they were, appeared weaponless.

Questions without answers. Life was full of them…

The two men followed the two aliens down a maze of damp and narrow corridors that glowed lime green on and off as they passed. Soon they came to a small oblong room. Not unlike being in a submarine, Kevin thought.

Kevin remembered touring the one in the Museum of Science and Industry in Chicago years before. A German U-505 captured by the Americans off the coast of Africa. Quinn had only been a couple years old then and immensely unimpressed.

Was she somewhere in this ship now with Sarah? Another question without an answer.

"You will join," said Sigma Six, pointing to the spot where a dozen other humans sat haphazardly around the floor. None looked happy. All looked frightened to the edge of death.

"Join what?" demanded Lance.

"I think he wants us to sit," replied Kevin.

"Oh, yeah? Why didn't he say so?" Lance fell to the ground and crossed his legs.

Kevin pointedly avoided sitting next to him and instead chose a place between an elderly male on his left and a woman in her twenties on his right.

"Welcome to Hell," quipped the woman. She was smiling but Kevin figured it was all false bravado. She had nothing to smile about. None of them did. Her crumpled MagnetIdent identified her as Nicolette Nelson, a mere 27 years young. Her cocoa brown hair was several inches longer now than in her ID photo.

"A hell Dante himself could never have dreamt of," added the man on Kevin's left. Henry Hemming according to his MagnetIdent, age 71. He looked just like his picture, with thick brown hair streaked with gray at the temples and deep creases in his forehead and cheeks.

"Well, if it isn't Mister Chocolate Bar!"

Kevin looked across the dimly lit chamber and saw the clerk from the store where he'd purchased his candy bar. "You came."

The heavy-set man shrugged unhappily. "It's all your fault. You got me to wondering what was going on outside. I mean, all those people, all going one way. What was that all about? I wondered. So, I closed up the shop, went outside and just sort of followed along."

He shrugged again. "I don't know why. Hell," the clerk said with a sad chuckle, "normally, I never give a damn what's going on outside, you know?"

Kevin nodded. He knew.

"But something like this...something so weird. I had to go see for myself." He looked at his brethren. "Now, here I am."

"Yes," said Kevin. "Here you are."

The man slid across the floor toward Kevin. "Say, where *is* here, anyway?"

"We're inside a spaceship," said Kevin.

"A tomb," said the young woman beside him.

"Hell's waiting room," suggested the old man.

"A spaceship? You mean," said the clerk, "like out of a science fiction novel?" He looked disbelieving and Kevin didn't blame him.

"We are about to embark on an amazing journey." Kevin was certain of this, though he had nothing tangible to base this belief on if pressed. Merely a sense he got.

Sigma Six waved his hands in the empty space and a holographic image of sorts appeared between his hands, floating. Magic. "This is your vessel." The Other clung to his side, as if supporting him. All the while, the hue of its pink skeletal structure strengthened and lessened in waves.

The scene changed. The vessel grew smaller and a galaxy of tiny stars appeared and engulfed it. One bluish star grew larger. A ring of brown spots orbited the star. Planets, Kevin supposed.

"When we reach destination," explained Sigma Six, "all will fight mighty enemy. Glory to all." He turned to the exit. "Thank you."

One human in a rumpled blue serge business suit jumped to his feet. "What the hell are you talking about?" he demanded, his fists balled tightly at his sides. "Fight? I'm not fighting anything you fat ball of glue." His MagnetIdent flapped against his inflated chest. Digsby Triump.

Sigma Six stopped and he and the Other seemed to be exchanging silent communications of some sort. "You are all defectives. Orders given."

The man laughed in the alien's face. "Screw you. I won't do it."

The Other said something in a tongue Kevin couldn't fathom but soon got the gist of as two sphinx-headed metal creatures appeared in the doorway, cousins of the sentinels by the looks of them.

On Earth, they'd call them the goon squad, Kevin realized.

The goons grabbed the businessman by the arms. When he started thrashing violently, two more identical things appeared and lifted him by his legs. The man's pleading eyes bored into Kevin's.

Kevin leapt to his feet. "Stop!"

Abject terror had turned the man's face into a contorted mask of pain and horror. "Help me, won't you? Don't let these monsters take me!" His face twisted around the room. "Which of you will be next?" he shouted as the things carted him away.

Kevin tried to follow but Sigma Six blocked his path. Lance pulled him to the floor.

"Let me go!" insisted Kevin.

"Stay put, you idiot. Are you crazy?" Lance held Kevin down. "Who knows what those tin cans are going to do to that guy? And do you really want to find out?"

Kevin pushed Lance off. "What's going to happen to him?" he demanded of his captors.

Sigma Six's lips vibrated a moment. "Defectives like you are not programmed properly. However, if agreeable, can be adaptable to service. Any noncompliants and unadaptables are removed from service."

"What's happening to that man?" Kevin asked once again. "What are you doing with him?"

"Creature has left the ship."

A cold shiver ran down Kevin's spine. "You mean you threw him out there—into space? Just like that?"

The room fell silent where up to then there had been murmurings of discontentment and mutiny.

"But that's murder!" oathed Lance.

"It is a long and costly war," interjected Sigma Six. "We must be efficient, economical." The Other stroked his side.

Efficient? Economical? The words bounced and echoed in Kevin's skull like jagged shards of marble. But he could think of nothing to say in reply. What do you say to a monster?

# 6

Lance muttered under his breath. "Those sons-of-bitches. Those lousy sons-of-bitches."

"They're sons of something," quipped the young woman whose bravado seemed to have melted away, "but God alone knows what."

"I don't believe in a god," muttered someone in the group.

"What do you think we're supposed to do now?" asked the clerk, addressing the remaining prisoners. "I mean, those things, they just left us here. You think we can leave?"

"Where you gonna go?" Lance scoffed. "You got an ion drive space escape pod under your shirt that you're keeping from us?"

"Shut up!" the clerk said with a frown.

"Make me!" Lance jumped to his feet and balled up his hands into fists. He was apparently a lot more fearless when it came to battling humans over their alien counterparts.

Kevin slowly climbed to his feet, dusted his threadbare trousers and headed down the dim corridor.

"Hey," shouted Lance, "where are you going, man?"

"To find my wife and daughter," said Kevin, without looking back.

Lance hurried after him.

"You get back here!" cried the clerk, mad, frightened and looking for someone or something to vent his fears and frustrations on. The young woman and the elderly man who'd been on either side of Kevin rose and followed after the two men.

Seeing this, the clerk reluctantly decided to go with them. Before he left, he turned to the remaining members of their small group. "What about you all? Aren't you coming?"

Several shook their heads, others gave no response.

The clerk snorted. "Look at you all, sitting there like a fat lot of Thanksgiving Day turkeys waiting to be stuffed in some giant gas oven."

"God will protect us," said a heavy woman with thin lips and a widow's peak.

"Yeah? He sure helped your friend, didn't he?" The clerk chuckled. "Gave him a ticket out of here—" He thumped his heavy hand against the wall. "A one-way ticket."

# 7

"So, your wife, huh?"

Kevin pushed through a throng of people listening to a bald-headed man. He was telling them to get organized, rebel, conquer. His listeners seemed uncertain of the wisdom of this. So did Kevin. "Excuse me?"

"Back there. You said you were looking for your wife."

Kevin turned. He recognized the woman from the chamber. Nicolette. There were others with her. Were they following him? According to Sigma Six, she was a defective like himself. Why? Did she hear voices in her head the way he did? She looked normal. "Yes. My ex-wife. And my daughter."

"You got separated?" she asked. "I got separated from my coworkers."

"Actually, we separated a long time ago. I rarely see them." He explained where he'd been when the whole thing started and how he'd gone searching for his ex-wife and daughter to see if they were all right.

"Same here," said the young woman, "sort of. I'm a school teacher. PS 147 in Brooklyn."

A glassy look passed over her blue eyes. "There I was, teaching social studies, when the entire class got up and left. I was in shock. I mean, I couldn't believe it. I still can't!" She shook her head in disbelief as the morning's memory played over in her mind.

"My whole class. They got up and left. I called after them but they wouldn't listen. They didn't even seem to hear me. I called the principal's office but it did no good. She'd left, too. The offices were deserted.

"I went outside and discovered all of them, the staff and the children, marching down the street in a ragtag bunch. It was weird. It was like they were—" She shrugged, apparently at a loss for words.

"A bunch of fuckin' zombies?" said Lance.

"Yeah, that's it. Zombies." She hugged herself. "I followed them to this-this place. Then one of those *things* snatched me up and made me go with it to that chamber where we met."

"And that Sigma Six thing called *us* defective," snorted Gig.

Kevin stopped, surveyed the untold masses surrounding them. "Maybe," he began, "it's because we couldn't hear the voices."

"What voices?" asked Lance.

Kevin tapped his skull. "The voices in here."

Nicolette nodded, touched Kevin's arm. "You mean they all heard some voice in their heads telling them what to do?" She chewed her lip. "That does makes sense."

Lance snorted.

"To drop everything they were doing and board these ships," added Kevin.

"Too fucking creepy," said Lance. "Impossible!"

"Not impossible," said Kevin. "I hear voices in my head all the time."

The old man, Henry Hemming, who'd also been following along, sighed. "But not those voices."

"No," admitted Kevin. "Not those voices." Was this what made him defective? The fact that he hadn't heard and heeded the aliens' calling? Was that what had made their entire ragtag group defective? Like the store clerk, Gig, for instance. He had been completely disinterested in what was going on outside when Kevin had gone into his store. "You didn't hear the voice, did you?"

"Nope." Gig shook his head. "Not so much as a whisper."

"What about the rest of you?" demanded Kevin. "Did any of you hear any sort of alien voice or voices in your skulls?"

The others shook their heads, except for Lance who laughed.

"I'm hearing one now," he said. "It's telling me you're loony tunes, man."

Lance rolled his index finger around his ear. "Real loony tunes. I mean, you don't even know that's what happened."

"Have you got a better explanation?" Gig demanded.

Lance tapped a stranger on the shoulder. "Hey, bro. What's going on? I mean, my friends and me are wondering—why did you come here?"

The muscular young black glared at Lance, his nostrils flared. "Is this your doing, fucker? Are you and your friends behind this bullshit?" He glanced menacingly at them all, then shoved Lance.

Lance fell against Kevin. "No, no!" said Lance, waving his arms in surrender. "Not at all, bro. I'm like you. Just trying to figure things out is all."

The youth throttled Lance, his thumbs digging savagely into the man's neck. "Go fucking figure things out on your own territory."

"T-territory?" said Lance.

"This," said the thug, "is our territory." He ran a red sneakered toe over the hard floor. "Go find your own."

"Okay, okay," said Lance. "No need for violence. We're all in this together." He held his open palms up in an attempt to placate the menacing figure.

The thug looked at him in icy silence.

"Let's go," said Kevin.

"Good idea," said Henry. He turned away, pulling Nicolette with him.

"Wait!" said the thug.

Lance gulped. "Yes?"

"Give me your wallet." He held out his right hand.

Lance patted his pockets. "I-I'm afraid I don't have it on me."

The thug frowned and took a step forward.

Lance took a long look at the extended hand, patted his pockets once more. "What do you know. Here it is!" He dropped his billfold in the youth's hand, turned and ran.

The youth and his gang melted back into the crowd.

"Do you think we've seen the end of him?" said Gig Shephard. He had been conspicuously silent throughout the exchange.

"Do you mean Lance or that petty extortionist back there?" asked Kevin.

"Well," said Gig, "I was thinking of Lance but now that you mention it..." He glanced back at the youth and his companions. An ugly bunch if ever there was one. Gangs were a growing problem in the cities. The rich were immune to them, living in so rarefied and protected a society. But for the rest of the citizens, gangs were deadly dangerous.

"Bunch of creeps," stated Nicolette. She laughed. "Those guys *and* Lance!"

Kevin looked through the crowd, trying to figure out a direction to go. He wasn't worried about Lance. He couldn't explain why, but he had no doubt he'd be seeing him again.

A piercing cry shot through the cold arid atmosphere. Loud and blood chilling. A woman's voice. The crowd surrounding their little group parted and a screaming woman in a torn white shirt ran into their midst. She took shelter behind Nicolette. She was shivering and nearly naked. Her white pants and panties were in a twisted knot wrapped around her right ankle. "Help me, please," she whispered, pulling on Nicolette. "They're going to rape me!"

"Who's going to rape you?" Kevin asked, his heart thumping rapidly.

"We are. Out of the way, asshole." A motley group of surly men in black leather ranging from middle age to mere teens descended on them. Their apparent leader was pointing a snub-nose revolver at Kevin's chest.

Kevin felt his chest pounding as if a bullet was already banging at the gates to his heart. Demanding to be let in. His jaw tightened and the inside of his mouth dried up. "You shouldn't do that."

The punk laughed. "What Jason wants, Jason gets." His tone

was cold, unyielding. His finger pressed the trigger ever so slightly.

Kevin's breath stuck in his throat. Death comes at the most unexpected and importunate times...

Nothing happened.

"What the fuck?" The gang leader squeezed the trigger again and again.

Still nothing.

He stared down the muzzle, grunted angrily, then shoved the useless thing back in his belt. Without warning, he took a step forward, toward the woman he wanted. She crouched lower behind Nicolette, never letting go and nearly taking both of them down in the process.

Kevin stepped in his path. He was no hero, but he knew right from wrong, or at least liked to think he did.

Nobody else outside their two oppositional groups was paying any attention to the little drama. The leader's fist smashed into Kevin's face and he keeled over in pain. He waited for the second blow—there was always a second blow—but it didn't come. So much for always.

When he looked up, Sigma Six or his doppelganger, Other, in tow, stood amongst them.

"You are not where you belong," said Sigma Six.

Was that a note of glumness in his voice? wondered Kevin. Kevin didn't know who Sigma was directing his comment to, himself or his assailant, but his assailant took flight. "Thanks," Kevin said. "I think you saved my life."

"You are not where you belong."

The near victim was leaning against Nicolette and struggling to get her clothes back on. Kevin hadn't noticed before just how beautiful she was. A shame that beauty could lead itself to such trouble.

"I'm Sequoia." She touched his nose. "Sequoia Jones."

He winced. "Ouch!" Sequoia. How apropos. She reminded him of a magnificent redwood, with her long red locks and dramatic green eyes.

"Sorry. Did I hurt you?"

Kevin shook his head. "I'm okay."

"Good. And thank you," Sequoia said. She very tenderly examined the fresh bruise on his jaw. "Can you move it?"

He wiggled his jawbone. "I guess so."

"Great. Nothing's broken."

"Way to use your face," said Gig.

"Shut up," said Nicolette. "I didn't see you doing anything to help."

Gig looked at his feet.

The Other chittered at Sigma Six who nodded slowly. He grabbed Sequoia. "Stay," he commanded. To the others he said, "Follow."

Sequoia gasped. Her eyes darted pleadingly at Kevin and the others. Nicolette slapped Sigma Six's hand from the girl. "Not a chance, slimeball. She comes with us."

Sigma Six and the Other exchanged a few indecipherable words then turned and began walking. "Come," he said once again in a bassoon-like voice.

Nicolette took Sequoia's hand. "You heard the man, er thing."

# 8

The small group walked single file down snaking passages that led nowhere, or so it seemed, then emerged on a catwalk looking down over the huge chamber that seemed to be the ship's main feature.

"Jesus," whispered Gig in amazement. He grabbed the low metal rail to keep from falling. "Heights make me crazy," he gasped.

Kevin nodded. He was not a fan of high places himself. And from up here, seeing all those people below, possibly millions of them, he could only gasp, too. Who were these creatures who had had the skill and the minds to build a ship large enough to hold so many people? Where had they come from?

Where were they going?

"It's incredible," Sequoia said, though they were all thinking it. "What's it all about?"

"We don't have a clue," said Nicolette.

Kevin leaned over the rail. "It looks like all of humanity swimming in a sea of emptiness." Were his ex-wife and daughter among them? "Where are you taking us?"

"I can answer that," spoke Henry Hemming. "Slavery."

"Huh?" Gig scratched his head.

"It's slavery, isn't it?" Hemming demanded of Sigma Six who stood silently by. "I believe we are all of us, all of humanity, being sold into slavery."

"They wouldn't—" started Nicolette.

"You mean they're carting us halfway across the stinking universe to serve a bunch of alien gooks coffee and donuts? Work in their cotton fields?" Gig shook his head. "That's crazy."

Kevin thought so, too, but he watched goosebumps spread up Sequoia's arms. She believed.

"Slavery is an extremely cheap and convenient source of labor," Hemming explained.

"Convenient for who?!" demanded Gig.

"No being here is a slave," said Sigma Six. "Except perhaps myself. For I serve without end."

Nicolette gave a quick sigh of relief. "That's good to hear."

"Amen," said Gig.

Hemming crossed his arms, and appeared unconvinced. "It's only words. You stopped our friend Kevin here from being killed by that thug because of his value as an able-bodied young man—as a slave," he insisted.

With an impossibly quick move, Sigma Six grabbed Kevin by the ankle and hurled him over the side. Kevin heard screams. One of them might have been his. He reached out wildly and felt his right hand wrap rudely around the stiff rail. The momentum swung him hard against the wall, knocking the air out of him and leaving him stunned. But he hung on dearly as hands reached for him and pulled him back to safety. He sank to his knees, gasping for air; waiting for his heart to quit screaming.

"What did you do that for?" Sequoia shouted.

"To teach," answered Sigma Six, matter-of-factly.

"Teach?!" Sequoia leaned over Kevin and asked him if he was alright.

"To teach that we do not save your lives. We act only to protect the vessel. And our mission. Your lives," he said firmly, "are to be given." The alien turned.

"Given?" said Nicolette.

"What the devil is that supposed to mean?" demanded Hemming.

"You shall shortly learn," said Sigma Six moving on.

"Wait!" shouted Kevin, climbing to his feet with Sequoia's assistance. "What are we to do now?"

"What you will," replied Sigma Six. "Do what humans do. Eat, drink, fight, sex."

Gig chuckled. "That last part sounds good to me."

"Shut up, Gig." Nicolette gave him a sharp look. "Are you saying there's food and water somewhere on this hellhole?"

"Of course. We do not wish you to become diminished. Or fail. That would serve no purpose."

"Meaning we're no good to you dead," said Hemming, his eyes narrowing.

"Yeah," said Gig. "And just think how a million dead bodies would stink up the joint."

Kevin spoke up. "You still haven't told us where we're going."

"To a large planet in what you call the Boötes Void," Sigma Six said without hesitation.

The words sounded vaguely familiar but what were they being dragged there for by these aliens? Was that their home? Was the Hemming fellow right? Were they being marched off into slavery? "And?"

The alien was silent a moment, lost in alien thought perhaps, looking out over the sea of humans below them. "And you will fight to defeat the enemy." The creature pointed in the direction from which they'd come. "Go back to your quarters. You are not like the others. You do not belong with them."

With that he departed.

"Fight to defeat the enemy?" gaped Gig. "What the hell does that mean?? He *is* the enemy."

Kevin's head pounded painfully. Had Sigma Six really intended to murder him by tossing him off the ledge?

Perhaps more perplexing, if Sigma Six was not the enemy, who was?

A vivid image jumped across his mind like a flash of liquid lightning. In that image, he saw millions battling and millions falling. And, though the image had come and gone in the blink of an eye, the fighting seemed to go on forever...

# 9

The aliens left and Kevin ran after them, leaving the others behind. He grabbed the big one. That one seemed the more solid, more real of the two. Not to mention he acted like the one in charge. But who knew? He/she/it was certainly the only one that spoke—at least to them. Maybe he was in charge of the whole shebang. The whole entire operation—whatever that was. He was going to find out.

Kevin tugged at Sigma Six's arm. A warm, mildly uncomfortable charge, like a weird electrical current, shot through his fingers and he let go.

The alien kept moving. Kevin jumped in front of him. "Stop!"

The thing's buggy eyes looked him over and seemed to conclude he was worth less than spit. Kevin ignored the unspoken insult. "I'm looking for my wife and my daughter. Ex-wife, actually." He watched those alien eyes watching him.

Sigma Six stared at him impassively.

"Sarah Kent? Quinn Kent?" Kevin said desperately. Who knew? Maybe they kept a list somewhere.

"This means nothing."

"Listen, frog face. They may mean nothing to you, but they mean everything to me."

Sigma Six pushed Kevin aside. "If these two heard the call they will be aboard one of the carrying vessels. If defective, like you, perhaps not."

"I've got to find them."

Sigma Six shrugged an alien shrug. "There is much time and what you do with yours on the voyage matters not."

Sigma Six stopped, turned. "Of course, there are millions of you scattered among our vessels." He'd said it like they were no better than an infestation of cockroaches he couldn't wait to be rid of.

Kevin gulped. "Millions?"

"Millions."

Sigma Six slid through a narrow doorway, then disappeared.

"Wait!" Kevin banged on the firmly closed door. "Have you got a computer I can borrow? Do you have a list of passengers?" He slammed his fist against the door. "Damn you! Get back here!"

"Well, that was pretty stupid. What are you, retarded?"

Kevin spun around. A girl with shoulder length blue-and-black hair clipped sharply off at the ends was looking him over with some kind of cross between amusement and disgust. But then, he got that a lot. Her violet eyes seemed to mock him.

She was dressed in a black T-shirt that read TRUST NO ONE in big white block letters across the chest, and a short Catholic school girl red-and-black plaid skirt with knee-high white stockings ending in yellow high-top sneakers. She'd painted her fingernails vomit green. A collection of tattoos ran up her left arm. A small tattoo of an ankh hung at the outside corner of her left eye.

The word MISFIT went off like a fire alarm between his ears.

"They're extinct," she said, rubbing her arm.

"Who's extinct?" Did she mean the aliens? They looked pretty lively to him.

"My tats. You were staring at them. They're all extinct species. Bald eagle, blue whale, dodo..." She rattled off a long list of species.

Kevin's head spun. "Uh, I'm sorry to hear that." He also wondered if she could soon add humans to that list.

"Yeah, sure you are," she said, rubbing her arm.

"Look," he said, sidestepping around her, "I've got other things to do. Goodbye."

"Sure," she called. "But you know you'll never find them."

Kevin blinked. "Who?"

"Duh, you're ex-wife and kid? Remember?"

"H-how did you know about them?"

"I've got ears, nitwit. What gave you the impression I was deaf? This snappy dialogue we've been sharing?" She crossed her arms over her chest. "According to that thing you were verbally abusing, it's a long way to wherever we're going."

"This Boötes Void." Kevin nodded. Whatever it was, it didn't sound like it was going to be just one subway stop over. "It could take years for all we know." He paused and thought a moment before adding, "I might find them."

"Right, like the proverbial needle in a haystack." She smirked irritatingly and rolled her eyes. "Good luck with that, doofus."

"Name's Kevin."

"Same thing."

Kevin pushed past the girl once more. She got under his skin, and not in a good way. Not to mention, she smelled like a patchouli and sourdough sandwich. "Nice outfit," he mumbled as he brushed by. "You pick up it up at the circus?"

She sucker punched him in the shoulder.

"Ow! What was that for?"

"Do I make fun of you?"

Kevin rubbed his shoulder. "Pretty much nonstop from the second we met, yes, you have and you do."

That seemed to stump her. "Oh, well. Okay, then. Let that be a lesson to you."

"A lesson?"

"Yeah, don't screw with me. Nobody screws with me," she said, her voice hard, her meaning ominous.

Kevin's shoulder throbbed. "I'll bet." He gestured towards a mountain-sized creature in a purple uniform standing only a few yards off. "What about our alien friends?"

She made a sour face and glared at the alien. "I'm making *them* my special project."

Kevin gave this some thought. The aliens were a complete mystery. But what the heck, life was a complete mystery and its purpose had long eluded him. This woman-child was a complete annoyance. But in some twisted sort of way, the tattoos, the aliens, she seemed to have given her life meaning.

He held out his hand and tried again. "I'm Kevin."

"So?" She looked amused as she curled up her lip and ignored his proffered hand.

"I'm going to find my...friends." Cohorts? Fellow captives? What were those people exactly? Whatever you called them, they were all in this together. "They should be in a room back there." He pointed. "You want to come join us?"

Her amethyst eyes sparkled with mischief. "Depends. Are they all as dumb as you?"

"Come on," Kevin smiled and spread his hands out, "Could anybody else really be as dumb as me?"

"You've got a point," she said, falling into step beside him.

Kevin backtracked his way to the room he and the others had been led to and sequestered within.

The girl followed him inside. "Well?" The room stood empty.

"They were right here." Kevin scratched his head.

"Got a real knack for losing things, haven't you?"

Kevin frowned. "Where did they go?"

"How should I know where they've gone? You tell me."

Kevin's hands fell to his sides. "I don't even know where my ex has gone. I don't have a clue where my daughter is." He looked out a triangular portal at a blur of light that moved faster, brighter, and then suddenly blinked out of existence. The universe had turned to black.

"I don't even know where I've gone," he said quietly, staring out.

"Whoa, old timer. Don't turn all deer in the headlights on me."

"What?"

"You know, all little baby sheep in the big bad wolf eye lights?" She raised her arms and extended her fingers like they were claws. She looked ridiculous as she growled.

Kevin slumped to the floor.

"Oh, great," she said, swallowing a yawn. "What a wuss."

Kevin forced his eyelids upward. "Feel so tired..."

# 10

"Grab as many articles as you can carry," repeated the inflectionless female voice. "Grab as many articles as you can carry."

"Grab what?" said Nicolette. "I mean, what is all this stuff?"

Kevin had awoken in the company of the other defectives, approximately three days ago by his reckoning, after succumbing to severe and spontaneous mental and physical overload. Sam had dragged him back.

The reason his fellow defectives had not been in the room earlier when he and the weird blue-and-black haired girl with the tattoos—whose name Kevin had learned to be Sam, Samantha Webster—had come looking for them was because they had been considering rejoining the main group of humans. Alien guards had forced them to return to their quarters after only a matter of minutes. Maybe the aliens were afraid Kevin and the other defectives would somehow contaminate the other *normal* humans.

Though they had been given free run of the upper portion of the ship, the small band had stayed mostly together in the small compartment provided to them. Nobody made a point of saying it, but it just seemed safer that way. The humans out in the main areas of the ship had turned into semi-feral packs, feeding off the wheat-smelling, gray mush for brains looking substance they'd been supplied with, while the most belligerent herded and cowed the tame and frightened.

The aliens, for the most part, did not interfere with the way the humans treated one another. Kevin and the others watched all this in uneasy silence from the high balcony that circled the great bowel of the vessel.

Now he was waking again and he couldn't even remember going to sleep. He suspected he and the others were being drugged. He awoke in a room the size of a two-car garage, disoriented but unnaturally hyper-alert, as if his blood had been laced with caffeine.

Bulky clothing, large and awkward looking, lay scattered across the floor and hanging from incongruously primitive looking hooks on the sleek buttery yellow walls. He had barely had time to catch up with his companions—during which time Kevin learned that the others had had a similar experience to his own.

They were pondering their fate and their options when the disembodied female voice came blaring from the walls. Repeating the same words over and over in various Earth languages.

"Landing will commence in fifteen minutes." Silence. "Be prepared to leave. Be prepared to fight. Your survival depends on this."

More silence. "Grab as many articles as you can carry. Grab as many articles as you can carry."

No one had any idea what was going on, yet they all knew that it wasn't likely to be anything good.

"What do you think?" quipped Lance, his nervousness showing through as he bit at his jagged fingernails. "Our trip to Intergalactic DisneyWorld about to begin?"

Nobody laughed. The floor quivered beneath their feet and they eyed one another nervously.

"Landing will commence in fifteen minutes." There followed several seconds of silence. "Be prepared to leave. Be prepared to fight. Your survival depends on this."

Then the loop began again. "Grab as many articles as you can carry. Grab as many articles as you can carry."

Hidden hatches in the ceiling opened and a variety of gear in all shapes, sizes and colors cascaded down on their heads. Some of the stuff was heavy and sharp and Kevin heard squeals of surprise and pain. Kevin caught sight of Sigma Six and his Other watching placidly from the corner of the room, saying nothing. Kevin looked at them wildly, hoping for some explanation. But their faces remained inscrutable.

Kevin and his companions were nearly crushed in the mountain of gear pummeling them. The aliens didn't seem to be disturbed or in the least concerned about that. But then, why should they? Apparently, humans were as cheap and disposable as dollar-store plastic butane lighters—to be used once or twice, then expended.

"What is all this?" Nicolette squeezed her hands together. "Camping gear?"

"And weapons," said Gig, eyeing a particularly deadly piece of metal.

Sam grabbed a sleek backpack and something that looked like the evil child devil spawn of a handgun pop and a bazooka mom. "Weapon, food, who knows?" She stuffed everything inside. "I say we each take as much different stuff as we can. Cover all our bases."

Kevin grabbed an orange bundle that appeared to be camping supplies and a pouch with a strap filled with clear liquid. He unscrewed the lid and sniffed. Odorless. He hoped for water but it could have been some alien incendiary fluid for all he knew.

"That's it?" said Sam.

Kevin shrugged.

"Better take a weapon of some sort, moron."

"I don't think so. I'm not much for fighting."

"Oh, yeah? How are you for dying? Being killed, slaughtered, without ever finding your oh-so-important ex-wife and kid?" Her sneer was maddening. "Besides, if you won't do it for yourself, do it for us. We've got to look out for one another."

"Yeah," said Lance, practically making love to a long-barreled alien rifle.

"Maybe this is only some sort of hunting expedition?" Sequoia said, eyes filled with distant hope.

"Yeah, and maybe it's us that these ugly aliens will be

hunting. Do you want a chance to defend yourself or not?" Sam retorted.

Sequoia seemed unsure and Nicolette helped her select some items from the floor.

"Hustle it up there!" Sam clapped her hands and snarled at Gig. "Pick up that pack!"

Jarred into action, everyone grabbed a weapon or two, even mild-mannered Henry. Gig and Lance struggled into some of the odd alien clothing, the rest ignored it.

Kevin looked at the others and knew that they were judging him now. Judging his worthiness, as a man and as a companion. Finally, he sorted through the alien weaponry and selected a small, practically weightless pistol and stuffed it into his waistband.

"Landing will commence in two minutes." A more commanding and strident voice filled the air. "Be prepared to exit. Be prepared to fight."

Exit? Fight?

Fearful looks passed between them. They were a small party, a mere few among untold thousands, perhaps millions, in a windowless flying cavern, clueless as to where they were, what they would be landing on and what enemy they would be facing when they finally arrived.

Kevin saw Gig's eyes roll up in his head. The big guy shook all over and it wasn't due to the gyrations of the ship. Before Kevin could say a word, Gig launched himself at Sigma Six, shoving the Other out of his path with his big open hand. The Other slammed into the wall behind with what might have been a look of surprise on its face.

Gig grabbed Sigma Six's arm and screamed. Over the noise of the ship and the stirring masses of humans, Kevin couldn't make out Gig's words.

Suddenly, Kevin's stomach dropped. Everything and everyone hung in the air a moment—complete silence descended on them like a curtain.

Then the floor gave way beneath them, and they were

falling...

# 11

Kevin flailed in emptiness. Air, hot, thick and red, blew over him. He tumbled for a lifetime, hit the ground hard, felt something smash into him and then felt no more. His last thoughts were that this was such a stupid, ignoble way to die…

"Wake up, moron."

Kevin groaned and opened his eyes. The world began to take shape. Blurs became objects though most of them appeared alien to him. "Samantha?"

"Very good. But call me Samantha again and I'll punch your lights back out for you." She wiped her dust-covered face with the back of her hand and scanned the alien landscape. "Can you get up?"

Kevin gave this some thought. The further edges of the universe began to pull together, sew up like a cheap rag doll coming to life. "I think so." He cleared his throat "…Sam." He struggled to his knees, bringing a bolt of pain across his spine. His knees complained too. "My god."

Nausea overtook him like a rogue wave. He vomited on his shirt. More spilled over the purplish-brown ground. A ground he now realized already littered with the bodies of thousands, tens of thousands, perhaps hundreds of thousands of the dead.

Most corpses, at least those still recognizable as corpses, appeared human–his shipmates. Former shipmates. Now lifeless occupiers of a strange world with a lavender-tinted sky and two small moons dangling in the air like movie set spotlights, shining brightly, even in daylight.

He saw other corpses, too. But these were not even remotely human. These oddly innocent yet ferocious looking corpses belonged to some sort of beasts that must have stood nine feet tall when alive. Kevin thought they looked like a cross between the Pillsbury doughboy and a baboon. He'd never seen anything like them before, not even in comics. They didn't fit any of the body types Kevin had seen aboard the alien ship either. What were they then? Where had they come from?

"You done heaving?" Sam handed Kevin a water bottle.

He drank tentatively, embarrassed that he'd vomited in front of the girl and afraid he might do so again. He handed the bottle back.

"You keep it," she said with a look of disgust.

"Thanks." Kevin climbed to his feet. "What happened?"

"I'd say the jerks dropped us right in the middle of a lousy hornets' nest." She spat. "And the hornets may have gotten the best of us. Humans, I mean."

Kevin nodded. It did look that way. "I don't remember anything…except falling," he said softly, apologetically.

She grinned. "That's because I expect you were out cold the minute you hit the ground. We both were. I'd say it's a good thing, too. Otherwise," she pointed, "we'd be like them."

Kevin shivered. The aliens had literally pulled the floor out from under them, dropping them from the sky like so much trash, unprepared for what lay below. A horrible pitched battle had obviously ensued. How many ill-prepared, untrained humans had died?

"You think this is it then? Do you think we're the only ones left?"

"Nah, I mean, there's a lot of bodies here. And I don't feel like taking a friggin' count. But I don't think there are enough bodies —" Sam squinted into the distance, "or parts, to account for everybody on the ships."

"So where are they?" He saw no moving bodies on the ground as far as the distant horizon, no ships hovering above in the lavender sky.

She shrugged. "I don't have a freaking clue. But unless you've got a brilliant plan that gets us off this freaking planet, on a first class rocket back home, where I can chill out and watch the tube like a good little vegetable—" Sam paused to give Kevin time to respond.

"Then," she said, grabbing her pack and her weapon and threading her way between a couple of lower limbs who'd strayed from their owners, "I suggest we start looking for them."

Kevin stood a moment. The sky was purplish, the ground red with blood where it wasn't covered by a thick low grass of some sort that pulled at the feet. Bodies were strewn everywhere like pine straw along the undulating plain. The horizon seemed foreshortened.

He took a slow breath, consciously filling his lungs, then letting the air slowly out. There was a slight sweetness, an odd alienness, to the air. His ex- and his daughter could be lying out there right now on this lifeless plain. Dead. A far off flock of a couple dozen large brown birds or what passed for birds on this world, swooped, tore pieces from the corpses, then swirled away with their awful prizes.

"Better take all you can carry," said Sam, jolting Kevin out of his morbid thoughts.

Kevin studied his pale dirty hands. "You don't understand," he said. "I can barely carry myself."

Sam rolled her eyes. "God, you are messed up." She kicked an abandoned backpack on the ground. "Get with the program, moron." She started walking toward a distant wood. "Or die!" she called over her shoulder.

Kevin watched her determined steps, her back growing smaller in the distance. He stood alone in a pile of alien and human meat. Sam was practically a speck now.

He chewed his lip, grabbed as much junk as he could manage, not caring what it was, and jogged after her, tripping over corpses left and right. It was as if the dead were reaching out and trying to grab him, take him down with them.

Kevin shuddered and raced on, breathless.

Unbeknownst to them, a small group of humans followed stealthily behind.

# 12

Kevin and Sam waded through a shallow stream wide as a four-lane highway. Unnaturally warm water, at least by Earth standards, sloshed against their knees.

Kevin hoped there were no bloodsucking aliens lurking in the mud. He imagined tiny, invisible creatures creeping over his flesh and up his urethra, devouring him from the inside out. "Are you sure this is safe?"

"No. Shut up and walk, weenie." Sam marched without caution through the murky water, stamped her feet on the far shore and waited for Kevin to cross.

Sam scratched her head. "It's a bloody jungle," she said, looking from the river to the interior.

Kevin nodded. If it weren't for the possibility that he might find his ex-wife and child out here somewhere, he would have wished himself back home in NYC, roaming the streets, roaming the days, roaming his mind, without a thought or care for what lay ahead or behind.

He'd given up caring long ago—or thought he had—until the aliens had captured his ex and his daughter, using their alien mind control, or whatever the hell it was, on them.

Kevin dropped to his knees on the muddy bank. They'd finally left the hideous circus of bodies behind them. That was something. But the two moons seemed to be marching in step with them.

The girl caught his gaze and said, "The moon's hollow, you know."

"How do you know they are hollow?"

"Not those moons," she said. "The moon back home. It's

hollow. That's probably where those alien goons came from. The way I see it, they've probably been up there spying on us all this time. I mean, they probably used to watch us from Earth, Atlantis would be my guess. But then people got smarter, got civilized." She studied the moons above. "So they retreated to the moon." She folded her arms and stared at Kevin as if daring him to challenge her theories. "My guess is that the moon's really a spaceship."

"So," said Kevin, wondering now which of the two of them was the crazier, "do you think those moons in the sky up there are spaceships too?"

Sam shrugged. "Could be. Who's to say?" She kicked his toe. "Come on, come on. Let's keep moving." She brushed a lock of hair from her face and shifted her backpack.

Kevin ignored her. "About what happened back there…"

Sam sighed the kind of sigh a child hears from a parent when they ask the same simple question over and over again. "A lot of people found Heaven, that's what happened. Come on, already. Let's march."

"They dropped us from the sky like so much useless trash." Kevin shook his head. "Ill-equipped, ill-prepared."

Sam laughed. "You got that right. Sick, huh?"

Kevin squeezed a fistful of mud in his hand and watched it ooze slowly out between his fingers. "Sheep to the slaughter."

"Yeah, well, *we* aren't dead yet, are we?"

Kevin shook his head.

Sam kicked him in the butt. "If you don't want to be next, I suggest you get your wet ass moving."

"What do you mean?"

"Are you dense?"

Kevin's face betrayed his confusion as she grabbed him by the head with both hands and turned his skull one hundred and eighty degrees, back across the stream. "See it?"

Kevin squinted. She was hurting him, but he wasn't about to let her know. Through the tears welling up in his eyes from the pain, he followed her gaze. It was late and the sun was setting on whatever hellish place they'd landed. "What is it?" A small, dark patch moved across the landscape.

She shrugged. "I'm not sure. A small group, twenty, twenty-five in number, is my guess." She let go of his head and wiped the wicked long blade of the sword she'd relieved a dead alien fighter of against her skirt. She'd also claimed a shorter but just as deadly-looking dagger. Gripping the hasp of the long blade tightly with both hands, she waved it through the air with convincing authority.

What was she, wondered Kevin, some kind of Amazon warrior woman? The blade looked sharp enough to slice the very molecules of air swirling around them.

"Whether they're aliens or humans, friends or foes, I couldn't begin to guess. They may be humans, survivors like us." She parried, thrust twice, spun and thrust again followed by a quick riposte. "Or they could be maniacal, blood-lusting aliens seeking to destroy any survivors," she paused and smiled, "like us. And then eat our entrails."

Kevin swallowed hard and swatted away a steel-jawed insect swigging a pint of precious blood from his cheek. Moving might be a good idea after all. He lurched to his feet and followed.

Their march was short-lived, however, as it soon grew so dark, not even the ever-so-annoying Sam felt it possible to continue. Standing in the center of a small depression surrounded by fifty-foot trees with yellow bark and broad flat pink leaves, she said, "We'll stop and make camp here for the night. Looks safe enough."

"Fine." Kevin sighed wearily. His clothes were torn, his calves throbbed and his ankles oozed blood. Throughout their march, the jungle had remained relatively quiet but for the occasional odd noises, like strangled laughter, sometimes coming from the trees, sometimes from the deep grass. They'd seen no signs of humans, or even aliens for that matter.

Kevin slumped against a flat brown rock. Sam planted her sword point-first in the red earth and settled beside him. She rummage through her pack and came up with a plastic sack filled with that same wheat-smelling, gray mush for brains looking substance they'd been supplied with aboard ship. Kevin frowned.

Sam silently broke off a chunk then handed the wet mess to Kevin. "Seriously? You're going to eat that?"

"You got something better?" Sam countered.

He pinched a small piece off, popped it in his mouth and chewed mechanically. "I didn't realize how hungry I was." His eyelids fell, then fluttered open. "Or how tired." He yawned to prove his point. "Think we should start a fire?"

"Go ahead, boy scout. What are you going to start it with? Magic fire drops?" She rubbed dirt over her hands to clean and dry them.

Kevin dug through his backpack. Lots of odd looking stuff he didn't recognize, but nothing resembling a lighter or even a pack of matches.

"It's just as well," said Sam, watching his feeble efforts. "Who knows who or what a fire might attract out here?"

Kevin thought about the weird noises that had seemed to follow them through the jungle. And the definite, though unknown, band that had been what? Following them? Stalking them? Since they'd left the battlefield.

Sam rose, stretched and stifled a groan. "I'll take the first watch. Wake you in a couple of hours." She picked up her sword and checked to make sure her pistol and knife remained securely tucked in at her waist.

"Is that really necessary?" Kevin didn't relish the thought of being awakened in the middle of the night only to stand watch over a bunch of cold rocks and trees. "I mean, it's dark. Don't you think whoever is following us will have stopped for the night, too?"

"Maybe. Then again, maybe not." She leaned in so close he could taste her breath on his tongue. "Maybe whatever those creatures are have extrasensory perception, or night vision. Maybe it's a pack of blood stalking, night hunting alien vampires." The corner of her brow arched upward. "Wanna chance it?"

Kevin gave in. NYC had its own vampires and he'd seen enough of those to last a lifetime. Besides, there could be other unseen, unknown and nastier beasties afoot. He shivered and felt for his own weapon, keeping it close to his side even as he fell into a deep slumber.

# 13

Kevin woke. "What? Sam?" He blinked. The stars above etched a pattern he'd never laid eyes on before.

He realized he wasn't alone. A couple dozen bedraggled and beaten down people confronted him.

At least they were human. Two of the humans toward the rear of the hollow seemed to be holding up something Kevin first thought was a large dirty white bedsheet. He then realized it was one of the aliens from their ship. Sigma Six? The alien hung between them like a listless sail. Its red eyes glowed dully. Kevin saw no sign of its Other.

The earthlings didn't look friendly, studying him with grim, dirty faces, balled up fists and drawn weapons.

Kevin slowly scoured the perimeter. No sign of Sam.

"Get up!" One of the men kicked him before he could comply or even respond.

"Hey!" Kevin complained, but got to his feet. Something about the wiry built man seemed vaguely familiar. And the tired looking group eyed him with open hostility. Why? They were human after all. Theoretically, they were all on the same side. Did they think he was some sort of alien morphed into human form?

Kevin counted five women with the group and they, like the men, were armed to the gills.

"Where's the girl?"

"Sam? I have no idea. Sure you didn't eat her?"

The man bared his teeth like a big jungle cat. Neck and arm muscles rippled in an unsettling fashion. He had shiny black hair and mean black eyes. "I don't care about any Sam. I want to know what you did with my woman!" He aimed a nickel-plated pistol at Kevin's face.

"Your woman?" Kevin frowned. "Do I know you?"

The stranger hooted hideously. A long, fresh gash cut along his face from the forehead, across his eye and down his cheek. The wound moved like a horrid, living thing and turned bright red as he laughed. "Don't remember me, do you?"

He glared at Kevin who could only wait and wonder.

"You stole my woman aboard that damn alien prison ship," he said. "She was mine." He thumped the pistol against his chest. His eyes went flat. "I should have killed you when I had the chance."

It was Jason. The creep who'd tried to rape Sequoia. A shiver ran up Kevin's arms.

"Don't worry, buddy. I know *this* gun works and there are no aliens around to save your ugly butt." He squeezed the trigger and Kevin involuntarily squeezed his eyes shut in reaction, although he'd told himself he wouldn't give Jason the satisfaction of showing his fear.

An explosion racked the clearing. White smoke filled the air. Through the haze, Kevin saw Sam jump down from atop the boulder behind them, swinging her sword menacingly. She brought the blade down across Jason's neck and held it there. Cold carbon steel pressing against his flesh. "Drop the gun, little man—or your headless body will drop it for you."

Jason coughed and the razor sharp edge bit into his Adam's apple. He dropped his gun. His mates stepped back.

"That's a good boy." Sam patted the top of his head with the flat of her blade. "Now, be a good little boy and run home to mommy."

He fixed her with an evil glare, fingers twitching. Unfazed, she poked him in the belly and he backed away. All his friends were gone.

"Go," she said. She kicked him in the butt just to speed up the process.

Kevin watched Jason slink away. He didn't imagine they'd

seen the last of him. "What was that explosion?"

"Some stuff I found in my pack. Plastic explosive is my guess."

"Good thing you knew what it was and how to use it."

"Hell, I didn't have a clue what it was. I thought it was food. I was only trying to distract them."

Kevin's jaw dropped to his knees. "Jason could have killed me."

"Always griping, aren't you?" She told him to collect his gear. "Time to move."

Kevin threw his pack over his shoulder. "Then again, a couple of inches either way and that stupid bomb of yours could've blown me to smithereens."

"Yeah," she said, smiling and scratching her cheek. "How about that—" She started up into the darkness ahead. "You can thank me later. Right now we'd better make some time."

"Wait!" cried Kevin. He suddenly noticed the alien lying limp on the ground like a wet blanket. He scampered over to it and peered at its body and near lifeless eyes.

"Careful!" warned Sam.

"I think it's alive." Apparently Jason's henchmen had dropped the alien in their haste to make their escape.

Sam approached, weapon drawn. She aimed for the thing's head. "Don't worry, I'll take care of that right now."

"No!" Kevin held up his hand to thwart her. "Don't kill him. I think it's Sigma Six."

"I don't care if it's Sigma Seven and Three-Quarters. That," she spat venomously, "is one of the monsters responsible for us being here." She leveled her gun at its head.

Kevin put himself between the gun and the alien. "We've got to take him with us."

Sam's face scrunched up as if in pain. "Why, moron? So it can kill us later?"

"He looks too weak to do us any harm, let alone kill us. Besides," said Kevin, "he may be able to tell us something—like where we are." He could see Sam's resolve breaking down like a sandcastle against the incoming tide. "Things that might help our survival."

Sam sighed and lowered her weapon. "Fine," she said finally. "But this thing is your responsibility. If I wake up in the middle of the night with this thing gnawing at my bones and sucking up my marrow, I'm gonna kill it first and you second. You got that?"

Kevin nodded.

"Okay, and remember, this thing's your responsibility. I want no part of it. If he, she or it can't walk, you're going to have to carry it. And if it needs to get up and go to the bathroom in the middle of the night, you're gonna have to take the thing out on potty patrol."

"Yes, Mom."

Sam snarled. "So what are you waiting for, moron? Grab your new pet and let's make some time. Put some distance between us and your best friend, Jason."

"What for?" growled Kevin, falling in beside her like some pathetic pup.

He'd picked up Sigma Six and carried him easily under one arm. The alien was surprisingly light, as if filled with helium. So far, Sigma Six, if that who it was, had made no attempt to communicate with them. Kevin was still only half-certain that the creature was even alive. After all, it wasn't a human, he had no means of judging whether this thing was living or dead. Only time would tell.

"I mean, it's not like we even know where we're going, what we're going to find or what we're going to do with whatever it is we do find whenever we get to wherever it is we end up."

Sam stopped in her tracks and put her arm out. Kevin walked right into her. "You're giving me a headache, dude. Are you always this negative?"

"Yeah," said Kevin, honestly. "That's always been a part of my problem."

"No wonder the damn aliens didn't want you," Sam said. "You really are defective."

"What about you?" asked Kevin, huffing. Sam had picked up the pace once again. "Did they get you like the rest of them? Like some sort of zombie? Or did you simply board one of their ships for laughs?" Kevin wasn't about to say so, but he wouldn't have put it past her.

"Neither," she answered, without stopping. "I'm just too smart for them. Too smart for all of them—human or otherwise. But," she added, "I'm also curious. I followed the pack of zombies, as you call them, to see what was going on."

Kevin wasn't sure how smart she was, but she certainly had bravado if what she said was true. But he kept these thoughts to himself and made no reply.

They walked in silence a ways until coming to a break in the trees crossed by a sandy path nearly three feet wide. Kevin shifted the alien creature to his opposite side. Carrying the alien turned out to be no more trouble than walking with a balloon. Kevin only hoped this balloon wouldn't pop when pricked by a sharp branch or rock.

"Which way now, boy scout?"

Kevin suggested left.

"Any particular reason?" Sam looked down the trail. It was impossible to see more than a half dozen yards in either direction.

"See the way these prints run and those ridges in the sand?"

"Yeah," said Sam, skeptically. She leaned in for a closer look. "So?"

It was Kevin's turn to smile. "So nothing," he said with a shrug and a fat grin on his face. "I went eenie meenie miney moe and the left won."

"Great," grumbled Sam, straightening, "serves me right asking an idiot for directions." Still, Kevin couldn't hide a smile as she turned left onto the path, holding her sword loosely at her side, scanning the brush and the treetops for hidden foes.

Kevin noted her wariness. "Are you really expecting trouble?"

She stared at him for the umpteenth time like he was some freak object washed up on the seashore. "You're kidding, right? I mean, has your life been anything but trouble since the last day you woke up on Planet Earth? Trouble is *all* I expect."

Kevin thought about the thousands of giant dead pasty

things lying back on the plain where he'd awoken, intermingled with the corpses of his human shipmates. The pasty aliens had a greenish crisscrossing of subcutaneous lines, an arterial system of some sort, he figured, that shone translucently and blood that quite evidently turned brown when spilled.

Was it them that he and his fellow earthlings had been flung across the universe to fight? Or were they only the first wave?

# 14

They followed the uneven sandy trail cautiously. A curious, sticky clear substance was sometimes in evidence mixed in with the sand. The annoying substance clung to their feet like epoxy and then stuck to their fingers when they tried to remove off. Both soon learned to leave it alone. It seemed to do no harm.

The ground rose slowly now and they could hear the sound of running water somewhere off to the right. But whatever river there was existed out of sight and they were sticking to the trail.

Rounding a curve, a chilling shriek from the branches above them froze them both in their tracks. They shared a quick quizzical look.

Before they even knew what was happening, a pack of howling quadrupeds, with faces and breath like jackals, pounced on them from the low hanging boughs.

Sam started swinging. The orange-furred beasts stood nearly four feet tall with lanky torsos and long, claw-like hands and feet. She took two of the beasts down to the two-foot level. They fell twitching and bleeding to the sand. She pulled out her gun and shot two more before a third sunk his teeth in her arm and another pounced on her back.

Sam shrieked in pain. "Help me, you idiot!"

She was too busy fighting for her very life to look at Kevin, but he knew there was only one idiot she could be referring to. Oddly, the beasts had left him and the limp alien he carried alone so far. Whether this was due to the fact that he hadn't moved a muscle and they mistook him for a peculiar tree, while Sam, on the other hand, had been moving actively, or the creatures simply viewed him as a lesser threat and so hadn't bothered to attack him yet, he couldn't say. Nor was he going to complain.

Sam, her sword drooping clumsily in her left hand, tried to reach the animal on her back, all the while attempting to shake off another on her right arm. "Kevin!" she screeched impatiently.

As if awakened from a dream, Kevin responded to the urgent crying of his name. He dropped the alien to the ground where it lay listless. Racing towards Sam, he grabbed the beast on her back with both hands even as it wrapped its long-fingered hands around her neck and squeezed her throat.

Sam gasped and said with a cough. "K-kill it—"

"Huh?"

"I said kill it, damn you!"

"But I never—"

"Now!" she gasped.

Kevin grabbed the short dagger in his belt and bit his lip. He plunged the knife up to its hilt into the beast's back and winced as if he'd just committed hari-kari.

The beast cried horribly and fell writhing to the ground. Sam sank weakly to her knees. She managed to smash the beast clutching her arm across its face with the flat of her sword. She felt her flesh ripping away as its teeth only stubbornly released their grip on her. The dazed creature spun in a circle, and she skewered the hideous thing before it could attack again or even think about escape.

Sam sobbed. That was the last of them.

"You're bleeding," said Kevin. That was an understatement. Sam was bleeding copiously from her arm and her neck.

She looked him up and down appraisingly. "You're not." With that, her eyes rolled up until only the whites showed and she fell to the ground face first.

Kevin rushed to her side. "Sam!" He felt her neck for a pulse and was relieved to discover she was alive, but perhaps only barely. Who knew how serious her wounds were or what infections might creep in on this alien world?

# 15

When she woke, Kevin was half asleep beside her. Some watchdog, she thought. She shook her head in disgust and immediately regretted the move—the pain it caused was intense.

The alien he'd been dragging along sat slumped against the trunk of a tree. It seemed to be watching her. So it was alive. The animals that attacked her and Kevin hadn't laid a finger on the creature. Why?

Then she noticed the tiny creature against Kevin's shoulder. It was a miniature version of the nasty creatures that had attacked them both and almost killed her. She painfully, slowly tested her arm. No problem. Stealthily, one eye on the little devil, she reached for her knife. She had to kill the thing before it struck. Its cold, yellow eyes followed her movements but the thing did not react. She cocked her arm and thrust straight into its chest.

But it wasn't there. The beastly thing had leapt atop Kevin's head. Kevin threw open his eyes and screamed at the sight of Sam aiming a sharp knife at him. "What are you doing?!" He winced, half out of fear that Sam was about to puncture his heart, half out of the pain the little bugger digging its nails into his scalp was causing.

"Killing it, you big baby. What do you think? Now sit still," she said, coming closer. She made a grab for the orange-furred creature. It easily dodged down beneath Kevin's armpit.

Sam scowled. "You're toast, fur ball!" The scowl morphed to a smile. "And I do mean toast. What do you say," she glanced up at Kevin, "fresh-roasted alien on a spit? Breakfast, anyone?"

She grabbed for it again. Kevin thrust out a hand and blocked her. "Quit that." He scolded. "You're scaring him!"

Sam's jaw fell. "Scaring? Him? What's wrong with you? You get bitten by one of these things?"

She looked warily at Kevin. "Don't tell me one of them did bite you? This one?" she said, pointing her knife at the cowering little fur ball. "Turned you into some sort of zombie, huh?" She nodded knowingly. "I should have figured. Aliens are like that." She edged closer. "Did you know that the earth has been populated with zombies since the time of the Black Plague?"

Kevin's brow dug deep.

"It's true. One of the first truly massive social experiments. It wasn't a plague at all. Of course, the government doesn't want us to know that. The hollow world government, that is."

"The hollow—" Kevin started to respond, then thought better of it.

Sam nodded. "And it's only a myth that they are afraid of the light." She made a half-hearted grab for the fur ball again and missed. "That's only vampires." She studied Kevin's neck and bare arms. "You sure this thing didn't jab you with some sort of alien mind control poison?"

Kevin wondered what she was talking about. Had she lost her mind? Had loss of blood left her delirious? She was making him nervous. "Of course not. Don't be ridiculous. And put that knife away." He swatted her forearm.

For a moment, he thought he was in trouble as her eyes grew large and her body tensed, but then she relaxed and lowered her knife.

"Freaking zombie," she sighed, wiping the blade along her naked thigh, all the while making threatening eyes at the scaled-down version of the creatures that had attacked and nearly killed her. She held out her lacerated arm accusingly. "You do remember what this little bugger's cousins did to me, don't you?"

"I remember." Kevin scooted away on his knees—to protect himself perhaps as much as the harmless seeming creature. "It's only a scratch."

"Only a scratch?! Rotten thing nearly bit my arm off. Now you're trying to make another pet out of it! It's bad enough we're dragging around the useless butt of the alien responsible for our being here in the first place!" Her face was livid.

"I'm sure it didn't mean it."

"Didn't mean—"

"Sure, you know. Probably just instinct."

"Oh, lord." She shook her head at the two of them. "You really are one screwed up moron."

Kevin grinned from ear to ear. "What can I say? I'm a defective, remember?"

Sam laughed. "Do I ever. And don't think I'll ever forget."

Kevin had never heard her laugh so genuinely, generally it was with a strong current of mockery and disgust. A regular river of rude attitude.

Sam reached a finger out to the creature. It had settled into Kevin's lap, its tiny hands clutching his shirt. "You two are pathetic." The little thing licked her finger and she flinched, afraid he was about to make a snack of her. But he merely licked a couple of times then fell back in Kevin's lap. "You called it a him. What makes you so sure it is a him? I mean, it could be a girl. Or, considering it is an alien, it could be an it."

"I don't know." Kevin shrugged. "I can just tell. That's all."

"Ooo-kay." She rolled her eyes and rubbed her forearm. "Thanks for bandaging the arm, by the way."

"No problem. Are you going to be okay?"

By answer, she stood. "Don't worry about me. We need to get going. Who knows how long it will be before nightfall around here and we don't want to be anywhere near here if those thugs from the ship come back for us." She pointed her sword tip at the small creature, "Or if any more of these things come raining down upon us. We'll need some sort of shelter before dark for protection. From the elements and the enemy."

"Fine," replied Kevin. "But first we've got to bury Huxley's family."

"Huh? Huxley?"

"Yes, you know."

Sam looked perplexed.

"It's a brave new world?"

Sam shook her head.

"Maybe I should have called him Cheetah," grumbled Kevin.

"In the first place," Sam said, crossing her arms, "you watch way too many movies. You know they plant subliminal messages in those things, don't you?"

Before he could reply, she continued "In the second place, I am not going to be your Jane. And," she said even more sternly, "I am not going to help you bury these-these things," she sputtered.

"Huxley it is," said Kevin, stroking little Huxley's belly. "Suit yourself, Sam." He'd been very tempted to say Jane, but wasn't fully convinced she wouldn't lop his head off with that silly sword of hers or bifurcate his tongue or some other equally important body part for doing so. "But I am not leaving here until these guys have had some sort of proper burial. I feel sort of responsible."

"You are *sort of* responsible. But hell, they were sort of," she said, making hash marks with her fingers, "responsible, too."

Kevin shrugged off her comments and started looking for a good spot to begin digging. In the end, the ground proved too hard and stubborn for them. They didn't have the proper tools to deal with all the solid rock they kept running into just beneath the surface.

He and Sam settled for piling stones atop the corpses. "A cairn for the dead," said Kevin, solemnly.

Sam made a face. "For all we know, covering their furry hides is sacrilege in their religion—assuming the alien buggers have any religion."

Kevin wasn't letting her comment get under his skin, he'd done what he'd determined to do. Better still, for all her complaining, Sam had helped him. Under all that electric blue hair and vibrantly-colored tattoos there just might reside a girl with a heart.

Kevin said a prayer for Huxley's brethren and their souls.

Though he'd never said a prayer before in his life, it seemed the right thing to do at the time.

Sam said a prayer for Kevin's goofy brains. It got her wondering about this oddball character who had through no wish of her own become her travelling companion on this crazy journey.

# 16

"So," she asked, wiping off the muck that had gathered on her hands as she'd collected stones for Kevin's ridiculous cairn. His pet, Huxley, had stood by without so much as lifting a finger to help. Same for that Sigma Six character. Typical lazy alien buttheads.

"So what?"

"So what did you do back there?"

"Back where?"

She tilted her head in the direction from which they'd come.

"Oh." He thought a moment. "Nothing."

"Nothing?"

"We fell out of the sky, I passed out and the next thing I know I'm waking up lying in a field of dead, butchered bodies."

"No, moron. Not back there. *Before*," she said, emphatically. She started up the trail of their interrupted journey. "On Earth, dumb-dumb."

"Oh, Earth?" He said the word as if it named a magical land that might never have existed. She nodded and he replied without pause. "Answer's the same—nothing."

"Everybody does something." Sam twisted her neck and shot him a look. Kevin kept pace, Huxley riding on his left shoulder. Sigma Six was now managing to walk on his own. She thought Kevin looked like some whacked out outer space pirate with limp-along first mate and a fur ball for a sidekick instead of a parrot.

"Not me. I didn't do anything."

"What do you mean you didn't do anything?"

"You mean like a job, right?"

She nodded.

"Well, I didn't have one. I didn't do anything."

"So what exactly did you do all the time, veg out?"

Kevin planted his feet mechanically, one after the other, in silence. He reached up and petted his newfound companion. "Nothing much. Mostly I walked around."

"Walked around?"

"Yeah. Just walked around."

"Ooo-kay," she said, drawing the word out like she'd pulled it out of an antique church organ.

"What about you?" he inquired, obviously wishing to change the subject.

"I'm a writer."

"Really?" Kevin liked books. "What have you written?"

"Lots of stuff."

"Give me some titles. Maybe I've read some of yours books."

"Nah. It's mostly investigative stuff."

"Investigative, huh? Sounds interesting."

"It is. But I can't get anyone to publish it. What I've got to say is too much truth for the world we live in. Stinking plutocratic state—plutocratic world! There's not a big publisher out there with the cajones to publish me." She spat. "Not even a small one."

True enough, thought Kevin, but nothing new. "Sorry."

"Don't be. I stick it all up on the web. Still, maybe if people had listened to me, and others like me, a million or more of our scrawny butts wouldn't have been scooped up and dumped here on Planet Death.

"What do you mean? You knew this would happen?" How could she?

"Oh yeah. I knew."

"About the aliens?"

"Oh, I know all about the aliens. They've been watching us for a million years." She stopped and looked Kevin in the eyes. "From the moon."

Kevin's confusion showed.

"It's hollow. One freaking massive space station disguised as a rock. And they watch our every move. Yeah," she said, tapping her skull with a fingertip, "I know a lot of things. The things I could tell. If anybody would listen."

"I'm listening."

She told him how the aliens listened and observed everything the earthlings did, from what they ate for dinner to how they tied their shoes and screwed one another, both in bed and in business.

"In the meantime," she added, bitterly, "I serve drinks at a bar in Greenwich, keep the bloated rich sotting drunk."

Could she be right? Was the moon a hollowed out rock cum space station? Were telescopes and listening devices being aimed at them around the clock?

"I always thought," said Kevin, "that if I was still doing nothing by the time I was sixty years old that I'd learn to play the saxophone."

"Become a musician?"

"No. Just stand on the street corner and play it. Badly, probably."

"They destroyed Atlantis, you know."

"Huh, who did?" Atlantis—was that even a real place?

"The aliens in the moon. Haven't you been listening?"

"Oh, yeah. The aliens in the moon." His words sounded as hollow as the moon she described. Were those the aliens that had kidnapped them?

"That's right. You see, the people of Atlantis were getting too smart, too fast. Sooner or later the aliens figured the Atlanteans were bound to figure out what was going on on the moon and discover the aliens watching them. So they had to go."

"The aliens killed them?"

"Destroyed their entire civilization," replied Sam. "The Atlanteans had come here from Titan. That's one of Saturn's moons. It's mostly water ice. The Atlanteans thrived there until their ecology went wacky." She waved away a bug. "Who knows why. Anyhow, they came here on a fleet of ships and built Atlantis on what was then the edge of the great sea."

She stared into Kevin's eyes. "But the extra-solar aliens, the guys inside the moon, they didn't like it. Like I said, I figure they were afraid they'd be discovered or that the Atlanteans would become too strong.

"So," she said, glibly, "they wiped them off the face of the earth. Drowned them in the ocean. It's all in my book, *The Rise and Fall of Atlantis*," she added, nonchalantly. "It's part of a series I did."

"Your book?" Kevin was getting lost in her words, a forest of darkness and confusion, paranoia maybe.

"It's all true."

"I believe you." He wasn't sure he did, but it seemed the right thing to say.

"No, that's the title of the series. *It's All True*. The history of Atlantis is one of the books in that series. I've written lots of books, actually, but the one where I discuss things like the aliens is called *It's All True*. The other two titles are *You've Been Drugged* and an expose on how the church conspired with the world government to trap God in an antimatter flask and rule the universe in his or *her*," she said with emphasis, as if daring Kevin to disagree with her use of the pronoun, "stead. I called it *The God Gambit*.

"You see," she said, her voice dropping to a whisper though there was no one around to overhear, "everything you ever heard, all those crazy conspiracy theories?"

Kevin nodded.

"They are *all* true. They ALL happened. Ancient alien invasions and visitations, Loch Ness monsters, the Kennedy mob-Russian assassination connection, engines that will run forever without a drop of gasoline, tires that will never wear out, even if you drive a million miles—"

Kevin asked, "The Holy Grail? Dragons?"

"Hey, don't kid around. Dragons used to be real, moron. If you could find a fossilized dragon egg, I'd bet you could conjure one up in a lab. Hey," she said, cocking her head, "who knows? The Chinese might be doing that in secret right now, for all we know."

Kevin nodded and grunted occasionally as they marched to let Sam know he was listening as she prattled on, expounded one crazy conspiracy theory after the other.

The path soon spilled out onto a broad rolling savannah. "Look." Kevin pointed to a long dusty line near the horizon.

"What is it?" Sam shaded her eyes with her hand.

"Something or someone is moving."

"Yeah, more like somethings or someones. There are a heck of a lot of them."

The line seemed to extend for miles. They were moving to the left, based on the way the dust was rising and settling. "Could be humans." As much as Kevin had never particularly cared for his own species, he found himself hoping so.

"Could be. We'll have to intersect their line and follow them from a distance until we figure out who or what they are." Sam crouched and slid down into a dry creek bed.

She looked up at Kevin. "Stay low. With luck, we can follow their trail from here. It should bring us close enough to see who or what we're dealing with. This dried up creek seems to go in that direction."

Her plan worked well for the first hundred yards or so when Sam let out a squeal. "Hey!" Something brown, multi-legged and sharp-toothed was clinging to her ankle. Some sort of mud lizard. She hacked it away with her dagger but before it hit the ground there was another to take its place.

Three more popped out of nowhere and swarmed her like bloated, misshapen toads. "I could use a hand here, moron!"

But Kevin had troubles of his own. The lizards were crawling all over him and for each one he killed, two more seemed to take its place.

Sigma Six appeared to be holding his own. A blue glow emanated from his body extending out six inches from his skin from head to toe. The critters bounced off it screaming in agony and quickly learned to ignore the big alien.

Huxley was screeching and bouncing from shoulder to

shoulder, sometimes blocking Kevin's view. "It's the creek bed," said Kevin. "I think our walking in it is stirring them up!"

Sam nodded grimly and fought her way up the side of the bank. Kevin was close at her heels. The mud lizards clung to them like blood-swelled leeches. But in a few tense moments they'd managed to destroy the last of them.

And no more followed. Kevin's hunch appeared to be correct. The lizards did not seem to want to leave the creek.

"I think it's time for plan B," Kevin said, sponging blood—his blood—off his arms with a scrap from his tattered shirt.

"Sure," agreed Sam, cleaning her own wounds with sand. Only Huxley appeared uninjured. Either he was too small for their taste or they didn't go in for monkey alien meat. "You got one?"

"You sure that stuff's sanitary?" Kevin asked, ignoring her question, and wincing as his shirt scraped over a nasty scratch.

"I'm not sure if any lousy thing on this planet is sanitary. Let alone this sand. Any single molecule of this place could be viral to us. Could be poison. Could be turning us into marrow sucking leeches.

"We could be as good as dead already, our clocks ticking, simply from breathing this frigging air. But what the heck," she said with a grin the Kevin thought looked altogether too crazy, "we're probably good as dead anyway."

# 17

Staying low and moving stealthily, Kevin, Sam and company followed the caravan for many hours as the sky turned from orange to red to black. When the caravan stopped for the night, so did Kevin and Sam. Kevin was all for starting a fire. If tonight was a repeat of the last night, it was going to be near freezing, made worse by the frigid twenty to thirty mile per hour winds that had kicked up as night fell.

Sam vetoed the idea. "We have no idea how far the flames might be seen or how good their alien eyes are."

"We still don't know they are aliens. Let alone enemies."

"Fine. Take a chance. Light a fire. Light yourself on fire and go running up the hill to them brandishing a torch in each hand for all I care."

Kevin rolled his eyes in the dark. Sam could be the queen of melodrama. The sound of falling stones and earth stopped their argument. Kevin looked up. A dark shape was sliding and tumbling down the hill towards them.

The dark shape turned into a human figure followed by a seven-foot, four-legged manner of beast that ran easily down the hill on four human-like legs.

Sam pulled her gun. Kevin jumped to his feet clutching his knife.

"Hey, careful! I surrender!"

It was a human voice. And it sounded vaguely familiar. "Lance? Is that you?" A wicked snarl cut the air like a rusty knife.

Lance, half-running, half-falling, yelled, "We've got company! Run!"

"Run, hell." Sam planted her feet and fired several rounds

into the approaching creature. It slumped to the ground, legs twitching.

Lance sighed loudly. "Thanks, dude." He twisted his long hair into a knot, then turned to Kevin and draped his hands over Kevin's shoulders. "Hey, Kevin, my man. Good to see you, bro."

Kevin stepped back. He needed his personal space. "Lance, it is you. What are you doing here? How did you get here?"

"Never mind all that. No time for explanations," replied Lance, glancing nervously over his shoulder.

"Make time," said Sam.

"Chill, dude."

"And stop calling me *dude* or I'll empty the rest of these cartridges in your mouth."

"Oh," said Lance, apparently only now recognizing his mistake as he looked Sam over. "My apologies, milady. Tis quite dark this night and I did not recognize thy beauty. But," he said, pointing to the four-legged carcass whose legs were still twitching as if it was not quite ready to face death yet or perhaps that death itself was not a good enough reason to give up the hunt, "you see that thing?"

Sam cocked an eyebrow and aimed her gun at his fat lips.

"Well, there are about six of his buddies not far behind. And I don't think they're interested in joining us in singing campfire tunes and eating peanut butter Girl Scout cookies."

Sam growled and ordered them to move out. She snatched up her meager belongings.

Lance was softly whistling. She recognized the tune as *Momma Told Me Not To Come*. She'd have shot him for making so much racket, but the tune was just too damn apropos.

They flew through the darkness. The sounds of blood lust snarling chased after them like a menacing shadow beast.

"There's no way we're going to outrun them," gasped Sam.

"Yeah? Well, there's no way you're gonna kill all the things either," said Lance.

Sam wasn't so sure. After all, she'd killed one already. How hard could it be? They'd reached the edge of a body of dark water.

How big and how deep, there was no way of telling. And it was too dark to even venture a guess.

Sam was about to say they had a choice to make—fight the four-foots or risk being swallowed up in the big black sea, but Lance was already splashing his way into the unknown.

Sam planted her feet at the water's edge and turned to make her stand. She yelled at Lance to get back.

Kevin hesitated at the edge, but when little Huxley jumped off his back and darted with a small splash into the water, Kevin followed suit. Sigma Six waded in after him, barely stirring up a ripple. "Come on, Sam. Hurry!"

"Are you all nuts? You don't know what's out there. Could be prehistoric-type giant killer fish with razor-sharp teeth!"

The snarling was growing to a frenzied roar in the darkness and she began to make out large blurry black shapes coming towards her. "Get your butts back here and help me, cowards!" But she wasn't feeling so sure of herself, or their chances.

Kevin waded out to Lance. Huxley leapt from Lance's leg to Kevin's chest. "Come on, Sam," Kevin urged. "Look, Huxley jumped into the water. He must know something we don't. Something about the water and something about those creatures."

A black blur on four legs flew at Sam and she jumped out of the way and into the water.

The thing's talons dragged across the air, passing so close to her cheek that she felt the air move. A cold chill ran through her. That was close, too close.

Kevin called out, "Sam, you okay?"

She said she was fine but backed up another yard into the water. Several of the things barked at her from the water's edge. But they didn't follow. "I think they're afraid of the water."

"Not me," said Lance, with a tremble. And it wasn't from the icy waters. "I think they're afraid of that."

Kevin turned. A mass of heavily armed warriors swarmed the opposite bank. A half dozen or so were sloshing towards them like black demons. They appeared alien. They sure as hell weren't human. He squinted but couldn't make them out clearly. Friend or foe?

"Rock," mumbled Sam, "meet hard place."

One of the aliens opened fire with a small blue weapon of some sort. A flash of white light was followed by a whistling noise. Lance screamed and ducked under the water but there was no need. A thick stream of fire flew over their heads terminating in a ball of flame that exploded over the heads of the four-footers. They turned and scattered into the blackness from which they had come.

One of the aliens waded further out, approached them, and gestured with his weapon for them to follow.

Rather than be charbroiled, Sam suggested that they follow. Kevin tried talking to the alien but no response was forthcoming. In fact, none of the aliens attempted to speak to them. They only barely spoke to one another.

The bank rose steadily on the opposite side, then leveled off as they marched. Flaming torches tied to rough-hewn posts showed them to have entered a camp of sorts. Nearly a dozen dull gray tents stood under the canopy of trees. Off to the left stood a wooden rack from which some unrecognizable skins had been stretched out to dry.

Kevin could only hope they weren't human skins.

As they entered the camp, those within stopped and glared at them. There was a lot of jabbering but it was all incomprehensible to them. Their captors seemed to take a special interest in Sigma Six.

"What do you think they're saying?" asked Sam.

"I don't have a clue," replied Kevin.

"That's talking? Sounds more like somebody's slamming both their elbows down on the lower octaves of a piano." Lance clapped his hands over his ears. "And it's driving me nuts. How can you two stand it?"

The alien who'd jumped into the water towards them first appeared to be the group's leader. He disappeared into one of the larger gray tents on the left and the flap fell shut behind him.

Kevin and the others remained where they stood, afraid to move, surrounded by the armed band of aliens who'd brought them in.

These aliens were different from any they'd encountered before. Tall and thin, not one of them stood under seven feet tall and none appeared over eight foot. Their skin was the color of red maple and they all wore layers of jewelry around their sticklike necks. Their dark blue clothing appeared to be uniforms, with small gold insignia of uncertain meaning in the center of their chests. But these uniforms were dirty and in tatters, as if they had been fighting long and hard.

Whatever these creatures were, they were not the same aliens whose corpses they'd seen scattered across the battlefield. What that meant and whether it portended good or bad, there was no telling.

Soon the tent flap lifted and their captor strode out followed by an eight-foot creature with waist-length black dreadlocks. He leaned on a gnarled stick for support and wore a similar uniform, torn off just below the knees.

The two figures stopped in front of the humans and conversed among themselves. All the while, the creature with the stick kept its eyes on them.

Kevin shifted nervously.

"Holy Bob Marley," whispered Lance. "Who does that guy think he is? Some sort of intergalactic Rastafarian or something?"

"Shut up," hissed Sam. "How do you know he can't understand you? You could be insulting his honor or his religion or something. You want to get us all killed over some stupid comment of yours?"

"Oh, please," said Lance. "Maybe I'll just ask him if he's got any good ganja."

"Fine. Insult him. Insult his religion. It's not like anybody's ever gotten angry and killed somebody because of something so minor as that," she said snidely.

It was a good point and Lance took it.

The alien who'd brought them into camp motioned for them to follow and they did. The tall creature with the stick bent its bony form, holding the tent flap open with his back. Using the stick, he indicated for them to enter.

Kevin stepped forward.

"What are you doing, moron?" Sam looked mortified. "You have no idea what that thing is going to do to you in there!"

"Sam, we have no idea what these creatures are going to do to us if we remain out here." He disappeared in the dark opening with Huxley clinging to his side.

"Sonofa—Come on!" Sam grabbed Lance by the arm and, despite his protests and struggle, shoved him through the door with her.

# 18

The floor was bare and the interior smelled as musty as his grandmother's old fourth floor walkup with its windows that had been frozen shut for forty-one solid years. His grandfather had jumped out of one of those windows to the street below and an instant death and his widow had had the windows nailed shut afterward, never to be opened again until her death forty-one years later. If she'd come through the tent flap just then carrying a tray laden with sugar cookies, Kevin would not have been surprised. Come to think on it, it would have been quite nice. He could use a good sugar cookie about now.

Sigma Six collapsed to the ground. The alien looked more pale than ever.

"You okay?" asked Kevin, not really expecting an answer.

"Time stops soon."

Kevin gasped. "I-I wasn't even sure you were alive."

"Without my Other, I am not. I shall pass soon. The Other supports me. The Other is necessary to my survival."

"What are you doing down here, anyway?" demanded Sam. "Decide to see how the other half lives?"

He looked at her a moment in silence. "One of you humans attached itself to me. We fell together before others could intervene."

Sam snorted.

"Tough break," said Lance, without compassion.

"Who are you, anyway?" Kevin asked softly. "Why have you brought us here to this planet?"

"I do not bring you here. Beings greater than I are responsible for this. I am but their servant." Sigma Six let out what Kevin could only consider an alien sigh. "Back when your universe was young, your world like many others was seeded. What you call mitochondria was introduced into the cells of your bodies. When your race, like so many others, reaches a level of development and in sufficient numbers, you are collected."

Lance scratched his head. "Mitoc-what?"

"Mitochondria," spat Sam. "Fucking organelles. I should have known." She snapped her fingers. "It's so simple. I should have seen it. To fight your stupid battles, am I right?"

Kevin smelled another conspiracy theory coming on.

But Sigma Six nodded. "It is a long, hard war. The war for this region of space consumes many. You had no choice but to come when called. It is in your genes. I am merely a collector. One of many."

"What region of space exactly are you talking about?" Kevin asked.

"As I stated aboard the vessel, you would call it the Boötes Void. Though it has not always been such a void. It was once populated with millions of stars." Sigma Six shifted against the ground. "Many stars have been consumed in the waging of war as well."

"Great," muttered Lance. "They drag our asses out here to some godforsaken empty space to fight a bunch of Booties, whatever the hell they are, in some freaking intergalactic turf war!"

"Be quiet, Lance. How do we get out of here?" Kevin asked Sigma Six softly. "How do we get home?"

Sigma Six's red eyes pulsed silently for a moment before he answered.

The tent flap flew open and two of their alien captors approached silently. One of the two grabbed Sigma Six by the arm and pulled the alien to its feet.

"Hey!" shouted Kevin.

"Let it be," warned Sam. "You want them to grab you, too?"

Kevin looked from Sigma Six to Sam. "We don't even know what they want with the thing," Sam said. "Maybe they're going to crown him their new king. I mean, they've probably never seen anything like him before. He could be like their god."

The two captors led Sigma Six away and the tent flap dropped down behind them.

"I could use a sugar cookie. I bet you could use one, too," Kevin cooed, stroking Huxley's furry hide.

"So, looks like it's just us" said Lance, slinking across the floor towards Sam. "It's dark, it's quiet. We're practically alone." He shot a look at Kevin's shadowy hunched-over shape. Kevin appeared lost in his own sugar cookie mind. "What do you say we make the best of things?"

"What?"

"I mean—if you can't be with the one you love..." He left the rest of the lines unsung.

But Sam knew her oldies, though she preferred them with a little twist. "Then kill the one you're with," she said, her voice flat.

Lance frowned as Sam slid over to Kevin. "Who the hell is this guy and can't we feed him to the natives as some sort of tribute and get our butts out of here?"

"Sam," said Kevin, with a wave of his hand, "meet Lance. Lance meet Sam."

"A true pleasure to meet you, sweet thing." Lance thrust out his right hand.

"You want me to slice that stumpy hand off or bite it off one finger at a time, sleazeball? Your call."

"Whoa, touchy, aren't we?" Lance snatched his hand back quickly. "I'd say I'd prefer the biting option but you appear to be much too literal, dear. Besides," he added with evident affront, "what do you mean calling my fingers stumpy?" He looked at his hands with admiration. "I've got great hands, long fingers. I'm a musician, you know."

"Well, fa-la-la." She turned once more to Kevin. "Really, Kevin, I mean, who *is* this guy? How is it you even *know* him?"

"We met aboard ship. Lance is a defective, like me."

"No kidding," snorted Sam.

"He's not so bad, Sam."

"Yeah, he's not so bad, Sam," echoed Lance.

"Shut up, will you?"

"Hey, give me a chance. To know me is to love me."

"Oh, brother." Once more she looked to Kevin, her knife drawn. "Couldn't I just run him through a little bit?" She tossed the blade deftly from hand to hand. Lance watched with worried eyes. Clearly he thought she was nuts. Which she didn't mind one bit.

"Careful with that thing, Sam," cautioned Kevin.

"Yeah," whined Lance. "No kidding around now. What is it with you and that pigsticker? I mean, it's practically the twenty-second century, who carries a freaking dagger? Who do you think you are—the freaking Empress of the Eastern Empire?"

Sam lunged at him and Kevin held her back. "Quiet, both of you. Do you want to draw more attention to us?"

"In case you haven't realized it yet, moron," said Sam, "I think we've already got their attention."

"So," said Lance, "I see it's not just me."

"What do you mean?" asked Kevin.

"I mean our friend Sam here abuses everybody."

"Listen, maggot, I've already warned you—"

"If you two would shut up for one minute," growled Kevin. "I'm trying to tell you both something."

Sam let out a long, slow breath in an obvious attempt to calm herself. "What is it, Kevin?"

"If you two would stop bickering long enough you would have realized what I realize."

"We're waiting," hissed Sam, never one for patience. And the whole calming down thing was obviously not working.

"No one is guarding us. We are all alone here," Kevin stated emphatically. He folded his arms over his chest smugly. The big alien had simply held the flap as they entered then retreated. "Who or what is to stop us from pulling up the back edge of this stinking tent and sneaking out of here?"

To prove his point, Kevin lifted the back edge of the tent about six inches off the ground.

"Careful," Lance and Sam said simultaneously.

"Don't worry," said Kevin. "No alarms went off. No whistles. No barking dogs."

To prove his point, he sprawled out on the ground and stuck his head outside. Holding his breath and praying he didn't get his head chopped off or shot off, he waited for his eyes to adjust to the darkness. Except for a glowing cube of light atop a tree stump near a tent similar to their own about twenty yards to his right, there was no other illumination but that feeble light coming from the scattered stars above. He strained his ears, listening. It was weird how few stars there were in this alien sky.

"Well?" demanded Sam.

"Shh. I'm trying to listen." He slipped back inside. "The coast's clear and the woods isn't ten feet from this side of the tent. I'm for getting out of here. Who's with me?" Without waiting for an answer, he scooped up Huxley and shimmied under the fabric of the tent with a slight rustling sound that he hoped wouldn't attract their captors.

Sam quietly gathered up their gear and followed after him.

"Hey," whispered Lance, "you guys crazy?" He watched Sam's feet disappear under the canvas. As much as he thought it was nuts to go running out into an unknown jungle full of unknown dangers, he hesitated only a moment before running after them.

After all, they were the only humans within miles. Better to take his chances with them than some oddball looking critters who might consider his eyeballs something of a delicacy.

"Wait for me," he said, scrambling out of the back of the tent on his hands and knees.

Kevin skirted around the edge of the camp. A large group of their captors stood around several of the glowing cubes he'd seen as they'd been brought into camp. In the center stood Sigma Six. The big alien with the walking stick was jabbering at him and waving his stick.

"What's going on?" whispered Lance.

Sam told him to keep his mouth shut. "You want them to

hear us? And keep your head down."

"Do you think that Sigma Six character is a friend of theirs?" Lance asked, ignoring Sam's order to keep quiet.

"I wonder," Kevin replied, quietly pulling down the low branch obstructing his view. The large alien pointed at a shorter version of himself and waved him forward. The creature bore something in his hands that looked like a cross between a single-barreled shotgun and a light saber.

"What is that thing?" Lance asked.

"I don't like the looks of this," Sam said, pulling at her lower lip. Kevin noticed her right hand reaching for her own weapon.

The large alien grabbed the long barreled object. He held it waist high in Sigma Six's direction. Sigma Six stood silently unmoving. A sudden bright burst of platinum light shot noiseless from the tip of the device.

Kevin lurched forward. "No!"

Sam pulled him back down hard. "Quiet, moron! Do you want to be next?" She shook him and held him to the ground, one dirty hand firmly over his mouth. "Because I don't."

Kevin watched. All in one instant the platinum light had flashed out in an egg-shaped pattern. Sigma Six dissolved before their eyes. Kevin twisted and struggled to pull free but Sam was having none of it. "There's nothing you can do."

She stared into his eyes and slowly removed her hand from his mouth. "Nothing. Besides, he's responsible for us being here in the first place. Good riddance."

"Yeah," muttered Lance. An involuntary cough erupted from his throat and several of the aliens ceased their murmurings and looked the tiny groups' way.

They held their breath. "Come on," said Sam, her voice barely a whisper. "We can't stay here any longer."

Huxley had chittered madly and fled into the jungle when the alien fired its weapon. Kevin decided that now would be a good time to follow. He pushed through the stiff brambles hoping the noise wouldn't raise any sentinels. He heard Sam and Lance at his heels. He really had no idea where he was going but followed the path of least resistance—hoping it wouldn't lead to their recapture.

Sharp-edged leaves lacerated their arms and faces but they feared stopping on the chance that their captors were close behind. He'd watched Sigma Six die. It was not the way he wanted to die. Besides, he had not found Sarah and Quinn yet.

He couldn't die.

# 19

It was towards morning and the orange sun was rising to their left when Lance decided he couldn't take it any longer. He collapsed against a granite boulder. "That's it," he said. "I've had it. We must have walked a hundred miles."

"More likely five," countered Sam.

"Whatever," said Lance. "I'm beat and if those brutes are looking for us, fine. They can have me. I'm pooped."

"They may not even realize we're gone yet," said Kevin. "Maybe they won't bother to look in the tent till morning. In which case, we've got an excellent start on them." He scanned the woods. All was quiet.

"Yeah," said Sam. "Maybe they'll come looking for us for breakfast—their breakfast."

"Big friggin' deal." Lance sprawled across the ground and drizzled water over his scraped and dirty face.

"You want to get caught?" Sam asked. "You didn't seem so keen on it last night when I stopped those four-leggers from making a midnight snack of you."

"Yeah, well. I'm beginning to have second thoughts." Lance propped himself back up. "I mean, what the hell are we going to do now?" He looked from one to the other. "Have either of you given even a minute's thought to that question?"

He didn't wait for an answer. "I mean, we don't even know where the hell in the universe we are. I mean, Sigma Six and all that alien crap about mito-mitocodia—"

"Mitochondria," Kevin corrected.

Lance waved his hand. "Yeah, whatever. Mitocs, Booties... what the hell!" His eyes danced with fatigue and maybe a hint of madness. "Freaking gobbledy-gook! All we know is that some crazy aliens dropped us here on this dirtball," he slammed his fist against the ground, "to fight their enemy. Dropped us like some cheap, disposable bug bomb. Use once, then discard." He let loose a long string of invective punctuated with the sound of his open palm slapping the granite boulder. "Face it, we're lost." Lance grimaced. "Screwed." He faced Kevin. "Don't you see? What are we going to do next? Run around this awful planet until something catches up to us and kills us because it thinks we're the enemy? Or maybe decides to eat us because it thinks we look tasty?"

"It may not even be aliens," said Sam.

Kevin smothered a groan as he plopped to the ground.

"What?" said Sam. "I mean, he's slime, but he does make a good point."

Lance stopped. "Huh?"

"I mean, this could all be a conspiracy."

Lance appeared dumbfounded and his jaw dropped like the ramp of cargo plane preparing to unload.

"A government conspiracy." Sam waved her arms. "This could all be some secret bunker or we could all be hallucinating, high on some top secret drug. Being experimented on by our government."

Lance rolled his eyes. "Oh, brother."

All the while the two of them were ranting, Kevin was thinking. Finally, he spoke. "We have to find other humans."

"They're all dead," said Sam. "Remember? Except for Jason and that gang of hoodlums of his that tried to kill us."

A picture of the mad battlefield jumped into Kevin's brain and he pushed it out. "We don't know that. They can't all be dead." He shivered at the thought. *Please don't let them all be dead.* Not all of them, not those he loved.

"Of course they're not all dead," said Lance.

"What's that supposed to mean?" Sam grabbed Lance by the collar. "What are you holding back from us?"

"Hey," whimpered Lance. "I'm not holding anything back

on you guys. I mean, we've been kind of busy. Running from monsters , getting captured by aliens, running some more. And, I've got to say," he knocked Sam's hand away, "I'm getting a little tired of the way you talk to me."

"Stop whining and tell us already," replied Sam.

Huxley climbed into a thick, round bush with yellow-green leaves. He pulled slender purple carroty looking growths from the nearest branches and nibbled at them.

"Where are the people then?" Kevin asked softly. "Do you know?" Were his ex-wife and daughter among them?

Lance shrugged. "Yeah, I know. Sort of. The aliens captured some of us defectives. Took us to a city somewhere near here I reckon, though I can't be sure."

"A city?" said Sam. "A real city?" She seemed surprised that such a thing should exist out here in this strange region of the universe.

"Real enough," answered Lance.

Kevin asked, "Can you lead us there?"

Lance chewed his upper lip. "I don't know. I mean, this isn't New York and we've been running all over the place. And it was dark when I escaped."

Sam's eyes narrowed. "How *did* you escape?"

Lance avoided her eyes. "We were being held in a jail-like building. It got hit when the city was bombed. I got myself out in the confusion."

"What about the others?" Kevin wanted to know.

"I don't know," replied Lance.

"Oh, brother," said Sam.

"Hey," said Lance. "Like I said, it was dark, there was smoke, fire. It was every man for himself."

"I'll bet," said Sam, shaking her head. "You abandoned them there."

"Who was it?" asked Kevin. "Who was there with you? Tell me their names."

"Sequoia, Nicolette, Henry," Lance paused, "Gig and some guy named Xian."

Those were the defectives Kevin had been with aboard the alien ship. "Were there any other humans?" Like Sarah and Quinn?

Lance shook his head. "Not that I could see."

"We have to go to the city," said Sam. "How about it?" she asked Kevin.

Kevin said yes immediately. He'd already made up his mind to go whether the others followed him or not.

"Good." Sam kicked Lance's feet. "Come on, get up. You've had enough rest."

"Go back?" Lance rose to his feet, complaining. "I already told you—I don't think I can find the city again. You ever hear of the word disorientation?"

Sam took a step towards Lance. "I'm going to disorient your head from your—"

"Please," interrupted Kevin. Huxley offered him one of the orange fruit and absentmindedly he popped it into his mouth and bit into it. It tasted surprisingly sweet and he swallowed it with pleasure. "We have to try. Which way, Lance?"

The erstwhile musician looked slowly around the clearing.

"Well?" Sam said.

He shrugged. "I don't know. Could be that way," he said, pointing lamely to the right. "But I don't know. We've been running in circles all night and I was running in circles myself before that."

"Yeah, yeah. You've made that abundantly clear." Sam hurried to match step with Kevin who'd already taken off in the direction Lance had indicated. "Try to keep up," she told Lance.

Before long, they'd left the woods and were marching single file through an endless appearing expanse of neglected or abandoned farmlands. The horizon was doing strange things. Giant purple plasmalike monsters coalesced out of the air and set the earth to shaking like a sheet of cheap light gauge steel.

"I don't feel so good," announced Kevin. He was having a hard time maintaining his balance and his breathing was becoming more labored and pained with each step. He turned to see how

Sam and Lance were doing, but they had turned bright red and were grinning evilly at him.

# 20

When Kevin awoke, he was lying on his back with an unfamiliar sun staring down at him. His head throbbed like somebody was beating on the side of his skull with a wooden mallet.

His ears picked up the sound of loose pebbles and then Lance was kneeling over him. "What happened?" whispered Kevin, his throat dry and burning.

"You tell me. One minute we're walking along like it's Sunday in Central Park. The next thing we know, you're teetering over and then fall flat on your face."

Kevin struggled to his elbows. "Where are Huxley and Sam?"

"The little bugger is skittering around here someplace. Sam's reconnoitering. She'll be back soon." Lance shook himself. "That girl gives me the heebie-jeebies."

Kevin felt a wet nudge against his fingers. It was Huxley.

Lance handed Kevin the water flask and told him to drink.

Sam returned and said she'd found an abandoned farmhouse a couple of miles distant. She thought it was as good a place as any for them to get some rest. Even she had apparently reached her physical limits. "Think you can make it?"

"I guess so," answered Kevin. "I still feel a little woozy though."

"I warned you not to eat those magic carrots," retorted Sam.

"Is that what happened?" A vague memory of munching on some carroty thing Huxley'd handed him came to mind.

Sam nodded once.

"Well, you never told me."

Sam opened her mouth, then hesitated a moment. "Well, I

meant to," she snapped back.

"Besides, we don't know that's what made me ill."

"We don't know that they didn't, moron. And you're the only one flipping out and keeling over." She pulled him up. "Come on," she said, " the farmhouse is this way."

Kevin walked slowly, gingerly, as if the ground was nothing more than a thin, moving crust. Sam may have been right about the plant, but he wasn't about to tell her that.

Besides, Huxley ate the plantstuff without any apparent ill effects. Then again, maybe the little thing enjoyed the hallucinations. Nonetheless, Kevin vowed to be more careful about what he stuck in his mouth from here forward.

Sam was right. The farmhouse certainly appeared abandoned. The windows were broken and debris was strewn everywhere in the yard—as if a tornado had bullied its way through—and a layer of dust covered it all like a cheap movie set. Only the front door looked reasonably solid.

Initially, Huxley refused to enter the ramshackle, one-story building, but once Kevin carried him inside he settled down and seemed to accept being there.

Staying together, they carefully searched all the rooms and found nothing of particular interest. At least, nothing they could understand.

They discovered some documents scattered about the farmhouse on an exotic paper that felt more like skin than an paper they'd ever handled. All the chicken scratching and crazy swirls meant nothing to them and they tossed it aside.

They ate and slept. No one even suggested keeping watch. They were simply too tired to care.

Towards dark, as Kevin lay looking out the big uncovered window in the front room nearest the door, he noted a bluish glow in the distance. "Take a look," he said to Sam who was stirring around in what might have been the alien's kitchen. She was fascinated with all the strange appliances and marveled openly at their queer cutlery.

"What is it?" She popped her head out the window.

"The glow of a city, I'll bet," replied Kevin. "There's no way to tell if this is the city where Lance had been taken, but it's a city—it could be."

"Probably," agreed Sam. "But don't get your hopes up, dude. Like you said, it might be a different city. Who knows?" she said, studying the faint glow. "It may not be a city at all. It could be a natural phenomenon or some kind of radiation that blisters and boils all our skin so bad that it falls off in big chunks."

Sam's way with words and imagery made him nauseous. He didn't know if he'd ever get used to her *unique* personality.

"We have to remember—we're on a strange planet. We can't judge what we see on this world based on our notions of our own world," she continued. "Besides, there's a war going on."

Sam was right and Kevin said so. After all, even things and people back on Earth were often not what they seemed. Why should things here be any different?

They agreed to wait until completely dark before venturing a closer look. Despite the inherent dangers lurking in the dark, they figured they were also less likely to be spotted and captured by their many and ever-present enemies if they clung to the darkness like a baby clinging to a security blanket.

When the time was right, Sam and Kevin woke Lance and laid out their plan to him.

"I said I'd lead you to the city. I did not say I'd lead the freaking parade down main street," Lance stated firmly, wrapping his arms across his chest. He made it clear that he was quite content to stay put. Except for the fact that all the exterior walls of the farmhouse tilted out a good ten degrees, it was a cozy retreat, practically earthy, he claimed.

He'd even discovered a weirdly atonal saxophone-like musical instrument—he assumed it was a musical instrument —it could have been a device designed for giving alien back massages or calling dragons in for dinner for all he or any of them knew. Sam had voted for the dragon signal and warned him not to play it for fear of what fire-breathing winged creatures it might bring down on their heads.

He'd ignored her and spent hours happily noodling away on it and would be happy to spend many more doing just the same. It was the musician in him dying to get out, he explained.

"It's the moron in you," Sam had countered, "trying to get us all killed."

"Come on, Lance," Kevin said. "We need you to show us the way."

"You want to know the way? Just follow that glow in the sky," replied Lance. "You'll find what you're looking for." He paused. "Sooner or later."

"But if the city's as big as you say it is, we won't find who we are looking for—"

"And probably end up captured or killed," interjected Sam.

"Listen," said Lance, idly fingering his newfound instrument. "I'll draw you a map. Anybody got a pen?"

"You're coming," stated Sam. "Even if I have to cut you up in little pieces and stuff you in this pack." She dangled her backpack in his face.

Lance had a smile on his face, half-playful, half-frightened. "Fat lot of good I'll do you then, beautiful."

Sam growled.

"I'll tell you what," said Kevin, eager to avoid bloodshed, "take us to the edge of the town." Lance started to object and Kevin raised his hand. "You don't have to go in, just point us to the building where you were being held. Sam and I will do the rest. Once we get the others out," he hoped, "we'll meet you back here at the farmhouse." Kevin turned to Sam. "What do you say?"

"I say I could use a new outfit and your buddy Lance here would make a nice snakeskin suit."

"Sounds like somebody's hot for the feel of my flesh," taunted Lance, with a leer.

Sam's fingers whitened around the hilt of her blade.

"What do you say, Sam?" Kevin said again, more forcefully.

She nodded once.

"How about it, Lance?"

"I don't have to enter the city?"

"Not if you don't want to."

Lance reluctantly agreed, partly out of fondness for Kevin, partly out of fear of Sam. After all, sooner or later he'd have to sleep and who knew what the crazy broad would do?

An hour later they stood silhouetted among the trees on a small hill overlooking the city. At night and from this distance, the city appeared only half-alive, bombed out. Lights shined sporadically across the valley the city below occupied.

Kevin turned to Lance with questioning eyes.

"Yeah," whispered Lance, "that's the place."

"It's big," noted Kevin, taking it all in. Maybe not NYC big, but big enough. Tall glittering spires rose from the ground, edging toward the sky. Big enough to get lost in. Big enough to hide some prisoners in.

"We need to get closer," Sam said.

"Go ahead, get as close as you like," replied Lance. "But we had a deal. My bus stops here."

"How will we find them?" Kevin turned towards Lance. "This is the place, isn't it?"

"Yeah, I recognize that cluster of buildings there with those minaret kind of towers. I think there's an airfield of some sort nearby. Lots of flying vehicles coming and going."

Kevin nodded. The whole place looked quiet and peaceful enough now.

Lance pointed. "You see that tower there, to the right?"

"The tall tripod?" Sam asked.

"No," Lance shook his head, "the one next to it. That's where you need to go. At least, that's where I was—we were. There's a long bunker beneath that tower." He paused and looked at Kevin. "That's the last place I saw the others."

"Then that's where we'll go."

Sam agreed and checked her weapons.

Lance agreed to wait for them back at the farmhouse. He promised he would stay as long as he could, so long as it was safe. Which he hoped would be a long time.

"You're not taking that thing, are you?"

"Huh?"

Sam pointed at Kevin's shoulder. "It could get in the way."

Kevin frowned and transferred Huxley to Lance's shoulder. "You go with Lance," he cooed. "You'll be safer with him. I'll be back soon."

Kevin rubbed the creature's little chin and took a step. Huxley jumped from Lance's shoulder back to Kevin's. Kevin tried again, admonishing Huxley to stay put. But the results were the same. Each time he tried, Huxley refused to obey. In the end, against Sam's vociferous objections, he just decided to let the little guy tag along. After all, who was he to decide anyone else's fate?

# 21

Moving cautiously, Kevin and Sam worked their way downhill in a zigzag fashion, keeping in the shadows as much as possible. They came to a slow moving river nearly a hundred feet wide by the look of it. Bordering the river's edge on the other side several docks jutted out. Improbably top-heavy vessels clung to a few of them. Beyond, a narrow road led past what looked like the single-story warehouses he'd seen so many times near the harbor in New York.

There wasn't a soul moving about.

"Lance didn't mention the river." Sam cursed him.

Kevin scanned up and down. "Looks like a bridge over there. We'll have to cross it."

"And be sitting ducks for alien target practice?"

"We don't have any choice. We could spend hours looking for another way across. It will be light by then."

"Fine. Let's get this over with," said Sam. "Though I'm not sure why I'm even doing this. They're your friends, not mine."

"Shh."

"What is it?"

"Get down!" Kevin flattened himself against the ground. "Don't move," he cautioned.

Spreadeagled in the grass, Sam strained to look up. A dull thrumming was soon followed by a helicopter-like flying vehicle with two rotating flood lights that turned in every direction, up, down and around in no apparent pattern.

The vehicle scanned the opposite side of the river, along the road and the buildings, then veered suddenly in their direction. Coming closer and closer.

Kevin felt Sam tense beside him. They were sure they'd be spotted. The dancing spotlight passed within inches of Kevin's nose. He held his breath as it hovered overhead, then turned sharply and took off downriver like an owl who'd spotted its dinner.

"Come on," urged Kevin, scrambling to his feet once he was reasonably certain they were beyond the range of the lights. "We have to get across that bridge before that thing comes back."

They took off in a mad dash. The helicopter unexpectedly changed course and was coming in their direction once more.

"Sam, hurry!" Kevin shouted as he glanced backward, surprised to see how far ahead he was of her and how close the lights were getting to them both.

The blazing lights were almost on Sam now, the helicopter almost directly above her.

Kevin hesitated. The bridge was merely a few yards away. "Sam!"

The helicopter was on her now, swooping low like a raptor on the attack. It's beam of light locked onto her.

"Sam!" He screamed over the thrumming of the helicopter. Why wasn't she running? Why wasn't she even moving?

Two dark figures jumped from the vehicle. Kevin took a breath and ran for the bridge. There was nothing he could do now.

"Sam," he panted, as he came to a rest along a waist-high white wall on the opposite side of the bridge. He watched forlornly as the flying vessel took to the air, hovered a moment, then headed deep over the city, where he soon lost sight of it. And Sam.

Because Sam was gone.

# 22

Kevin heard a bleating siren in the distance. After thirty seconds or so, the tooth rattling noise ceased. The streets were eerily quiet, though he could make out a few lights behind covered windows.

Sticking to the shadows and the edges of the buildings, Kevin worked his way towards the tower Lance had pointed out.

Twice he got mixed up in the maze of streets and lost sight of the tower. When he'd spotted it next, he was even further away than he had been minutes before. He groaned in frustration.

How long would it be before he was discovered and captured like Sam? Was she still alive?

But the landmark was clearly visible now and it was only a matter of a short time before he stood beneath the overhang of a bombed out looking skyscraper. The portcullis was shattered and scarred by flames now dead.

A squat bunker-like building stood nearby, just as Lance had said there would be. It was still four stories tall, but dwarfed by the giant standing beside it. The skyscraper's windows were dark. Had it been abandoned?

If it had been, what chance did he have of finding his shipmates? It was a big city. An alien city. And it was a big, alien planet.

Kevin stood staring at the lifeless looking building. If the humans had been moved, they could be anywhere. Maybe not even still in the city. And he wouldn't have a clue where to look next.

And with Sam gone...

Kevin drew a long breath. He didn't know what to do but

knew he had to do something.

Pressing a finger to his lips and motioning Huxley to keep quiet, as if the gesture meant anything at all to the furry marionette, he stealthily crossed the open street, not knowing what to expect—police, helicopters, laser attacks, slicing machine gun strafes, pies in the face from angry clowns with painted faces violently demonstrating man's inhumanity to man...

But nothing happened. Weirdly, he felt a little let down.

Kevin didn't know if this was a good sign or a bad one. But the nothing unsettled him. It would almost have been better if something had happened.

Three windows occupied each side of an approximately eight foot tall and four foot wide door. Kevin could only hope it was something and not someone that was meant to go in and out that doorway that large.

The windows were high but, by standing on tiptoes, Kevin was able to reach them. He peeked over the windowsill to no avail. Useless. It was simply too dark to see anything within. He gave up and navigated around the building, stepping over and between the rubble surrounding it. A section of wall had fallen completely away at one of the corners. That fit in with the bombing that Lance had described.

Kevin caught sight of a more human-sized interior door about ten yards inside, past the rubbled remains of what had probably been an office of some kind. The door itself had been damaged and hung askew.

Kevin's hopes for finding his shipmates or any humans in the damaged building at this point were diminishing by the minute. Yet he had no choice but to move forward.

He had nothing to go back to.

Stealthily threading his way through the debris, he pulled on the door's recessed handle. It groaned gently, like a youth tossing in her sleep.

Kevin paused, waiting and listening. No cry of alarm rose from within. He pulled the door open further and stepped inside. The instant he did, the small cube-shaped room was bathing in sterile white light.

Kevin froze.

A creature, the twin of the white giants whose corpses equally littered the battlefield with those of the humans who had been unceremoniously, unexpectedly, and unpreparedly dropped there, sat in a broad, bowl-shaped chair, apparently guarding the room.

The humanoid leapt with incredible speed, hands outstretched. Huxley screeched madly and leapt from Kevin to the floor, running between the white giant's legs, distracting it, but only for an instant. Then the white giant's gaze was back. It glared at Kevin with malice-filled eyes. Large hands reached for him.

Kevin drew his weapon and fired. The white thing hit the ground with a thud that sent a shock wave through the floor. Kevin grunted in surprise, looking blankly at the gun in his hand. He hadn't even realized that he had pulled it out—that he had been holding it at all.

That he had shot something, *someone*.

The gun fell from his hand and Huxley climbed up his right leg. He glanced nervously back the way he'd come. The sound of the skirmish was bound to bring others. Kevin was surprised there weren't more of this thing's reinforcements pouring in already.

He had to move swiftly now, search the building for the human captives and get out.

He scooted around the dead giant and quickly pulled open the next door in.

# 23

Like before, the lights flicked on instantly. But this time, instead of a white giant in a bowl-shaped chair, Henry Hemming sat on the edge of a flimsy-looking cot, hands clutching the side.

"Henry!" Kevin swung the door shut behind him. "Am I glad to see you!"

Henry looked startled and bewildered. His face bore remnants of sleep. "Kevin? Is that you?" He leaned forward and rubbed his eyes. "How on earth did you get here? He glanced at the closed door. "What's going on out there?"

"There's no time to explain now," Kevin said quickly. "Get dressed, Henry!" Henry was both shirtless and shoeless. "We've got to get out of here—and quickly."

Henry looked at the door once more, as if expecting someone or something to come bursting in. "What about the guard?"

Kevin frowned. "He won't bother us."

"You-you killed him?"

Kevin nodded. "Yes. I didn't mean to. It just happened."

"Thank goodness," said Henry, visibly relaxing. "You have no idea what a living nightmare this has been." He slipped out of bed and shook Kevin's hand. His flesh was warm. "Thank you, Kevin. Thank you."

Kevin nodded again, uncomfortably. He wasn't used to people thanking him for doing anything—he wasn't used to doing anything to be thanked for. He really wasn't used to doing *anything* period. "Grab your things, Henry," he said once more. "We've got to get out of here quick as we can."

Henry threw on his shirt and shoes and grabbed his small Mitoc-issued pack. Oddly, his captives had let him keep it. It should have made Kevin wonder, but it didn't.

Henry made for the door through which Kevin had entered. "No, not that way," Kevin said. "There could be others coming to see what the shooting was all about. Is there another way?"

Henry thought a moment, then nodded. "This way. There's a storeroom. We can go through there. It has windows that face an alleyway."

Kevin grabbed Henry's sleeve. "What about the others?"

"Others?" Henry appeared baffled.

"Nicolette, Sequoia—the others who were aboard the ship with us."

"I have not seen them, Kevin," Henry explained, all the while leading the way into the storeroom. Unlike the first two rooms Kevin had encountered, this room remained dark when they entered. But Henry had no trouble leading them both through a maze of shadowy shelves and desks. He stopped under a pair of barred windows.

"But Lance said you were all together," Kevin whispered.

"Lance?"

"Yes, he found me, or rather, we found each other. He said you were all here together. That's why I came."

"Ah, I understand now," answered Henry, running his hands along the top of the window's edge. "There's a release here somewhere. Aha! Found it!" The bars swung inward.

"Yes, we were all together, initially. But during the bombing there was a lot of confusion. We were separated. I assumed all the others had made their escape." Henry motioned for Kevin to climb through, then followed.

Kevin fell to the ground and looked anxiously about. They were alone in silence. "That could be."

"So where is Lance?" asked Henry, looking up and down the dark, narrow alleyway. "Is he waiting nearby?"

Kevin shook his head and explained that the musician was waiting for them back at an abandoned farmhouse.

"Sam?"

"What?"

"You mentioned a Sam. You didn't come here alone?" Henry buttoned his shirt and pushed back his hair.

"No, there was a girl with me."

"Ah, Sam as in Samantha?"

"Yes, I suppose so." He really wasn't sure. Maybe Sam was all the name she had. He found it hard to picture her as a Samantha. It sounded so...girly. "She's been captured." Or killed. But he didn't dare say that aloud. It might make it real.

"I'm sorry," said Henry, laying a hand on Kevin's shoulder.

"I've got to try and find her." She was annoying and then some, but he felt he owed her.

"I agree," said Henry. "But it's going to be light soon. This place will be bustling with Booties, then."

"Booties?"

"They are the dominant species on this planet, like homo sapiens back on Earth. Like that hominoid you killed back there."

Kevin nodded. That matched what Sigma Six had said, what little that had been before Sigma Six himself had met his end. "And they're hostile?"

Henry shrugged. "How do you suppose we Earthlings would feel if a million aliens fell on Earth with guns blazing?"

Kevin got the picture. Henry's words convinced him that the best thing they could do would be to retreat. Head back to the farm where Lance was waiting for them. Together, he hoped, they could figure out a plan that might have at least a small chance of success in finding Sam and said so. "Maybe the others as well," he added.

"Maybe," agreed Henry. "But don't get your hopes up, Kevin. The Booties might have moved them out of the city. On the other hand, if they have escaped, they could be anywhere at all."

Kevin led the way back. The way he had come. He got lost a few times but, with Henry's assistance, they managed to get back on course.

Just as dawn was rising on the horizon, they arrived at the bridge he'd crossed in the night. Alone.

Minutes later, as the sun hit their backs like a warm hand,

they were climbing the hill where he and Sam had last seen Lance.

On the hilltop, Huxley leapt from Kevin's shoulder and shot after a small winged insect of some sort. Snatching it out of the air, Huxley swallowed it down in a single motion and his eyes darted about the small clearing for a second helping.

"What exactly is this creature?" Henry squatted closer and reached for Huxley. The little animal scurried out of his way as if afraid of the earthman.

Kevin shrugged. "I found him on the trail. We've sort of adopted one another."

Henry smiled. "Congratulations, Kevin."

"For what?"

"You have succeeded in making a friend a world away." Henry's knees cracked as he stood. "That's quite an accomplishment."

Kevin smiled back. Kevin supposed it actually was something of an accomplishment. He held out his arm. As if trained, Huxley jumped onto his elbow.

"Now," said Henry. "Where's this farmhouse where you are to meet Lance?"

"That way." Kevin pointed. "I think." They overlooked a broad field filled with scattered trees below. Narrow roads skirted the edges of croplands. Tall, slender Seussian vehicles sped along the road in both directions without regard for which side of the road they belonged. Still others wandered up and down the furrowed fields.

"I don't see a farmhouse."

Kevin explained that it must be over the next rise. "I'm not sure, to tell you the truth. I could easily be off by a mile or two in either direction." He hoped not. "But I am certain it is in that general direction." He waved his arm around vaguely.

"We'd better get going then," said Henry.

"I'm not so sure," said Kevin. "It's light out now. We'll be awfully easy to spot." Easy prey.

"Still, the sooner we meet up with Lance the sooner we can

rescue your friend Sam." He raised an eyebrow meaningfully. "Before anything happens to her."

Kevin frowned. He turned and studied the alien city they'd left behind. Even from this distance, he could see the place bustling with activity now. Was Sam back there? Were the others there too? Had they escaped perhaps?

Worse, were they all dead? They could easily be lying dead somewhere or have been gobbled up in some alien feast the night before.

"Maybe we should wait until dark," Kevin thought out loud. "Yes, I think we should wait until dark."

"Sure," said Henry, with a broad smile. "I guess that makes sense. I certainly don't want to get captured again." He shivered visibly.

They settled down in a shallow depression between two trees and tried to sleep. Kevin hoped that Lance and Sam were okay— wherever they were.

# 24

Sam felt like killing somebody. Anybody. But who to start with?

Not to mention, she still felt like a walking bowl of mush. Whatever kind of whacky beam the aliens in the copter had locked onto her with had locked her up tight. The instant the beam hit her, her muscles turned rigid as steel and a wave of nausea had coursed through her body from her toes to her nose.

Two of the aliens had jumped to the ground and carried her helplessly and ignominiously aboard their flying vehicle. They'd whisked her off to some military-looking dude in a black uniform waiting arms folded for her at a landing pad lit up by a necklace of ground-level light globes.

He'd eyed her with something that resembled a frown and muttered some gibberish she didn't understand. Then she'd been hustled away again through the dark streets to a building bathed contrastingly in brilliant yellow light.

All the while, she'd felt like puking. But even for that, her muscles refused to cooperate. Inside they went, leading her in alien silence. Up elevators and down corridors until she felt like a hamster in a funhouse, forever lost.

They finally halted outside a locked door that one of the aliens opened with the wave of a small metallic keycard. Gripping her stiff, tingly arms, they pushed her roughly inside, stripped off all her clothes and sprayed her with some foul-smelling mist.

"Hey!" she protested. "What the fuck do you think you're doing?"

A seamless door opened in the wall behind her and with

another push, she was inside. And alone.

This room was dark but for the light spilling out from the sides of a brown tarp-covered window opposite the door. She ran to the window and pulled down the tarp, hoping it might lead to her freedom. She yanked on the window frame. Maybe these idiots would be like the ones back in the jungle who hadn't even bothered to keep an eye on them. Maybe she'd be gone before they returned to do whatever Island of Dr. Moreau type experiments they had planned for her.

Locked. She banged her fist against the window sill. Nothing, barely a shudder. Rats. So the alien buggers weren't as dumb as they looked.

It probably wouldn't have mattered if the window hadn't been locked anyway. She was a good three stories up. Even if the window proved breakable, there was no way she'd make it safely to the quiet street below. Only a few stars marred the night sky.

A movement in the alley across the way caught her eye. Two creatures came creeping up the small dark passage. As they fell into the light, she recognized them as humans!

As the two humans dodged across the street, she realized both of the humans were men, and one of the two was Kevin!

The other man she did not recognize. Who was he? How had that moron Kevin managed to stumble on another human in this alien hellhole?

She shouted and jumped up and down in front of the window.

Looking desperately around her cell, Sam searched for something, anything that she could use to break what felt like plexiglass under her fingertips.

But there was nothing but a lumpy mattress on the floor.

And it didn't matter anyway, for when she turned back and looked out the window again, Kevin and his mystery companion had gone.

Suddenly, she felt all alone.

Despite the chill, Sam was sweating like a heavyweight wrestler at the end of round three. Things were not looking good. And the aliens had taken her weapons and her clothes. What were they planning to do with her? Why hadn't they killed her flat out?

And what were Kevin and that other man doing? It wasn't Lance. She could tell that even from a distance. If he was one of the humans she and Kevin had come to rescue, where were the others?

Had Kevin failed and only managed to release the one? Perhaps the one man was all that was left of the group Lance had been sequestered with. The others could very easily be dead.

Sam's head hurt. She had so, so many questions. She shivered, hugging herself, and turned in a slow circle, her eyes taking in the room clearly for the first time. Except for the wobbly mattress, the room was barren and the floor hard.

She hurled the mattress at the wall and only then noticed the paneled door to the right of the window. There was no visible doorknob but she saw the faint impression of a recessed handle up high. She reached for it, stretching up on her toes, and tested it. Nothing happened. Her first thought was that it was locked.

"Of course," she grumbled, "why wouldn't it be?" Out of anger and frustration she slammed her shoulder into the door. Her eyes watered in pain and she would have regretted her impulsive action—but the door silently slid open!

As light rushed through the open door and into her prison cell, her eyes bugged out and she gaped. She was standing naked in front of a group of strangers—human strangers. They looked almost as surprised as she was.

"Well, well," said a pudgy and pasty looking yokel with a lascivious grin, "Fresh meat."

"Shut up," a long-haired young woman snapped.

Sam's first impulse was to cover herself—well, her first impulse was to kick the dumb yokel in his useless man parts — but she quickly recognized the futility of such efforts and abandoned the idea.

Opting to ignore her nakedness, she asserted herself. "Who are you people?" she demanded. For they were people after all, genuine, Made In America, five-toed, five-fingered, two-armed, two-legged, et cetera. Some may even have possessed brains, though it was too early to jump to any rash conclusions.

The young woman snatched a navy blue blanket from a cot and approached Sam. "Here," she said to Sam. "Take this."

Sam nodded and draped the scratchy blanket over her shoulders. She pulled the ends tightly together across her front. Without buttons or a belt, she was forced to hold it shut.

"So, what's your story?" purred Gig.

Sam immediately placed him in the pudgy/pasty ignoramus category. "I'm new to the neighborhood and dropped by to introduce myself and to see if I could borrow a cup of sugar cuz I'm baking some brownies, doughboy."

"She's funny," Gig said to the others. He threw out both of his chins. "But we'll see just how funny you think you are," he said, turning back to Sam, "when these alien sadists start poking and prodding away at your outsides as well as your insides like you were nothing more than a disposable lab rat." He snorted. "I wonder what they'll make of your tats."

Sam extended the fingers of her left hand, and pushed her long jagged fingernails into Gig's baby soft forearm. "I wonder how you'd like me to carve a few fresh ones for you."

Gig whimpered and pulled away. "Christ, bitch, you're crazy! Look what you did to my arm!" Tiny droplets of blood rose from his pasty white skin.

"And don't you forget it, fatso," snarled Sam.

Gig turned his back to her and skulked off to the other side of the room. He threw himself down on a cot and coddled his arm. The cot rattled angrily and threatened to give out but managed to hold despite the jarring and excessive load.

"What's goober talking about?" Sam asked the others. "What's all this talk of lab rats?"

"Don't mind him. That's Gig being Gig. He can't help himself. He's on edge. We all are." The young woman who'd given Sam the blanket held out her hand and Sam shook it. "My name's Nicolette." She went around the room introducing the others.

Sam smiled. "Kevin's friends, right?"

Every eyebrow in the room went up as if on director's cue. "You know Kevin?" Nicolette asked.

Sam nodded and laughed sadly. "Can you believe it? We were coming to rescue you."

"Coming to rescue us?" Sequoia asked. "How did you and Kevin know where we were? Where to find us?"

"We didn't, Lance did." Ignoring the groans that escaped several lips at mention of Lance's name, she told how she and Kevin had stumbled upon Lance, or rather Lance had stumbled upon them. And about how Lance had escaped and told her and Kevin of their predicament.

"Well," said Nicolette. "At least one of us managed to get away."

"What about the school teacher?" said Sam. "Lance told us one of the captives was an older gentleman." She scanned the room once more. There was no one here fitting that bill. "A school teacher. It can't be one of you, right?"

Gig suddenly sat up, his hands tightening around the frame of his cot. "You mean Hemming," he spat venomously. "Henry Hemming."

Nicolette and the rest nodded.

"He's working for them." Gig's voice was hard, his eyes sharp and filled with malice.

"Them?" asked Sam.

"Them," echoed Nicolette. "The boogie men."

"What's he talking about?" Sam asked.

Nicolette pulled Sam down onto her cot. "The Booties. Or boogies. Henry's helping them. And," her gaze fell to the floor, and her voice dropped several decibels, "and they're experimenting on us."

Sam nodded. The Booties again. That matched what that idiot alien had told them before being whacked by those other idiot bloodthirsty aliens. What kind of crazy nightmare had she gotten herself mixed up in? Was this all a nightmare anyway? Had the gov laced the water with something that was creating all these crazy scenarios in her head? Was this payback for her digging around and exposing all the gov's secret conspiracies?

"It's been horrible," whispered Sequoia, rubbing her arms as if to get the smell and the touch of the creatures off her skin.

"Treat us like bugs in a jar, that's what they do," interjected Gig from the cot.

"It has not been pleasant," said a man introduced as Xian. Xian worked on Wall Street. He had an actual job, according to Nicolette. He was a Chinese National and had been on the team brought to the US some years ago when the Chinese government finalized its purchase of the New York Stock Exchange.

"What would you know?" said Gig. "Booties took a pint of my blood yesterday. I don't know if they plan on studying it or drinking it."

He clearly disliked Xian. But then, like many Americans, Gig was undoubtedly frustrated that his country had been sold off in pieces. China just happened to be the lucky holder of many of those pieces. Not that it was any of Xian's fault.

It was the United States' own fault. Gig knew that and it only made him madder.

Sam asked the obvious question. "Why? Why not just slaughter us like they seemed to have no compulsion against doing back on the battlefield the day we got dumped here?"

"They want to know what makes us tick," Sequoia explained. Like all the others, she wore a simple, loose-fitting outfit comprised of off-white trousers and a long-sleeved chemise. The material looked to be paper or cellulose of some sort.

Sam nodded. "Know thy enemy."

Gig snorted.

"Something like that," replied Nicolette, giving him a cold stare. "The best we can understand it," she said, folding her hands in her lap, "is that the Booties want to know what makes us—" She hesitated.

"Go ahead, say it," Gig chided.

"Different."

"Different? Different from them?"

Nicolette shook her head. "Different from the other humans."

Sam's puzzlement showed on her face. "I don't get it."

"I did not get it at first either," said Xian. "None of us did." He looked at the others. "But we are *different*."

"Explain," said Sam.

"Don't you get it?" Gig said, impatiently. "Think about it. I'll just bet you didn't go rushing off all zombied up and climb aboard one of those moon-sized spaceships now, did you?" He aimed a fat finger accusingly at Sam's nose.

"No." Sam drew her answer out. Thinking. Wondering what was going on under the surface of whatever was going on here in the first place.

"None of us here did," explained Xian, waving his hand around the room.

"That's what the Booties are interested in learning more about, if they can. They want to know what it is that sets us apart physically in such a way that we did not—" Nicolette paused, searching for the right word, "respond to the programmed call of the Mitoc."

"Mitoc? As in mitochondria?" That word again. She pulled at her lower lip. "Booties and boogies!" Sam leapt to her feet and began pacing. A small black hole of a headache was eating up her brain. "What on earth are you all talking about?"

They were all nuts, every last one of them. Somehow she had to get out of here before she lost grip of her own sanity.

# 25

Kevin woke with a start. A bright orange sun hung like an engorged galaxy-sized fruit in an impossibly blue sky. His back rested against something hard. For just a moment, he thought he was on Earth, awaking from a nap on a slatted bench near the park. But his fingernails clawed the ground and he knew then that he was clutching earth, but not the Earth of his home. This was the earth of a distant land.

Did a map even exist that could tell him where he was?

Kevin rose to his elbows and yawned. How long had he been sleeping? "Henry, I don't know about you, but I'm famished."

Huxley scurried to Kevin's side and nibbled his fingers. "Henry?" Kevin slowly came to his feet, tired and stiff. He looked around uneasily. It was too quiet. And the mere rustling of his feet on the hard ground seemed offensively loud. Henry was nowhere in sight.

Through a break in the trees, Kevin caught movement far below. Soldiers looking for them? He inched away. A hand clasped his right shoulder and he cried out. Another hand shot forward and covered his open mouth.

"Quiet," whispered Henry, turning Kevin around. "It's me."

Kevin loosened. "Thank goodness. I thought you'd disappeared. I thought they'd got you."

Henry pulled Kevin away from the exposed landscape. "Better keep back. One of those devils might spot us."

Kevin nodded and retreated. "What's happened? What happened to you? Where did you go?"

Henry sat on a thick stump and took a sip of water from his canteen. "I couldn't sleep. I thought I'd reconnoiter." He wiped his lips with the back of his sleeve. "I wanted to get a closer look at them."

Kevin tensed. "A risky business, don't you think?"

Henry smiled. "Relax, Kevin. Nobody saw me. I kept myself in concealment. There are enough trees around for the job. Thankfully."

Kevin grabbed some food from his pack. He needed something to eat to steady himself. Pickings were slim. They'd have to find food somewhere. "Did you learn anything?"

Henry's lips flattened to a line. "Nothing good. Lots of aliens skittering over the countryside like misguided ants in search of their queen."

A sudden rumble and several sharp bursts of focused ruby light erupted over the horizon.

"What was that?" Huxley hid behind Kevin, clutching his calf.

"Sounds like another battle."

A chill swept through Kevin at the thought of the countless thousands of dead he'd first woken to on this infernal planet—and he wondered how many more might be joining them now.

"I'd say the fighting is a good twenty miles or so south of the city," estimated Henry.

"There could be humans there," said Kevin with a yearning in his voice that he would not have expected. There was a time, not long ago, when the presence, the very nearness of humans, meant nothing to him. Less than nothing.

"I'd bet money on it," said Henry. "The Mitoc probably dumped a shipload or two." He kicked the ground hard. "Like they did with us."

"Have you noticed how earthlike everything seems?"

"Sure. My guess? The Mitoc sent us humans here specifically because they knew we'd have a better chance of surviving here. Adapt better to the surroundings without need for protective gear."

"Like respirators? Or gravity boots?"

Henry chuckled. "Exactly."

Kevin gave some thought to the mysterious and seemingly all-powerful aliens. "Who are these Mitoc exactly?" asked Kevin. He repeated what Sigma Six had told him. "What can you tell me about them?"

Henry shrugged. "Who can say?" He smiled. "Them, I suppose. But they're not telling. I wonder if Sigma Six even knew. Hell, he might never have seen one himself. He was just as much a tool as we are. Mitoc isn't even their real name for themselves. Mitoc is just a moniker that's been tossed out and stuck." He chuckled, watching the lights of the distant battle.

If Kevin hadn't known a battle was waging and lives were being lost, it could have been a fascinating light show.

"Mitoc is as good as any name—and appropriate."

"Appropriate how?" Kevin felt there was so much more to know about what was going on. And Henry Hemming seemed to have at least some of the answers he sought.

Henry draped his arms over his knees and adopted the posture and professorial tone of voice he'd often used on his students. "Mitoc is short for mitochondria."

Kevin frowned. "That's what the alien said. But I still don't get it."

"Well, basically, mitochondria are these organelles, stuff in our cells, that produce energy—ATP—adenosine triphosphate. Have you heard of it?"

"I sort of remember a little from high school science," confessed Kevin. "But not much. It has its own genome, right?"

"Correct," said Henry, delighted. He cleared his throat. "I don't know much more than you. I'm not a biologist, after all. But mitochondria is pretty strange stuff. Believe you me. Standard Earth thinking says it probably had evolved from a bacteria, I believe. But we can throw all that out the window." He shook his head. "I wish I had access to a decent library."

"I don't understand," said Kevin. "What's so special about this mitochondria?"

Henry nodded. "The Mitoc—those aliens we call the Mitoc—seeded Earth with the stuff." He spread the fingers of both hands.

"They seeded a million Earths with the stuff, Kevin," he paused, "maybe billions…"

He leaned forward and took Kevin's left arm. "And they did it a couple of billion years ago!" His eyes went wild for a second, then he reined them in.

Kevin sat still a moment, lost in his own thoughts. "Why?" he finally asked. He feared he knew the answer, the answer that Sigma Six had alluded to, but hoped he was wrong or had been lied to.

"For this," said Henry, rising and circling the glade. "So a couple of billion years down the road we'd come flocking to the mother ship and gladly, gleefully go like sheep to our slaughter."

Kevin's confusion showed on his face like a carnival mask.

"Don't you get it, Kevin?"

Kevin shook his head no.

"The mitochondria made us what we are. Made us *human*. At the same time, the mitochondria enslaved us, programmed us to respond to our unknown, unnamed makers—who would come to claim their mastery over us in their own due time."

He spun round and looked wildly at Kevin. "To do their bidding," he said, "or die in the trying. To fight the great war, the great forever war."

Kevin's eyes went wide as Henry's words sunk in. It sounded farfetched. No, crazy! Had Henry Hemming gone mad? Had his alien captors done something to his mind?

Or had Henry snapped as a result of being snatched rudely from Earth and the life he'd known and hurtled to a dismal planet for who knew what purpose?

Or was Henry right? Had this all—all humanity itself—been nothing more than a result of alien science? All in the name of creating an unending supply of cheap, disposable soldiers for some impossibly long war that stretched across billions of years of time and billions of light-years of space?

"It's a war, Kevin," Henry went on. "A war like humans cannot even begin to imagine. And it's been going on for billions of years across billions of light years," the former teacher said, as if snatching the words from Kevin's mind. "And the Mitoc have created us and billions of creatures like us to use, to fight for them, to die for them."

"It's not possible."

"What isn't?" retorted Henry. "Life itself seems impossible on the face of it." He scratched the ground. "Yet here we are. You and me." He paused. "Wherever *here* is."

"You don't know? You haven't been able to figure out exactly where we are?" He had been hoping that Henry would have some idea. If they knew where they were then maybe they could find a way to get back home. How could they get home if they didn't have a clue as to where they were?

Henry frowned. "Not exactly. The nearest I can figure out is that we're somewhere along the rim of the Boötes Void."

"That's what Sigma Six said, too. What can you tell me about this Boötes Void?"

Henry explained that the Boötes Void was a two hundred and fifty to three hundred million light-year in diameter region of space that was relatively devoid of stars. "Think of it as a giant soap bubble in the starry froth of space," Henry said, poetically.

Kevin nodded, constructed the image in his head. It was an image he was well familiar with. A great, giant void. That's precisely what he felt was at the center of his mind. "How far away? From Earth, I mean."

Henry pursed his lips and shrugged. "My guess, and it's only a guess, mind you," he paused, tapping his index finger against his lips as if doing calculations, "four to five hundred million light-years from our Earth."

Kevin took a slow, deliberate breath. If he remembered correctly, a light-year was something like six trillion miles. Home was a long way away.

# 26

Sam was stunned. What this tiny group of captives had told her was a lot to absorb. Was this how she was going to spend the rest of her days? she wondered. Nothing more than a gerbil in some mad Bootie scientist's lab?

All so they could figure out what made her tick? Good luck with that. She didn't even know what made her tick. She'd tell them if she could, if it meant they'd forget about prodding her with needles. She did not like needles.

Then again, what did she care? Why should she care? She didn't know the good guys from the bad guys. In fact, from her perspective, and probably the rest of humanity's, they were probably each and every one of them—Booties and Mitoc alike—the bad guys.

Except that humans had been bred to side with the Mitoc —excluding the defectives, of course, like her. And that's what made the defectives so important a catch for the Booties, they or their masters, wanted to know what made them defective. Obviously so they could use this knowledge against the Mitoc in some fashion, maybe search out worlds that the Mitoc had seeded with mitochondria and reengineer them so everybody was a defective and immune to the instinctual call of the Mitoc. The Mitoc would lose a major source of meat for their army.

Mitoc, Booties. Sam ground her teeth. She'd trade them all in for a one-way ticket back to Earth. How crazy was that?

Sam tugged at the Ident dangling from her neck. "What am I still wearing this for?" She yanked, then yanked a second time even harder. The plastic strap snapped.

"You're not supposed to do that," said Xian. "It's against the law."

Sam couldn't help laughing. "Are you going to turn me in?"

"I'm just saying." Xian turned away.

"Listen, everyone. It's a new world with new rules. Forget about Earth. Forget the past." Sam looked at each of them slowly, deliberately. "We have to deal with today. We have to think about our survival. We can't just sit here accepting our fate." Sam rammed her fist into her palm with a smack. "The first course of action is escape. We have got to get out of here."

"Why?" shrugged Gig, sullenly, his voice drained of hope. He stared at the ceiling. "Even if we could get out of here, we've got no place to go. We're a bazillion miles from home in this Boötes Void you talk about, so I don't expect we'll find any train station or bus line running within a kajillion light-years, let alone one with a connection that stops anywhere near Earth."

"Right, face it," said Xian, nodding his head, "we're stuck on this planet."

"Maybe," replied Sequoia, "but we don't have to be stuck in this room, right?"

"That's right," Sam said firmly.

"I agree." Nicolette stepped forward. "We have to try." Conversation was interrupted by a soft pinging sound from without. Like a pack of Pavlovian dogs, all eyes but Sam's turned to the door.

Three Booties entered the room. They left again a moment later. Taking Sam with them.

"Watch the blanket," complained Sam, tugging the thin blanket back up over her shoulders. It was the only thing between her and prying eyes. "What is your problem? Never see a real woman's breasts before? Looking for some kind of peep show, perv?"

Her guards squawked incomprehensibly and pushed her down a nondescript corridor. The three thugs escorting her were similar in size and shape, all within a few inches of each other in height and a few pounds, she guessed, in weight. They were easily twenty inches taller than Sam.

Of course, she could have narrowed that height distance a little if she'd been decked out in stiletto heels instead of traipsing barefoot and buck naked except for the tissue-thin synthetic blanket that was trying desperately to abandon her.

Their faces were humanoid, but flattish, almost owlish. Each had dark gray pupils. Not a one of them sported an eyebrow. Fetish, fashion, or heredity? She found their rubbery-looking skin off-putting—weirdly white like an albino of Earth. She'd seen a pink-eyed albino alligator at an aquarium. But there was a weird greenish undertone to these things' skin that creeped her out.

Sam wrinkled her nose. They smelled like sheepdogs left out in the April rain three days past their expiration date. "What's wrong," she grumbled, "you dogs don't believe in baths?" No reply. "Or haven't you invented them yet?"

She waited again for an answer but again none was forthcoming. Either they didn't understand her or they were dissing her. Either way, she would have killed them all if she'd had her weapons.

See Mom, Dad, she thought, all that money spent on karate classes and time at the county shooting range wasn't the waste you thought. It's paid off in spades. "Yeah," she said aloud, "look at me now, Mom, Sam The-Would-Be-Alien Annihilator."

A door opened, a door closed. And Sam was on the inside.

The room was bare and dimly lit. A glass partition separated Sam from a much larger room across the way. Two Booties uniformly dressed in navy blue outfits that looked like scrubs, were consulting or maybe gossiping in the far corner.

One of the two stopped yammering long enough to look up in Sam's direction, then continued talking with his/her/its colleague as if she were as inconsequential as a bug.

Between the two Booties, on a simple white slab attached to the floor by a single pedestal, lay a naked human.

And from the gray complexion head to toe, Sam surmised that this was one dead human. Male and not one that Sam recognized from the ship or any time since; though for one second she'd half-feared it was Kevin, caught and slaughtered like a pig at this alien luau. But this guy's hair was black where Kevin's was brown mixed with a few strands of gray. And this guy was pudgier, definitely pudgier. And that was saying something considering Kevin was pretty much a doughboy himself.

The Bootie on the right nodded, unceremoniously tossed the corpse into some sort of over-sized hamper and left.

The other Bootie eyed Sam silently for a moment from afar, his icy silver eyes slicing spookily through her. He approached, his footsteps silent as shadows, and the glass between them melted away.

Sam watched him pocket a small metallic device he extracted from his coat pocket. Something some dopey steampunker might have cobbled together. He stopped then and loomed over her.

Sam jumped to her feet. No matter. He still loomed a good two feet over her. "Doctor Frankenstein, I presume?"

Sam figured the Bootie would have arched an eyebrow if he'd owned one, but he didn't. His fat mouth twisted into some uncomfortable looking shape resembling either a smile, a grimace, or an 'I'm going to eat you for breakfast, Little Red Riding Hood' sneer.

"You may address me as John." Without warning, he ripped away her blanket, leaving her naked.

"Hey!" she said. He'd spoken. English! Startled and naked, she grabbed at the blanket on the floor.

"No." He kicked it aside and planted his hand on her breast.

"Hey! What are you, some kind of perv?" She slapped his hand away. "Get your kicks from the alien chicks? Does your wife know about this little fetish of yours, John?" Sam folded her arms and covered her breasts. "And you are kidding, right? *John*? Give me a break. I mean, what kind of proper name is that for an alien?"

She snorted. "John! Shouldn't you have something—I don't know—more exotic, more alieny?" Sam knew she had to keep talking, gibberish though it was. Keep thinking. Keep the Bootie distracted.

And herself alive. Not end up like the corpse the Bootie's partner in crime had just wheeled out of the room.

She had to think her way out of this trap. Face it, there was no way she was going to fight her way out.

"I mean, shouldn't your name be Alpha Blaster, Beta Max, or, I don't know, Iggy Pop?"

"John is the designation you may communicate with me through. I'm told this is a common designation among your type."

Sam's lips turned down. It talked human but it sure didn't *sound* human. She snapped her fingers. "That's what I'm calling you—Ziggy Stardust."

The Bootie apparently ignored her, didn't care, didn't understand or, D, none or all of the above. He grabbed her none too gently by the arm and took her over to the lab side of the room.

"How is it you speak English, Ziggy?" Have you been watching our satellite TV?" Her eyes darted questioningly around the room. "How's the reception up here in spaceball land?"

"It is my occupation to study..." he paused, "invasive species such as yourself."

Well, *that* didn't sound good. "Is that what we are to you?" Sam asked as the Bootie pushed and pushed her until she was forced to sit her naked butt down on the same slab they'd just scraped the last dead guy off.

*Ewwww.*

She cringed as her butt hit the cold slab. That poor guy had spent his last otherworldly minutes upon this table. Was she about to do the same?

The Bootie reached for a sharp and shiny instrument on a shelf above her head on the side wall and set it between her legs. What was he planning to do with that thing? His back was half-turned to her. "If you think you're gonna stick that thing up my

—"

"You may think of me as an anthropologist, as your psychologist." He picked up instrument after instrument, all stuff that looked like it could easily have come from Dr. Mengele's little bag of tricks. He turned them over and over in his hideously long hands.

Was he trying to decide which one to use as a can opener on her brain?

"You may also come to think of me as your friend," he said, his voice flat as an unleavened pancake.

Sam cringed and slid back as far as she could to the edge of the slab, her back literally against the wall. After all, she'd seen firsthand how well this Bootie treated his visiting friends from Earth.

She snatched a cord dangling off the rim of the slab. Probably meant to tie victims down to keep them from squirming around. She couldn't imagine too many folks placidly lying here letting Ziggy Stardust poke, prod and stick stuff up their lady parts! The cord was slippery and slimy, like a snake struggling to free itself from her grip. She squeezed all the tighter while Ziggy kept yammering away, oblivious as a chunk of granite.

"Now," Ziggy Stardust continued, his back to her, "I am going to ask you to—"

It was now or never. Sam leapt atop the slab, slipped the cord around Ziggy's stupid neck and pulled with all her might and then some. He bellowed like a bull elephant and lurched forward, almost spilling her off. She planted her feet, braced her shoulders against the wall and pulled and squeezed and pulled and squeezed with strength she never knew she possessed.

Ziggy's fingers clutched madly at the cord around his neck. His head twisted impossibly around and he glared at her with eyes that seemed to show something like fear.

They hung like that, the two of them, eye to eye. Facing the uncertainties of death.

And then Sam heard a snap, like the sound of a balsa wood airplane whose fuselage suddenly snapped in two at the hands of a toddler. The Bootie went limp so fast that Sam lost her balance as he fell against her. She tumbled to the cold hard floor knees first and screamed in pain.

"Damn, Ziggy. You don't make it easy on a girl." She kicked him in the side then struggled to her feet, keeping her eyes on the fallen Bootie.

"Now," said Sam, looking down at her victim, "you may come to think of me as your killer." She extended a toe, thinking she'd give him a nudge, but couldn't in the end bring herself to touch the thing again. Still, she couldn't help wondering if the critter was really dead. Who knew what it took to kill a Bootie? Not her, that's who.

A cool draft hit her shoulders and set her shivering. It was coming from an overhead grill. Sam realized she was going to need some clothing. Not some stupid blankie.

A nearby cubby provided the answer. Several sets of scrubs lay neatly folded on three shelves. Sam helped herself to the smallest shirt and trousers she could find. Both were still humongous.

She rolled up the sleeves and the pant legs as far as possible. Looking at her reflection in the glass she thought she looked awful. Well, maybe not awful…

Godawful.

It would have to do.

She approached the doorway the Bootie's partner had gone through earlier and peeked slowly around the corner. She discovered a small anteroom with a closed set of double doors beyond. She also found the hamper abandoned. The human she'd seen earlier lay naked and exposed in the hamper. A rectangular shaped row of red welts rose from his chest, running from his collar bone to his navel like an angry red tattoo.

The guy was definitely dead and he was definitely not Kevin or anyone else she had ever laid eyes on. "Thank goodness for that," she muttered.

And there wasn't a damn thing she could do for him. Except one. She retrieved a blanket from a nearby shelf, covered the corpse and said a prayer for his mortal soul, if he had one.

Then she plotted her escape. She wasn't in favor of ending up tattooed like this guy.

If the Booties came in numbers her goose would be cooked. How would they react when they saw she'd strangled one of their own?

Sam thought it definitely wiser not to be around to find out. The glass partition that had been between her and the lab when she'd first been brought in was in place once again. She banged against the glass and ran her hands along the nearly invisible seams.

No luck. No clues.

Looking around for something to help, she spotted a mallet-like tool beneath one of the tables. She wondered what they used it for—breaking knee caps? Risking the noise, Sam slammed the mallet into the center of the glass. No luck again. No shattered glass. Not even a chip or a crack to give her hope that a second swing would accomplish anything more.

She remembered the slender metallic device she'd seen in her inquisitor's hand when he'd come for her. The glass had parted as easily as a flimsy curtain. He'd slipped the device into his pocket, hadn't he?

That was it. She'd have to get it. And that meant digging through dead Ziggy Stardust's pockets. Not the most pleasant occupation she could think of but it beat being dead herself by a mile. Or a lightyear.

Who knew what diseases this alien weasel might be carrying? Earth was bad enough. It was Sam's opinion that Earth's scientists create diseases just to create cures and make money in the process. The same way she swore that computer programmers create viruses and then create programs to fix them—all in the name of the Profit.

# 27

Lying there in sticky dense bushes that pulled at his skin, waiting in the relative safety of darkness, Kevin replayed Henry's words over in his mind. Could it be true? Could all of humanity simply have been created by some vastly more intelligent and powerful race? All so they could come back and harvest them like so much cannon fodder?

Out of the corner of his eye, he watched Huxley explore the forest floor. The creature seemed almost never to sleep. Henry, on the other hand, slept soundly.

Kevin wished he could close his eyes and sleep half as soundly. But he'd never been a deep sleeper. Less so since this whole crazy upturn of reality had shattered the world he once knew.

Besides, he couldn't stop thinking about these mitochondria Henry told him about. Now that Henry had so richly explained everything, Kevin felt like he could practically feel the millions of them in his body moving all around and through him, little microscopic alien invaders. It literally made his skin crawl like he'd been dunked in a dirty pond filled with leeches. Just the thought gave him the willies and he rubbed his arms as if he could rub them off. But he couldn't. But he also couldn't stop dwelling on them.

Then a thought struck him. If what Henry said was true, why hadn't he been compelled to board one of the ships like the others? He heard Henry stir and he asked him.

"Easy," answered Henry, rubbing his eyes. "You're different."

Kevin nodded. He'd heard that before.

"I'm different." Henry peeled open a bar from his pack and

chewed. "We are all different—our whole little group."

"You mean because none of us boarded the ship so unthinkingly, so—"

"Zombie-like?"

"Yes."

"That's correct." Henry tossed the empty wrapper to the ground. Something he'd never have dared do back on Earth; such an action there would have gotten him jailed. "That's why the Booties want us."

Henry tapped the side of his head. "They want to know what makes us tick. They desire to learn what it is about us *defectives* that makes our biology, chemistry, whatever, unique."

Kevin slowly digested Henry's words. "Because if they can figure it out, they might be able to use this against the Mitoc. Thwart their plans. Keep them from using the technique to continue raising these massive, disposable armies they keep throwing at their enemies."

"Sounds about right." Henry rose and dusted himself off. "You'll have to admit," he said, "no joke intended—but these Mitoc are pretty inhuman."

Kevin had to agree. But then again, he didn't know the good guys from the bad or even what the stakes were.

"We'd better get going," suggested Henry. "You ready?"

Kevin and Henry scrambled down the hill. Huxley rode shotgun on Kevin's right shoulder. They noticed few moving lights on the roads below and the bombing they'd witnessed throughout the day had slowly dwindled and then stopped altogether.

The stars overhead provided little light and less comfort. The stars here were different, too alien, so otherworldly. Besides, there were disturbingly too few of them. It seemed wrong, unnatural somehow.

After what felt like a couple of hours marching and probably a few wrong turns, Kevin stopped atop a rise and pointed. "That's it. That's where Lance said he would be." Where was Sam? Emotion tugged at his heart.

Henry strained to see. The farmhouse was nothing but a dark blur in a distant field. "Are you sure?"

Kevin nodded. "Yes. It looks quiet. Let's go." The scene appeared nondescript and ever so ordinary.

"Wait," said Henry. "Maybe you'd better go alone."

"Why?"

"You know how skittish Lance is, Kevin. If he sees two people coming he just might run—or start shooting."

"I suppose."

"Yes, I think you should go," Henry said. "He's expecting you, after all. I'll stay here. I can keep a lookout from here."

"Good idea." Kevin started down the hill and across the neglected field. He saw no visible lights on inside the abandoned house. Was Lance even there? He might have run away, or been recaptured.

Kevin stopped a couple hundred yards from the house and listened. Something sounded wrong. It took him a minute to figure out what it was—no bugs. No chittering, whistling, buzzing, pestering insects.

Moving forward, the shoulder high crop grass rustled as he waded through and warily approached the silent house. At the edge of the clearing surrounding the house, Kevin paused. Glancing back up at the hill where he'd last seen Henry, he thought he saw a brief, small flash of light. Other than that, he couldn't discern Henry's shape at all, lost as it was in the trees.

Kevin softly called Lance's name and watched the door and windows. Seeing and hearing nothing, he called a second time, as loud as he dared.

Nothing.

Kevin swallowed nervously. "Lance?" he whispered. "It's me, Kevin."

His eyes fought to see through the dark shroud hanging over the house. Still nothing. "I'm coming in," he said, sounding none too certain. Mindful of Henry's words regarding Lance's skittishness and the fact that Lance might answer the door with guns blazing, Kevin approached very slowly.

He stepped on the porch. The boards squeaked under his feet. So much for stealth. With a trembling hand, he reached out and touched the rough door. It fell open.

Inside, all was dark and the air dusty and stale. Kevin pinched his nose to stifle a sneeze. "Lance, it's me, Kevin. You here?"

He took a tentative step past the door, then another. A dark blur shot towards his unprotected face. Before he could react, he was on his back with something heavy pinning him down. A foul smelling hand covered his mouth, smothering him. Kevin fought back.

"Ouch!"

That was Lance's voice.

The stinky hand left his face and Kevin hastily took in mouthfuls of air.

"Damn thing bit me," Lance cried indignantly. "Right on the finger. Why don't you tame that beast of yours? Leastwise, put a leash on him." Lanced sucked loudly at his finger.

Kevin pushed him off. "What were you doing? Trying to kill me?"

"Quiet. Keep your voice down," cautioned Lance. "Of course, I wasn't trying to kill you, Kevin. More like trying to save your life. You oughta be thanking me."

Kevin could barely make out Lance's face in the dimness but the face he could see looked scared, tired, and more than a little crazy. "Why didn't you answer when I called you?"

"I had to be sure, didn't I? I had to be sure it was you. Sure it really was you, not some alien zombie."

Okay, he sounded way more than a little crazy. Like he'd gone over the edge. Kevin asked Lance if he was okay. The guy definitely did not look or sound okay.

Lance leaned in close. "We're not alone," he whispered ominously, so close that Kevin could feel his stale breath on his cheeks.

"What do you mean, not alone?" Kevin was more than a little skeptical. Lance sucked the blood from his bitten finger and spat.

"This house is haunted," Lance said, his voice trembling almost as much as his eyes.

# 28

The second to last thing in the world Sam wanted to do was to reach into some dead guy's pocket. The absolute last thing in the world that she wanted to do was to reach into the pocket of some alien dead guy that she'd only moments before strangled to death.

Nonetheless, she reached into the pocket of the alien dead thing and retrieved the small silvery locking device. She bounced it in the palm of her hand. It felt more like plastic and was practically as light as the surrounding air. It looked completely harmless and useless. But when she slid the tiny bar along its face upward the glasslike wall barring her passage melted away.

Before the door could change its mind, Sam hurried across the room and was relieved to discover the further door there was not locked.

About to toss the magic device to the floor, Sam had second thoughts. Who knew? The toy could come in handy. Besides, she was something of a self-confessed hoarder. Why get rid of something if you didn't need to?

The corridor was empty. Sam was pretty sure of the path she'd taken to get to the lab, so it was with confidence that she pulled open the door where the other humans had been being held. She was instantly struck by a wave of cold dampness. Thick fog filled the room. The humidity must have been hovering at about the three hundred percent mark. The temperature couldn't have been above fifty Fahrenheit.

And that wasn't the weird part. The weird part was that the room smelled like pancakes smothered in maple syrup—the real kind, not that horrid corn syrup imposter. An unanticipated wave of homesickness jarred her, reminding her of the times she and her parents used to get away to Bar Harbor up in Maine.

The room was lit a dull brown from spotlights in rows where the walls met the ceiling. "Ceiling meet walls, walls meet ceiling," muttered Sam. In the center of the room stood a wide table on wheels. Atop the table sat a sickly looking yellow lump of many folds. The gelatinous glob was a good meter in circumference and every few seconds a wave of white light pulsed weakly across its surface.

Definitely not the room her friends were being kept locked up in—unless this thing had eaten them or the aliens had gelatinized them all and turned them into this loose lump of jelly.

Sam's first thought was a quick escape but, as she was about to step out the door, the voice popped into her head, yammering nonstop.

"Pancakes. Buttermilk pancakes with blueberries. But you can't get blueberries anymore. They're too expensive. Only the elite get fresh blueberries. Only the rich get anything real at all. Reality is..." There was a short pause. "Too costly."

Sam clenched her fists and squeezed them against her temples. Despite the frigid air, perspiration rolled down her forehead. Where were these...thoughts coming from? Were they her thoughts? They seemed so alien.

Or, she wondered, was that slab of gelatin on the table actually speaking—communicating somehow—with her?

No. Not speaking to her in a way that two people might speak to each other, rather an inserting of thoughts into her head, through to her thought center. And her thought center was translating these intruded thoughts into words she could understand.

She felt invaded. Attacked by an invisible knife blade that wounded her far worse than one of steel.

Sam backed to the door.

"No," it said, reading her mind. "I am not one of the natives of this planet. Not related to the other that you destroyed."

Sam gasped, and a cloud of fog escaped her lips. She cringed warily and took a step backward. This thing knew that she had strangled Ziggy Stardust? What else did it know? More importantly, what was it doing here? And what did it want?

"I am a tactician," it explained in answer to her unvocalized questions. "I belong to the Mandos who belong to the Mitoc. Like you."

Sam's face muscles tightened. "I don't belong to anybody, jelly boy. And I don't like aliens poking around in my brain."

She glared defiantly at the blob. "You know what I did to the last one that tried." Though looking at this thing, she couldn't begin to imagine how she'd manage to strangle it, supposing she could even find some spot remotely worth strangling. Did it even have bones?

"Anyway," she said, "don't think I won't do the same thing to you, jelly brains." Surreptitiously as possible, she glanced around for a weapon to back up her threat but her eyes came back empty-handed. What do you kill jelly brains with? A tub of peanut butter?

"Acid would do the trick."

"What?"

"Acid. A chemical compound that, when dissolved in water yields a solution with hydrogen ion activity exceeding pure water. A sufficient quantity of hydrochloric acid would suffice. However, it would require a large, uneasily contained quantity and quite a bit of time. You do believe in time, don't you? I have sufficient time. You, however, do not."

Sam's blood was at its boiling point. The only thing worse than an alien jelly ball invading your brains was an alien jelly ball that wouldn't shut the hell up. She was about to speak when it started up again without even waiting for her answer to its question.

"No, I would suggest a mixture of fluorosulfonic acid and antimony pentafluoride. I do not know if you can secure such a solution here, however. I do not know of a nearby facility or supply."

"Would you just shut up for a second?" Sam pounded the sides of her head with her fists. Great," she winced. "Now my ears hurt." There was that sudden memory of pancakes again. Buttermilk pancakes and Vermont maple syrup. Sam's salivary glands went into overdrive. "What are you doing? Stop that!"

"I am counteracting negative thoughts with comforting thoughts. You like pancakes."

Sam growled. The image of a young girl riding a chestnut brown pony trotted across her brain, accompanied by the scent of dewy fresh morning air. "Cut that out!" shouted Sam. "I never had a pony!"

"My pardon."

The image popped like a soap bubble and Sam sagged to the floor, exhausted both mentally and physically. Her brain felt battered. Bruised and wrung dry like an old kitchen sponge. "What do you want?" she said wearily, hands on her knees.

Jelly brains didn't answer right away. Didn't even pace around the room getting up his/her/its courage to speak.

"Well?"

"I must leave this location."

"Leave this location?" Sam thought about this. "You want me to push you somewhere? Like under a nice shady palm tree in the sun? Maybe leave you with a five-gallon jug of sunblock and a good book? Maybe a light summer read?" Jelly brains was a hoot.

"I must leave this location. You must take me with you."

Sam's jaw dropped. This thing was crazy. Biggest brain she'd ever seen, but completely loco. "Are you out of your mind?" From the look of him he was more out of his body and she would have said so, but she didn't want to be rude or anything. "I can't do that."

She sat up. "How am I going to do that?"

# 29

"Your brain is haunted," snapped Kevin, instantly regretting his words. After all, if anybody's brain was haunted, it was his own. It had been as far back as he could remember. And this crazy world he was now living in wasn't helping it any.

Even in the dim light, Kevin could see the look of hurt on Lance's face. He sighed. "Sorry. What makes you think it's haunted, Lance?"

He'd humor the guy. Besides, who knew? Maybe this old alien farmhouse was haunted, maybe the whole planet was haunted. Who knew what was possible in this place? Kevin had never believed in ghosts, but then he'd never believed in aliens either.

Lance scooted across the floor on his knees, peeked around the doorway, then returned. "I don't think, I know." His head bobbed up and down. "Believe me, I know."

"Lance—"

"No, listen, Kevin. You haven't been trapped in here with her the way I have."

"Her?" said Kevin, half-tempted to lick the skepticism that was no doubt drooling down his chin as he spoke.

"Yeah," Lance said, excitedly, "I hear her talking. And she's watching me. All the time watching me." He glanced nervously over his shoulder. "She's watching us now. Bet on it."

Despite himself, Kevin shivered. He didn't like being watched. If there was anything good at all about being flung across the universe to this rock on the edge of nowhere it was the relief he felt in not being watched. Back on Earth, everybody, practically everybody—the elite stood immune to the law, like they were immune to everything else that applied to the masses

—was watched. It was a fact of life. Life, death, taxes, and watch out because *we are watching you.*

Kevin heard a sound, nothing more than a soft rustle, yet he flinched. Lance was getting to him. "What was that?" he whispered.

"The ghost."

"No," Kevin dropped to the ground. "It sounded like it came from outside."

Lance crossed to the window and stuck his head up.

"Keep your head down. You never know who or what might be lurking about." Kevin was concerned and didn't want to take any unnecessary risks, but he was not overly concerned. After all, Henry was keeping watch from the hilltop. Henry would find a way to warn them of any approaching danger.

"No problem," said Lance. "Coast is clear. I'm telling you, Kevin. It's here we've got to worry about—inside. This is where the ghost is."

"Get out of the window anyway, before someone or something spots you," ordered Kevin. "And don't worry about your ghost. We'll be out of here soon enough. I just want to give Sam time to get here."

"Yeah, whatever happened to Sam?" Lance asked, still looking out the window, despite Kevin's wishes.

"Long story. I'll explain it to you later." Kevin groaned. "Lance, would you please get out of the window. You're making me nervous."

"Yeah, yeah," chided Lance, "look who's skittish now." He turned his face to Kevin. "Not scared of the dark, are you?"

Lance was obviously feeling quite full of himself all of a sudden. Kevin was about to put him in his place when all the windows exploded at once and giant white aliens began leaping through the shards of glass before the pieces even hit the ground.

"Run!" yelled Kevin. But there was no need to shout, Lance was running as fast as he could.

One of the aliens tripped over Kevin, sending them both

sprawling in a tangle of arms and legs. Out of the corner of his eye, Kevin saw three of the brutes grappling with Lance. They pinned his arms behind his back. He valiantly kicked out at them. Sadly, to no avail.

Strong arms grabbed Kevin and he was yanked laterally and downward. His head slammed against something solid and he momentarily lost consciousness. When he came to his senses, his vision was blurry and he saw little in the small and dusty confined space. As he raised his head, the sounds of struggle continued for a few more moments then ceased altogether.

Alien voices shouted and alien feet trampled through the farmhouse, then scattered in all directions. A coarse hand smothered Kevin's face. He couldn't see and he could barely breathe. Instinct told him not to scream. After all, except for being roughed up a bit, unable to see and barely breathing, he was in pretty good shape. He tried working his jaw to speak and tasted hand—and it wasn't his.

He spit it out. It tasted like a well-worn baseball mitt that had been seasoned with peanut oil. He tried again. "Hefmorfmoferingme" is what came out. What he was desperately trying to say was "Help, you're smothering me!"

And if this thing that held him didn't remove its hand soon, there wouldn't be much more coming out. He needed air. Now!

Maybe the thing understood, or maybe it had only gotten tired of holding him, but Kevin felt the hand slowly withdraw. A high-pitched voice said but one word and not one in Kevin's lexicon.

The voice repeated itself.

Kevin twisted on his side with a grimace. There wasn't room to stand, barely room to turn around. He was trapped with this thing, whatever it was, in this small enclosed space; dark and hard. Kevin was thinking *they*, but in truth had no idea who or what *they* was.

Two brilliant blue eyes the size of golf balls locked onto him. Bright white flecks floated in a sea of blue, rotating round and round, sometimes coming together, sometimes fanning out, living creatures themselves. And moving. Always moving.

This was not one of the Booties. Booties did not have eyes like these. "Who are you?" Kevin whispered, fearful not of this strange creature, but that there may be Booties yet lurking nearby, and much preferring his present situation, provisional sanctuary that it was.

The voice with the blue eyes and the floating white islands spoke again, high and soft. Kevin sensed a catlike quality in its timbre. He heard footsteps that seemed to be coming from above. His breath caught in his throat. He felt his heart pushing against his chest. Moving feet shuffled overhead. He was surprised and confused to realize he was inside a tight space beneath the floor.

"Kevin?"

Kevin flinched. The thing with the big blue eyes smothered Kevin's face with its hand again. It seemed to be pleading with its eyes. What was it afraid of?

Kevin tore the things fingers away from his eyes and strained his neck to peep through a slit in the floorboards. It was Henry. He knew he recognized that voice. He started to rise but the alien was stronger and held him down.

Kevin watched helplessly as Henry carefully searched the room. Henry's eyes fell on Kevin's pack which lay where he'd dropped it. The schoolteacher picked it up, shook it, then let it drop to the floor. "Kevin?"

Kevin squirmed but the hands were unyielding and the eyes still pleading. As Kevin watched, three armed Booties burst through the front door. He wanted desperately to yell, to warn Henry to get out while he could. *Run, Henry, run*, he thought.

But it was hopeless. One of the three aliens barked at Henry and waved his arm toward the door.

Kevin's eyes widened. Henry didn't look frightened, not even a little bit scared. In fact, he didn't seem the least bit perturbed by this sudden armed alien invasion. Rather, he barked something back in monosyllables that sounded weirdly alien— and the three Booties left!

What was going on?

Henry took one last slow turn around the room then followed them out.

Kevin lay still. So stunned that he hadn't even realized that the strange creature keeping him had now released him.

Their eyes met.

Kevin saw the outlines of a hatch in the floor and pushed. Dust hit his eyes as the hatch rose. He coughed. The creature made no attempt to stop him. The alien had dragged him into some underground compartment or shaft of sorts, like some kind of troll living under a bridge neatly snatching its next victim. Kevin could only guess what the contrivance had been used for by its owners. Grain storage? Tornado escape hatch? A refuge from alien hunters? Who knew?

And why had the troll saved him from the Booties? Did it want Kevin all to itself? Was it going to eat him like all good trolls must? Troll unions could be rather fussy about such things.

Of course, the thing could even be the homeowner. How else could it have known about this underground chamber?

The trapdoor lifted silently and no sound but the beating of his heart came to his ears. Kevin's pack lay abandoned under the windowsill. What few things he possessed—food and weapons —were in that pack.

And where was Huxley? Had the Booties taken him? Kevin squirmed out of his hidey-hole and crawled on all fours to the window. He glanced over his shoulder. So far, the creature in the basement still wasn't stopping him. If it tried, there probably wouldn't be much Kevin could do about it. He was beginning to think the creature might not be so dangerous after all.

Maybe it was the family pet. And maybe that cramped space was its lair.

Kevin glanced back again. The hatch hung open, held up by the creature's head. Big blue eyes watched him. Actually, now that he saw him in better light, the creature didn't look like a troll at all, more like a pink, furry humanoid—on a very large

151

and muscular scale.

Kevin's ears picked up the sound of voices outside. Not too far distant. Some Booties, some human. He peeked out the edge of the window. Henry was returning to the house!

Kevin scrambled back to the hatch and dove into the crawl space, knocking the creature in his path to one side. The hatch fell shut. Alien and human froze, glanced at each other, then fixed their eyes on the crack in the floorboards.

Kevin flinched as Henry appeared in the open doorway. "Kevin, you here?" His voice sounded so smooth, so soothing. So innocent and caring. "It's me, Kevin. Henry." He flashed on a brilliant flashlight and played the beam around the room. "It's okay, Kevin. There's nothing to fear now. The Booties are long gone."

Kevin clenched his teeth. What was Henry up to? Whose side was he on? And what was going to happen to Lance now that the Booties had him? He feared there was nothing he could do to help.

Kevin felt his companion's grip tighten on his arm. Was it for support or to keep him from exposing them? It didn't matter. Didn't the creature understand? Kevin wasn't about to give himself up to Henry. He wasn't going anywhere.

The narrow beam of light danced along the walls and floor like a firefly. Henry went from room to room, came back to the front room, called Kevin's name once more then left.

Kevin sighed with relief. Even the alien must have been scared because Kevin felt its strong grip on his arm release once Henry was gone. Kevin twisted over and put his hand up to push open the hatch just as Henry suddenly appeared in the door once again. It was all Kevin could do to keep from crying out loud. Ever so slowly, he let the top of the hatch down the inch he'd already raised it.

Henry stepped in the door and flicked on his light. Kevin watched through the crack. The schoolteacher was frowning and moving the brilliant light more slowly this time, back and forth, up and down.

Had he heard them?

Frowning some more, the schoolteacher scratched his head and turned to leave. Kevin and his alien companion watched anxiously. Kevin prayed Henry would this time leave for good.

Henry was halfway out the door when he turned yet again, light in hand, his brow furrowed, his face pinched. He shined the light on the big window in front then slowly worked the beam down to the floor.

Henry stepped toward the window, keeping the light on the floor, frowning, always frowning.

Kevin wondered what Henry could see—what he was looking at—that could possibly be so interesting or perplexing. Of course, Henry had to be wondering furiously where Kevin had disappeared to. If only Henry knew he was mere inches away.

Kevin squeezed the strap of his pack. He'd pulled it inside after Henry and the Booties had gone the first time. Damn. Henry might be remembering seeing the pack on the floor. After all, he'd picked it up from under the window and then dropped it only minutes ago.

Kevin's heart revved. He glanced from Henry to the alien at his side. And then everything happened quickly though time seemed to be going in slow motion. Henry was barking words, alien words, that Kevin could not understand, but they were ugly words and surely meant Kevin no good.

Henry ran to the door, shouting. At the same time, Kevin felt alien hands grabbing him from behind and sliding him across the hard ground.

# 30

"This is stupid." And crazy, Sam thought. Stupid and crazy. So why was she doing it? Probably because there were so few real choices. Real! That was a hoot. Sam wasn't sure if any of this was real. Probably all some insane world government experiment taking place in a bunker buried deep on an atoll in the South Pacific. "Probably a bunch of geeks and spooks watching us right now," she muttered.

"Not so," replied Jelly Brains.

Sam jumped. She'd forgotten the thing could read her mind—was constantly reading her mind. Very annoying.

"Though there will be two scientists arriving shortly to renew their researches on me."

"How lovely."

"If they discover us together, they will summon security."

"I know, I know," Sam said impatiently. She couldn't help glancing toward the door. "I'm still not convinced you're real, you know. I'm not even convinced any of this is real." She waved her arms around. "You, this place, the Booties, the Mitoc—" She made a face. "Probably just some chemical-induced fantasy foisted on me by government thugs with nothing better to do. They're like that, you know."

Sam didn't believe in Santa Claus but she believed in government conspiracies. Believed a lot. Sam explained her theory about how scientists on Earth created diseases just to invent cures they could then charge millions for, computer programmers created viruses just so they could write and sell programs to thwart them.

"The government lies and lies big." She was on her pedestal

now. "I'll bet you didn't know that the Earth is really hollow?"

"Your home planet? No, I did not."

"Well, it is. And it's where the real elite hide out. And," she added, "it's full of alien technology. But then, they have problems of their own. The Vril also live in the subterranean Earth. They're an advanced matriarchal society responsible for the fluoride in our water. It makes us all docile and subservient to their will, you know."

"Is that a fact?"

"Fact." Sam snapped her fingers. "And so is the moon— hollow that is. Hollow as a beachball. Just all covered with rock and dust. Camouflage." She leaned in closer to the thing on the table. "It's an alien spaceship, you see."

"Yes," said the thing on the table, "I do see."

Sam pinched her brow. Was this goof mocking her? This thing with no arms and no legs? Oh well, at least he wasn't one of those shape-shifting alien lizard things that she had reason to believe occupied the bodies of the world's top leaders. Though that theory seemed to be on shaky ground now in light of Earth's most recent alien invasion by the Mitoc.

"I am not mocking you at all."

Sam squeezed her eyes shut. "This mind reading has got to stop. She balled up her hands and pounded the sides of her head. "It's invasive. It's rude."

"There is no other way for us to communicate," Jelly Brains replied. "Besides, it is unavoidable. It is what I am."

Sam had no good retort to that, fact that it was, and said, "I still think you're some sort of delusion, part of some unholy experiment by the gov." How else do you explain a wheelbarrow full of talking jelly?

"If so, it is quite a good one. And," it added, "if this is true, what have you got to lose by playing along? And I might add that Jelly Brains sounds rather pejorative."

Oops.

Once again the smug lump of goo had to be right. Sam felt like smacking him, but what good would that do? Her hand would probably sink harmlessly into its body a good six inches and come out covered with sticky alien goo. And she'd probably contract some sticky alien disease.

Nonetheless, it irked her terribly when spineless, legless, jelly creatures got the better of her, not to mention called her out.

"This is really stupid," she said, having come full circle. Did this thing really expect her, the four other humans trapped here, and it to escape this place?

"Time is short. I estimate five of your minutes before the Bootie scientists arrive as per their normal schedule."

"Five minutes! Why didn't you say so?" Sam was going to have to hurry. Worst of all, she was going to have to touch dead Ziggy Stardust again. "Be right back!" She stuck her head out the door, saw that the coast was clear and raced down the hall. She popped into the lab where her victim lay sleeping the sleep eternal sprawled out on the floor. Her plan was to use the cart the dead human had been rolled out in to carry her new friend off. But first that meant dumping Mr. Dead Earthling, he of the hideous red welts.

Happy to see that Ziggy was indeed still dead, she sailed past him, through the lab and out the other side. The human lay naked where she'd last seen him, too, inside the deep cart that looked more like it had been designed to transport soiled hospital gowns and towels rather than people.

Cringing, she grabbed the dead Earthman by his freezing wrists and pulled. His head fell forward against his chest but he came no further. Planting her bare feet and yanking harder, she managed to get his butt off the bottom, but only an inch or so.

This wasn't going to work. And there was no time for niceties. Not if Jelly Brains was right in his estimate of when the Booties would return. Sam grabbed the side of the cart and shoved. The cart hung in the air a moment then fell on its side, sending the dead Earthman's body to the floor with a slapping sound that made Sam want to vomit.

"Sorry," she said. "Emergency."

Pushing the cart in front of her, Sam raced back to Jelly Brains who waited passively. Then again, it wasn't like he had a choice.

She came to a screeching halt next to the table on which the tactician sat, if you could call lying around being a blob sitting. "Now what? Do I simply plop you in?"

"Slide me off the table and into the cart. Quite simple."

"What if you land on your, ah, head?" Not that she could tell what particular spot of goo might be the thing's head.

"Not a problem."

Sam shrugged and nudged the alien into the cart. The creature fell with a *fwump* and a jiggle and then was still. "You okay?"

"Yes. Hurry now, please."

"Yeah, yeah." Sam pushed her alien catch in front of her, and went searching for her friends. The first two doors she tried were locked and the device she'd taken from Ziggy did nothing to change that. The third door opened to reveal an empty office of sorts.

She looked up the hall. Doors and more doors. How many doors did this place have anyway?

"Footsteps," said the cart of jelly.

"I hear them!" Sam whispered sharply. This was definitely not good. She was weaponless and wouldn't stand a chance if there was more than one of the Booties. And what good was her new companion going to be in a fist fight?

She hastened to the next door. Thank goodness it was open. She pushed the cart through and closed the door quietly behind her. Pressing her ear against the door, Sam made out the sound of footsteps passing in the distance.

As she caught her breath, she turned and took a look around. She'd stumbled into what appeared to be a locker room of sorts. A row of open-faced lockers with storage bins along their bottoms filled three of the walls. She ran her fingers over the glossy material of a shirt suspended from a hook. She pulled the shirt off the hook and held it against her, sizing it up.

"These are human clothes," she said, with surprise. She riffled through the lockers. "My things!" She grabbed her clothes, filthy and torn though they were, and smiled. Her pack and weapons had been tossed into the bin below.

Sam shot a look at her companion, only the tip of his/her/its gelatinous head was visible above the lip of the cart. "Keep your eyes to yourself," she warned as she began peeling off her alien clothing. "I mean it. No peeking."

# 31

Alien hands with the strength of thick steel fingers relentlessly dragged Kevin backward through the narrow tunnel. After a few futile efforts, he'd given up fighting, stopped flailing his arms and legs and focused on keeping his head from banging against the low ceiling. He was going to end up with a concussion, he was sure of it. Maybe two. Whether that was possible or not.

After about ninety seconds of this wild and slightly upward sloping ride, they came to a sudden stop. Kevin felt himself being lifted helplessly up as if he weighed nothing at all. The back of his skull cracked against a hard wall. "Hey!" he protested, before the catcher's mitt-sized hand smothered his face.

Furiously, Kevin summoned up the courage and strength to yank the hand away. He'd had just about all he could tolerate. Miraculously, it worked.

Stunned, it was a moment before Kevin spoke up. "Listen, whatever you are. I am not some sack of potatoes. You can't go hauling me around like so much produce."

The alien's eyes seemed to implore him. It placed its hands, gently this time, on either side of Kevin's face and twisted him to the side. He found himself staring at a small slit, no more than four inches long and barely an inch tall. But from it, he could see out.

They were in a squat silo in the midst of a field some distance from the house, that much Kevin could deduce. And that long tunnel must have been some sort of chute meant to carry whatever crop the field yielded up from the field to the house.

As his eyes adjusted to the dimness, he discerned the roof of the farmhouse a few hundred yards away. He heard voices and saw wickedly bright flashlights. Any brighter and they'd have left tracks of scorched earth.

How long could the two of them remain hidden here?

Kevin couldn't yet see it, but he recognized the ominous sound of one of the alien flying machines. It sounded like the same type that he'd watched helplessly snare Sam.

Poor Sam. Was she alive or lying slit open and pickled in a jar in some alien high school classroom being ogled by giggling teenaged alien biology students?

Kevin studied the alien beside him. The alien tilted its head and pushed against the lower portion of the silo. A square hatch opened opposite the side facing the farmhouse. The alien pushed its hand through. There was no mistaking the alien's intent. It meant for them to run.

Kevin could not have agreed more. They were sitting ducks if they remained where they were. Being caught was only a matter of time—and time was not on their side. Henry and the Booties were tearing the house apart and swarming every inch of the grounds. It wasn't a matter of being discovered, only a question of how much time it might take them.

Kevin nodded and, gripping the sides of the hatch to keep from landing on his face, pushed through. The alien followed and though Kevin first thought the thing too large to squeeze through the opening, it did so with ease—as if it had done so a hundred times before.

The alien blinked and looked at him and Kevin could have sworn it was smiling. Then, with a look of unmistaken grim determination, it took off in the opposite direction from the hill atop which Kevin and Henry had recently stood together like brothers-in-arms.

As Kevin ran to keep up with the alien, looking back, he saw the halo of liquid light in the sky that was the dozen or so Booties' search craft.

Their combined light built menacing shadows on the ground. Kevin spotted his own gangly, spasmodic shadow out in front of him and fought to outrun it.

Kevin's lungs screamed, begging him to stop. They seemed to be running in circles. He'd followed his alien companion through a sloping rutted field of tall grass, into an uneven field of brambles that plucked at his clothes and bit at his skin, then through another field of tall grass that made him sneeze and brought tears streaming from his eyes.

Kevin was beginning to wonder if this creature he had placed his trust and his life in really had any notion of what it was doing or where it was going. His calves ached and sharp pains banged out a dissonant tune up and down his ribcage. All he wanted was to lie down for a while, but his companion pushed relentlessly on.

They crossed a narrow road. Kevin tripped jogging up the steep side of the ditch on the other side. The alien looked back, seeing that Kevin had fallen, and waited. Its blue eyes twinkled like distant galaxies.

Kevin struggled up the side of the ditch and stood. Pain shot up his leg. He winced and fell down. He tried to stand again but his left ankle was refusing to cooperate and stung like he'd stepped ankle deep in a beehive.

He stooped and rubbed his ankle, hoping to drive away the pain. A distant thrum in the air grew louder. Like a freight train rumbling through desolate and forlorn hills, moving forward inexorably and ominously.

The alien said something and gestured towards the sky. Kevin saw nothing out of place but the alien continued pointing. Then Kevin saw it. A solitary light moving against the background of stars. And it was headed their way.

Kevin pulled in a deep breath, then let it out slowly. There was nothing to be done. He was beaten, tired to the point of collapse and now as hobbled as a horse. He yelled for the alien to run. "Go, leave, run!"

He waved the alien off. But the alien simply stood there, looking at Kevin, the ever growing light in the sky and the distant hills. "Bad leg. Sprained ankle," Kevin explained, as loudly as he dared. As if speaking more stridently would make him more understood.

The alien jumped into the ditch beside Kevin. Without warning, Kevin found himself cradled in the alien's arms like a baby. "Hey, put me down!" he protested.

The alien took off at a trot along the bottom of the ditch, the wet ground squishing beneath its feet.

"How far do you expect to get hauling me around like this, anyway?" stuttered Kevin, feeling like a complete and utter idiot.

The alien jogged along. "This is ridiculous," groused Kevin. "I'm not a baby and you're just going to get both of us killed. Oh well," Kevin said, "it's your own fault. If you get killed—if the Booties kill you—don't say I didn't warn you."

The alien ran silently on another couple of hundred yards. The light of an airship was clearly visible now, like the light of a lamppost on a distant street corner. And the thrumming was growing louder, whatever it was.

Without warning, the alien came to a stop and dumped Kevin unceremoniously to the ground. "What? Was it something I said or have you run out of juice?"

The alien stepped over Kevin. Kevin dodged, thinking for a moment that the alien was going to stomp him out of existence. Had the indecipherable alien carried him all this way only to make a meal of him?

Instead, the alien hand grabbed a dimpled metallic cover built into a concrete base that Kevin hadn't even realized was there. The alienish manhole was rusted, coated with dust and blended into the side of the ditch. The cover was a good three feet in diameter and riddled with two-inch holes that no doubt allowed water in and out. Snakes, too, he feared.

Kevin glanced up. The airship wasn't more than a couple of hundred feet away now, moving in slow circles above them, like a hawk circling its intended prey. They didn't have much time.

The alien stuck its fingers in the holes and tugged the cover free. It lifted with a squeal of protest. The alien set it aside, then gave Kevin a shove that sent him sliding headfirst into the muck-filled tube in protest.

The alien fell atop Kevin and pulled the cover back in place from inside, its lips turned down in a frown.

# 32

She didn't really feel clothed until she had her weapons in hand. Even then, Sam still felt mentally naked since her alien cohort could obviously read every thought in her head from the moment she was born up to the present. Sometimes it seemed it knew what she was thinking before she did.

She wondered if it could even see her future—tell her where and when she would die and what she'd be thinking when she did. And she couldn't help wondering if that was years away or only moments.

"No."

"Huh?"

"No, I cannot read what is not there."

"Cut that out," Sam said sternly. She stuffed the pistol into her waistband, then threw her discarded alien clothing over Mr. Jelly-For-Brains.

"I can still see your thoughts."

Sam bit her lip and pushed the alien clothing around, making sure the Jelly Brain was fully covered. "I know that," she snapped. Truthfully, she'd been hoping the drapery would provide some sort of protective shielding between her brain and this spineless voyeur. "I'm only covering you up so no one sees you. It's camouflage. It's for your own protection." She tucked the ends in at the corners.

The alien made no reply, apparently deciding that silence for once was golden and discretion more precious than letting her know that it knew exactly what she was doing and why.

Sam approached a door to the left of the lockers. It fell open easily. "Nothing but a closet," Sam said, with obvious disappointment. "Any ideas?"

"We can attempt to leave. But if you choose to search for the others of your species it becomes a question of finding them before the Booties find you."

"Oh, thanks. You're a great help." Sam waved her hands in the air. "Look at me, the great strategist!"

The brain in the basket refused to rise to the bait. Okay, so he was legless and couldn't rise if he wanted to, that was no excuse. Besides, it wasn't her fault or her problem. Getting out of here alive. That was her problem.

And after that?

Who knew?

She pushed her crippled charge out the door and up one hall after another. Every once in a while she caught the sporadic sounds of fighting and wondered what was going on outside.

Rounding a corner, she caught herself just in time and pulled back. A Bootie occupied the next intersection, sitting behind a semicircular desk, its back to them.

Sam braced herself.

"It is not a good idea," said the alien in the cart.

Sam ignored him and his feeble protests. She summoned up all her strength and launched the cart at the Bootie.

Jelly Brains had gone silent.

By the time the Bootie behind the desk heard and responded to the sound of the cart's rubbery wheels racing up the hall, it was too late. As he turned, the cart struck him in the chest. He was picked up and flung backward, hitting his head against the top tier of the station.

Sam was on him before he could blink. Assuming aliens could blink, of course.

"That was quite unnecessary."

"Quiet," complained Sam. "I'm trying to think." The Bootie lay sprawled across the floor like a broken doll.

"I might have been killed."

"You might be yet," quipped Sam with a touch of warning. She could see flickering, moving images behind the alien's head.

She gently slid his skull to one side, unsure if he was dead or not. A monitor came into view. The camera focused on a small room, filled with weary looking cots and even more weary and worn looking occupants. Humans.

"It figures." Sam shot a dirty look at the unmoving Bootie. "Spying on them like they're goldfish in a bowl, eh?" She poked the alien with her toe. "Shame on you."

"I don't believe he can hear you."

Sam was about to say something smart-alecky, then stopped herself, mouth agape. "Hey, can you tell? I mean, can you read this thing's mind?"

She wrinkled her nose. It wasn't the first time that Sam had noticed that Booties smelled like overcooked boiled cabbage, and that didn't make them any more pleasant. She wrinkled her nose. She imagined what humans might smell like to them.

"Yes. Its mind is clear."

"Is it alive?"

"Yes. The Bootie functions. But at the moment is not reasoning."

Sam nodded, making a mental note. Jelly Brains might be of some use after all. She returned her attention to the flickering console. Lots of dials, lots of knobs. No instructions. Sure, why make things easy?

She noticed what looked like a schematic of the floor of the building they were on etched into the countertop to the right of the monitor. Five corridors and probably twenty rooms. Not good. A lot of doors to open, each time wondering who or what she'd be facing.

She was beginning to think the whole thing was hopeless when she noticed the tiny red dot of light on one of the doors marked on the schematic. A recessed light diode marked each door. But only the one particular light glowed red. She ran her finger over the light, thinking. The light was cool to the touch.

It had to be. She looked again at the sullen-faced captives on the monitor, but it wasn't their faces she was interested in. It was the tiny red glowing light on the upper left side of the screen.

A smile broke across her face. A quick glance at the schematic told her where she was. The little command center, or whatever this was, was clearly marked. The captives were only two corridors over and three doors down.

"Easy as pancakes on Sunday morning," she muttered and was instantly hit with the stomach-arousing scent of buttermilk pancakes and warm maple syrup. "Cut that out!" she said, grabbing the cart. "If I wanted special effects, I'd order them."

Fearful they'd run into more Booties, Sam forced herself not to run. Finding the room that held the captives was no trouble. Opening the locked door with her handy-dandy locksmith-in-a-box gizmo was no problem either.

Stepping into the room, tired and beaten down, the humans barely looked up. Even when they realized Sam was alone and not being led in by armed Booties, they regarded her with suspicion in their eyes and questions on their tongues.

"What's going on?" asked Nicolette, her eyes wide. "Are you alright?"

Sam nodded. "I'm fine. Come on. We've got to get out of here."

"What?" Surprise blossomed across Nicolette's face.

The others started yammering. Gig's voice rose above the others. "What's in the basket? You bring us lunch?"

The cart was over-brimming with everything Sam had managed to squeeze in. It hadn't been easy what with an overgrown bulbous brain taking up the lion share of the space.

"Your brain," quipped Sam. Gig she could live without. "Now, come on." She scanned the corners of the tiny cell, knowing there was a spy camera there somewhere. And where there was one watcher, there could be two. Maybe a watcher had been watching the watcher.

"We really have to get moving." Sam was making herself nervous. She glared with annoyance at Gig as he dragged himself off his cot—she'd have sworn she'd heard the cot sigh in relief—and lifted the edge of a crumpled blue shirt atop the pile in the cart so he could peek into the basket.

"Where will we go?" asked Sequoia.

"Does it matter?" replied Nicolette.

Sam had been about to say the same thing.

"I say we go," said Xian, "no questions asked. I do not savor ending up in some elementary school classroom sliced open navel to sternum like a frog."

Good point, thought Sam. She slapped the edge of the cart. "As you can see, I grabbed all the gear that I could find. Take what's yours and let's get moving."

Everybody began riffling through the clothing and gear. This was no time for modesty. In a couple of minutes, they were dressed, armed and ready for action.

A shrill whistling sound rose from without and penetrated the walls like a demon. "What's that?" Sam asked.

"You get used to it," shrugged Nicolette. "We figure it's a warning alarm. I expect we'll hear fighting soon." She sounded sad and looked up at the ceiling, chewing her lip nervously.

But Sam took this for good news. The more distracted the Booties were the better chance this motley troop had of escaping.

"Let's go!" Sam pushed the cart out the door.

"What are you bringing that thing for?" whined Gig. "We've got all we need. It'll just slow us down. Dump it!"

"I told you," snapped Sam, impatiently, "it's got your brain in it." She whipped back the pile of Bootie clothing hiding her cohort. "See?"

Gig's eyes bulged and his face turned yellow. "What is that?" he squeaked. He appeared ready to faint.

"Somebody catch Gig before he falls on his face," snickered Sam—or after, she thought—"and follow me."

She stopped and faced her tiny troupe "And stick together," she added sternly. "No lollygaggers and no detours."

No one challenged her.

# 33

Kevin woke leaning against a storm drain looking out over the river below and the alien city lying like a dormant beast on the far side. He hadn't even realized he'd blacked out except that he couldn't remember anything beyond being pushed into the other end of the storm drain back in that ditch.

He shifted uncomfortably. The storm drain cover was rusted and wet, leaving streaks of orange and red stains along his shirt and hands. The river churned below, brown and menacing. A few Booties were moving up and down the docks. Some walking, some driving small open vehicles that motored slowly in all directions.

Kevin couldn't be certain but it looked like the same city he'd come to with Sam. The one where he'd so famously managed to rescue Lance and lose Sam all in one night.

And now he'd lost them both. Kevin Kent, Warrior Extraordinaire. No wonder he hadn't been fit for Mitoc fodder. Even his little pet, Huxley, was gone.

Kevin took a swig of water, offered his bottle to his companion, who refused. Rummaging in his satchel for food, he came up with a packet of the same gray stuff they'd been fed almost exclusively aboard the Mitoc spaceship.

Not only did his new alien friend refuse to share, he shook his head vigorously, as if Kevin shouldn't eat the crud either. Kevin ignored him and took a bite. It wasn't tasty but he moved his jaw resolutely. He was that hungry.

Kevin watched curiously as the alien withdrew a slender blinking oval device from a deep pouch in his trousers. "Dodder."

Kevin raised an eyebrow. The pilose alien's mouth was

moving though it sounded like his voice was coming from inside a vacuum cleaner—and there was a catlike quality mingled with it.

Figuring he had nothing better to do with his time, Kevin replied. He said his name slowly, tentatively, as if he was hearing it for the first time himself. He tapped his chest as he said it, like they did in the movies.

The alien nodded. "Dodder."

"Got it," said Kevin. Not even attempting to get the crazy vacuum cleaner cum cat inflection, he repeated "Dodder." He smiled.

The alien nodded once more and scratched his finger on the pad. At least it looked like scratches to Kevin. When the alien was done scratching, he touched a button on the side of the device and the device said "Dodder" with the alien's accent. The alien looked at Kevin expectantly but Kevin had no clear idea what he wanted.

"Kevin," he said more loudly. What more could he do?

The alien appeared to think a moment, letting the word sink in, then ran a finger atop the pad. A moment later the pad said "Kevin" or at least something that came remarkably close to it. Clear enough for Kevin to understand. He leaned closer.

The alien beamed and pointed to the device.

Kevin examined the squiggles crossing the screen. They looked like nothing more than gibberish but put it all together and somewhere in there, in that scramble of lines that might as well have been hieroglyphs, it spelled his name.

Dodder, if that was this guy's name—after all, the thing could just be telling him the name of his planet or what he had for lunch yesterday—handed Kevin the pad. Startled, Kevin glanced at the pad then wrote out Dodder's name as best he figured.

The alien studied the letters on the screen and tapped his fingers atop the screen in a flurry of movement that would have bested the best word processors on Earth.

They spent hours scratching and trying to communicate. It was baby steps but it helped to pass the time. Besides, Kevin realized, it was nice to have someone to "talk" to—even if that someone had psychedelic eyes, teeth twice the size of his own, and skin almost translucent blue, as if there was nothing but veins beneath the surface.

The creature's feet and hands matched the proportion of its teeth. Big.

Its name was something close to Dodder, at least that was as close as Kevin could come to pronouncing it. It. He had to stop calling *her* that. Dodder wasn't an it, turns out Dodder was a she.

And, like Kevin, she seemed to be a long way from home. She'd shown him her voodoo, at least that's the closest approximation Kevin could make out for the name she'd given the palm-sized device—(her palm, not his—her version of a portable computer, though about a bazillion times more powerful than the latest-greatest back on Earth.

Dodder was from a planet she called Tura. Her planet was impossibly far away. But then, so was Earth. Kevin yawned. The Turan's eyes were closed. She had apparently fallen asleep.

He quietly watched the Booties across the river for a few minutes then closed his eyes, too. Might as well try to get some rest, he figured. It was hours until nightfall and they'd stay hidden until then.

A boat was moored to a banged-up dock this side of the river. Though he and Dodder were still a long way from fully understanding each other, Kevin knew the boat was their destination. Yet what Dodder intended for them to do afterward, he had no idea.

All that mattered to Kevin for now was finding Sam, Lance and the others. After that—well, after that, he didn't know. Would he ever find Quinn and Sarah, his daughter and his ex-wife?

# 34

The far side of the building melted away like butter in the summer sun, sending bricks and Booties spilling over the edge and into the street below. Sam cursed. All hell had broken loose. The six Booties chasing Sam, Jelly Brains and the other humans stopped in their tracks, weapons wavering.

Several more feet of the destroyed building collapsed and the hallway reverberated. One Bootie was pointing at them, but several others were pointing in the other direction. One Bootie remained neutral, his back against the wall for support. The hall shook again and a fire burst out through live power lines overhead. The Booties apparently favoring advancing to the relative safety from which they'd sprung won out and the unit raced back up into the darkness.

Sam ducked as a live wire went hissing and snapping past her shoulder like a venomous electric eel on steroids. She hastily wheeled the cart around and pounded after the Booties.

"What are you doing, Sam?" asked Xian.

"Yeah," said Gig, "the Booties are back there. Are you trying to get us killed?" Nonetheless, he ran to keep up with her and the others. At this point, he would have followed her off a cliff. There was nothing else to do.

"I'm trying to save your life," puffed Sam. "Would you rather take a flying leap off the edge followed by a short cut to the street? Or maybe you prefer being electrocuted or burned to death?"

Nicolette grabbed hold of the cart and helped Sam push. Sequoia jabbed Gig in the ribs to keep him moving at speed.

"Trust me," said Sam, projecting way more confidence than

she was feeling at the moment. "I'm trying to keep us *all* alive."

Whether she would succeed or not was an entirely different issue. Hopefully, the Booties were running to safety and not simply running blind like scared hens running in circles and ultimately to their demise.

But then, what did she know about Bootie behavior or survival instincts? A Bootie suddenly popped around the corner grinning, weapon in hand.

Sam screeched to a halt but the Bootie kept going, slamming into Gig and sending him bouncing off the wall in its haste. Everybody screamed at once.

But mostly it was the sound of the Bootie they heard, it's nightmarish screaming filling the hall like sonic blood. The alien wasn't smiling after all. It was grimacing. An alien rictus of pain. Having your back eaten alive by liquid fire and molten plasma could do that to a creature—human or alien.

Sam shuddered as the thing dropped its weapon and clawed futilely at a locked door before sliding to the floor giving one last cry of agony.

As the alien became still, its spell was broken. The small group of humans looked at one another. Each pondering his or her fate. The building gave a shudder and moaned, as if it too knew it was dying.

Sam grabbed the cart. "Let's move, people!"

# 35

Kevin felt his whole body weirdly vibrating, as if it didn't even belong to him as he pulled himself up from a deep and dolorous sleep.

He discovered Dodder shaking him. "Wake, wake."

Kevin blinked his eyes into focus. He could hardly see in the light. It took him a few moments to remember where he was. For a second, he'd thought he was back on Earth and had improbably ended up—whether he'd crawled into it on purpose or someone had dumped him there—in some sewage tunnel.

So he was half-right.

Kevin peered out the grating. Night had come again. How many days did that make it now since he'd been on this planet? How long since he had been home on Earth?

He could only guess.

Time had lost all meaning as had life itself. Funny though, Kevin had never thought life had much meaning or significance in the first place.

Now it seemed so much less.

He supposed the grass always was greener, even when it was brown. And alien.

A streak of light shot overhead, past the city and beyond the mountains.

"Mitoc," said Dodder, knowingly. "Mitoc ship."

"From Earth?" asked Kevin.

Dodder shrugged. "Can come from any world Mitoc seed."

"Your world?"

Dodder appeared sad. "Too late for Tura. The Mitoc have taken all there was to be taken."

Kevin was sorry he'd spoken.

"To boat," said Dodder, tugging at the grating.

"Are you sure?" Kevin looked down towards the river. There was more activity going on there now than he had ever seen before. Booties were quickly loading vehicles and all appeared to be heading in one direction out of the city. Were they abandoning it?

Dodder nodded and pulled the grating inside and laid it against the side of the tunnel. She slid over the edge and dug her feet in. Loose dirt and rock rolled down. The hillside was steep. It was all Kevin could do to concentrate on keeping his weight against the hill to keep from becoming a one-man avalanche.

Despite his best efforts, Kevin slid face down the last ten yards and would have ended up in the river if Dodder hadn't prevented his plunge.

"Hurry," cautioned Dodder, leaping nimbly aboard the flat decked boat.

Kevin looked nervously across the river, spitting dirt and blood from between his teeth as he scrambled up. "Aye-aye, Captain!" he saluted.

Dodder looked at him questioningly.

"It means let's get going," explained Kevin, hoping, number one, that Dodder knew how to work this craft and, number two, that she knew where they were going.

In the case of question number one, Kevin quickly had his answer, for no sooner had he planted his feet on the deck when Dodder untied the lines that held the thirty-foot vessel to the dock, and grabbed the joystick jutting up from the helm that apparently controlled the boat. She pushed a silver-topped button recessed atop the joystick. Kevin heard the boat roar to life beneath his feet.

He wasn't a big fan of boats but he was loving this one. And Dodder was handling the thing admirably. All she needed was a pair of size twenty boat shoes and a triple X-sized sailor's hat with a gold anchor stitched on the front to complete the picture of the perfect ship's captain. Once more, he was tempted to salute. But he needed both hands just to grab the rail and steady himself.

Kevin squeezed his fingers round the rail as the boat catapulted away from the dock. The night sky shifted overhead, as if all the stars were mere grains of sand in a cosmic sifter and some prospector had just given it a brisk shake.

Kevin fought to keep his stomach down while the contents of his stomach—meager though they were—fought to rise up.

Dodder, on the other hand, looked positively radiant and in her element. Maybe she'd been a river pilot in another life. And this river was dark and fast. Dodder pushed against the current.

A small Bootie patrol skirting the opposite bank came driving along in their direction but sped past Dodder and Kevin without so much as a second glance. Kevin could only wonder why. Given their speed and the fact that they were speeding without running lights, their lack of suspicion was curious.

Several hundred yards up, the sounds of fighting erupted from between two low warehouses. Purple and white laser light flashed like a Chinese New Year display. As they watched, a small group emerged by the water's edge being doggedly pursued by a considerably larger force along the dock.

Kevin couldn't imagine who was fighting who and hoped neither side decided he and Dodder were also the enemy. The two of them were poorly armed and very exposed on the open water. And the craft was making slow headway against the strong current.

Why had Dodder chosen to fight the current rather than flow with it?

Kevin lowered his head as they neared the loud fighting. With no working lights along this section of the dock, the only light to see by came from the flash of weapons.

Dodder glanced at Kevin briefly as she struggled to push the boat to the far side of the river, away from the fighting. But the river curved here and the current obstinately kept pushing them closer towards the battle.

Fortunately for them, neither group of fighters was paying

them any attention. The small group was pinned down behind a wall of heavy equipment lying dockside.

From a bluish glow spilling from a waterside warehouse, Kevin now recognized the larger group as Booties. They spread out along the street in a broad swath, obviously intent on slowly trapping their victims.

Kevin wondered what sort of creatures the others were. Were they Booties too? Were they in the middle of a Bootie civil war or were they fighting some other enemy?

He stood at the bow and took a last look at the city and the battle being waged at the edge of the river. As they rounded the river leading them to the relative safety and silence beyond, Kevin shouted at Dodder. "Go back! Turn around! Go back!"

He grabbed Dodder's hand at the joystick. "Hurry!"

# 36

Sam crouched behind a smelly black bulk of machinery, cursing. They were all going to die. Or be recaptured. And she wasn't sure which she feared and hated the most.

Part of her wanted to believe this whole thing was not real, just a galaxy-sized figment of her drug-affected brain. All part of some wicked dream the plutos had dreamed up. The plutos being her name for the plutarchs who ran the Earth. She blamed them for everything.

However, the taste of blood in her mouth and death on her hands made her suspect this was all too real. But not for long, because soon she and the others she'd hoped to save would be lying dead in these streets—finally joining the millions of dead she'd seen when she'd first wakened in this awful place.

Either that or she'd soon be in a cage or a test tube. Somewhere with Booties picking at her body and her brain. And maybe that was what she feared the most after all.

"What are they waiting for?" complained Gig. "The Booties have got us pinned down and they outnumber us three to one."

"Yes," agreed Xian, slapping a bandage over a badly scraped knee. "Why don't they attack and finish us off?"

"Are you both in such a hurry to die?" asked Nicolette, sitting shoulder to shoulder with Sequoia, who had just seconds ago picked off two more Booties who'd made the fatal mistake of lingering too long in the open. Sequoia discovered she was a pretty decent shot.

"You are all forgetting something," said Sam. "They don't want us dead like the others. We're all defectives, remember?" She heard a deep hum coming from the river and feared the worst. Probably a Bootie patrol boat. "They want us alive. They want to pick us apart and study us. See what makes us tick. What makes us different from the mindless masses that came so willingly to this party, at the Mitoc's beck and call, to be slaughtered."

She didn't add what she was also thinking, that one day their brains would probably all end up pickled in jars somewhere on a dusty lab shelf. Oddities to be ogled by alien eyes, passed around in alien elementary school classrooms.

"I'd rather die," said Sequoia. "Let's attack. Go on the offense."

"Are you mad?" gasped Gig.

She shrugged. "If we turn the tables on them and rush them, they'll have to fight us, won't they?" She was looking at Sam for the answer.

But Sam wasn't so sure. "They have other options besides killing us," she said, remembering how easily she'd been completely incapacitated and rendered utterly helpless when struck by that crazy beam from the Booties' flying ship.

The hum coming from the river was growing louder. It could be a patrol boat with such a paralyzing weapon at its disposal. Sam peered out across the water but could only make out a dark, blurred shape headed quickly towards them. Their hopeless situation had just grown worse.

Xian aimed his flashlight out over the water and hit the black bow of the boat.

Sam slapped his hand. "No lights," she whispered. "You'll give us away."

Xian nodded. "Sorry."

Sam looked overhead. A large gantry extended above and out over the river. If she could manage to get up there without being seen, maybe she could take the Booties on the boat by surprise. Maybe they could even capture the boat. Escape up the river.

She quickly outlined her plan. "Stay put, whatever happens." Her eyes locked on Gig. "We haven't much time." The boat was almost upon them and the Booties on shore had drawn up some reinforced shields that protected them from everything the

Earthlings threw at them.

"Be careful, Sam," urged Nicolette.

Sam nodded. "Give me some cover."

Sequoia and Xian fired toward the shielded Booties, sending flashes of shrapnel into the air like spinning fireflies.

Sam grabbed the side of the gantry frame and started climbing. Halfway up, she realized the boat had reached the dock ahead of her. She'd hoped to be high enough to get a clear shot down at them—surprise and confuse the enemy. That was the plan.

So much for plans.

Someone was calling her name.

She looked down. Her companions were climbing aboard the boat and weren't even putting up a fight. So much for sticking together, she muttered glumly. Had they finally lost their minds as well? Did they prefer capture to death after all?

"Sam, hurry!"

Someone was calling up to her again. Idiot. Probably Gig. Did he really think she'd join them? Lambs to the slaughter? She watched the cart being lifted into the boat. She did feel sorry for old Jelly Brains. His future wasn't looking too bright in the hands of the Booties.

"Sam, come on. Jump!"

Who was that man's voice she was hearing? Why did it sound familiar? Sam frowned, gripping the hard metal with quickly tiring fingers. The boat rocked violently at the dock's edge.

Hands beckoned. "It's me, Sam. Kevin. And I can't hold this thing here much longer. The current's too strong. You've got to jump."

Kevin?

Sam's eyes doubled in size and she lost her grip. Oops, she thought, as she realized that she was suddenly and helplessly falling.

# 37

Sam opened her eyes and peered into the face of a hairy monster whose eyes spun like cosmic whirlpools and threatened to suck her in. "You can put me down now," she snapped.

Oddly, the muscular creature appeared to understand her remark and, even more surprising, complied. Weird. Her feet hit the deck and she teetered off balance. The boat was moving fast. Sam wobbled to the rail. The Booties that had pinned them down were now swarming the deck in frustration, probably looking for a vessel of their own so they could launch a pursuit. Tough, she thought, wrapping her knuckles around the rail, with luck there wouldn't be another boat for miles.

"Sam."

Someone or something tapped her shoulder and she spun around. "Kevin! What's going on? How did you get here? How did you find me?" She pointed at Dodder. "And what the heck is that thing?"

Kevin's grin spread across his face. "Sam, meet Dodder. She's from a world she calls Tura. Dropped here courtesy of our friends."

"The Mitoc?"

"The one and only. Seems like they've got fields of flesh planted all across the universe. Just waiting to be plucked, shipped and slaughtered in the line of Mitoc duty."

Sam looked the odd creature up and down. "Thanks for catching me. I suppose you saved my life," she said reluctantly. She'd made 'never trust, or thank, an alien' her latest motto. Her ribs protested as if they'd been crushed in a vise. Still, who was she to complain? Better than lying flattened on the deck like one of those pancakes old Jelly Brains was constantly reminded her of. "So are you one of those cat aliens, like on Earth?"

"Sam?" Kevin was looking at her funny.

She shot a look from Kevin back to the big catlike alien. "You know," she said, "like cats on Earth."

Kevin looked befuddled.

Sam sighed. "You do know that all the cats on Earth are aliens, don't you?"

Kevin's mouth fell open.

"Sheesh, don't you know anything? Have you ever even had a cat?"

Kevin nodded. "Once."

"Have you noticed how most of the time, well, they're there." She paused dramatically. "But, sometimes, you go to look for them—all around your house—and they're nowhere to be found?"

Kevin waited. He had no idea where Sam was going with this. "And?" he said finally.

"That's because cats slip through another dimension. And before you ask," she said holding up a hand, "I don't know what dimension that is."

She glanced over at Dodder. "All I know for a fact is that they disappear into this other dimension. Probably going back to their home planet, wherever that is, to file their reports on human activity." She crossed her arms as if daring Kevin to refute her. "I mean, I expect they have to file a report now and again. Am I right?" She aimed her question at Dodder.

Kevin finally found his voice. "Sam, I think—"

The boat lurched and Sam suddenly found herself in Kevin's arms. Dodder was steering as close to midstream as she could and they had rounded a bend in the river that had removed the city's lights from view.

Sam extricated herself from Kevin's arms and avoided his eyes. She felt awkward. Weird. For a second, only a second, she'd had the sudden impulse to kiss the moron! What was going on? Had she sustained a concussion in her fall?

Nicolette interrupted her thoughts. "Where's Lance, Kevin? Sam said he was with the both of you. Is he back at the farmhouse she spoke of?"

It was Kevin's turn to look about. Somehow, he'd just assumed that Lance would be with the others. But now he looked at every face twice and Lance wasn't one of them. Rats. He shook his head. "I'm afraid Henry—"

"Henry!" gasped Nicolette and Sequoia in unison.

"That louse?" said Gig, who seemed uneasy and kept an equal distance between himself, Dodder, and the edge of the boat. "What's Lance doing with Henry? Did Lance turn traitor, too?"

"No," said Kevin. He explained how he'd found Henry in the city and been taken in by him. "So, you see," Kevin concluded, after describing how he'd been responsible for leading Henry to Lance and how Lance had been recaptured. "It's all my fault that Lance was taken."

Nicolette stroked Kevin's arm. "It's not your fault, Kevin. You couldn't have known."

"Yeah," Gig was forced to agree, "that scumbag. What a piece of work. Started collaborating with the Booties practically from the start." As Gig spoke, his hands went to the cart and he pulled back a tangle of clothing, his curiosity having gotten the better of him. It was only half a second more when he screamed and jumped back, slamming into the low rail. He tumbled backward over the side. Dodder threw out a hand and snatch him midair. "What on earth is that thing?" Gig was pointing to the laundry cart.

"I told you before, it's the brains of the outfit," quipped Sam, who couldn't stop smiling at Gig's discomfort and fright. "You didn't believe me, did you? Shame on you."

Gig looked uneasily at the cart, to Dodder and back again. "I think I'm going to be sick."

"Well, be sick that way." Kevin pointed toward the rail.

Gig obligingly bent double over the railing and started heaving. He looked pale as any ghost. Xian bravely assisted him. Sam moved downwind as the craft sped into the night.

The landscape was an inky blur with a few scattered lights in the distance. The sky was alien and unsettling. Kevin didn't think he'd ever get used to it.

"Any idea where we're headed?" asked Sam. They'd been cruising for hours now.

"Not a clue," replied Kevin, peering into the inky blackness ahead as if it might contain some answers. He could only hope Dodder knew what she was doing and he said so. "She's managed to keep me alive so far."

Sam had to agree. "What about your pet?"

Kevin shrugged. "Huxley ran off or got taken with Lance."

"Why would the Booties want that little fur stick?"

Kevin looked insulted.

"I'm just saying—he's not even an alien, is he? I mean, not to them. The thing is probably from this planet. It's not like us. The Booties won't want or need to study it." She patted Kevin's hand. "I'm sure he's okay. Probably ran off to be with some of its own kind again. You know, family."

Kevin nodded. He missed the little thing, but he knew what it was like to miss family, too. He missed his family. Hopefully Sam was right and Huxley had found his. Kevin had come to the conclusion that he could not hope for that for himself.

"Uh, what's that thing doing?" said Gig, with alarm.

"No!" shouted Sequoia. "We're headed straight for shore."

Nicolette screamed and ran to Kevin. "Can't you make her stop?"

Kevin watched the shore coming closer. They'd meet in mere seconds. He shouted for Dodder to slow down or change course, but, if anything, Dodder started pushing the boat to go faster.

"For heaven's sake, Kevin," said Sam, "make her stop. She's going to get us all killed! Has she gone crazy?" Sam ran to the cart and thumped Jelly Brains. "What about you? You've been awfully quiet."

"All this jostling is quite disturbing. I prefer a more fluid, cushioned existence."

"Yeah, well, your existence is about to be cut short."

"What can I do?"

"Can you read that thing's mind? Tell me what she's thinking?"

Kevin clung to Dodder and tried to force her to move the joystick and guide the boat back to midstream. But his strength was no match for hers.

"Don't worry," Dodder repeated over and over. "Don't worry. Soon."

Soon was what Kevin was fearing.

Jelly Brains said, "Dodder is thinking that her world is dead, her people are all dead, and that she wants to help you humans."

"Help?" screamed Sam. "She's going to help get us killed."

"She does not seem to think this."

"Can't you do something?"

"For instance?"

"I don't know," said Sam in frustration. "Make her think about pancakes or something."

"I do not believe that would help."

Sam fingered her weapon.

"I would not do that."

"Why not?" she said gruffly. She was hating mind readers more and more by the hour.

"Kevin Kent would not be happy if you took that action."

Sam frowned. "What do I care?"

Kevin stopped struggling with Dodder. "Everybody brace yourselves!" he shouted. The shore was fifty yards away, then thirty, then ten.

"I can't swim," worried Xian.

Somehow, Kevin didn't think that was going to matter. Either Dodder knew what she was doing or they were all going to die. And he had no complaints. Dying was what they had come here to do, after all.

Dodder gazed fixedly at the shore.

Kevin stole a look at Sam. She was wrestling with that cart of hers, trying—foolishly, he thought—to keep it from flying around the deck like an out of control bumper car.

Kevin smiled.
Sam smiled feebly back.

# 38

The bank sloped about forty-five degrees and the boat must have hit it going at least forty knots per hour. Kevin figured there was some sort of math in there somewhere, but he also knew that he wasn't very good at math. So he didn't even try to calculate whatever it was that might be calculable. Besides, whatever number he came up wasn't bound to be good.

All this flashed absurdly through his mind in the moments that the small boat hit the shoreline and flew into the air with a roar like somebody had just stepped on a million crows toes, commingled with the sounds of six humans and one Dodder screaming like they were riding the world's tallest rollercoaster.

Kevin's stomach fell to his ankles. One minute he was floating, the next he was lying on his back, looking up at the stars, at least what he could see of them with Nicolette lying on top of him.

Nicolette pulled herself together and laughed self-consciously. "Sorry about that." She stood and stuck out her hand.

"No problem," squeaked Kevin, feeling a bit giddy himself. "Thanks." He climbed to his feet. Miraculously, he still had all his limbs, and they were functional. And everybody was still alive.

Even more miraculously, the boat was still moving, cutting through the field of grass as if it were the Sargasso Sea.

Dodder maintained her grip on the joystick, faithfully manning the helm.

Kevin squinted over the side. So that was it, they were riding some sort of hovercraft! He grinned in Dodder's direction and shot her the thumbs up. Dodder smiled back. Kevin shook his head. He should have known that Dodder knew what she was doing. "Everybody okay?"

Gig and Sequoia complained about being a little banged up, but said they were otherwise okay. Nicolette went to offer them aid.

"How about you, Sam?"

"I'm fine," she said rather icily. "You and teacher have a nice snuggle?"

"Huh?"

"Never mind." Sam grabbed the cart, which had tipped to one side and was lying across her legs. "Help me right this thing."

"Sure," said Kevin. He pulled the cart off her legs and peered inside. "What have you got here? A science experiment?"

"You explain," said Sam, coming to her feet tentatively and testing her legs for breaks, tears and lacerations.

"What?"

"I'm talking to him, not you." Sam waved at the cart.

"Him who?" Kevin looked at the blob in the cart. "That goo?"

"Say something already," snarled Sam. "You want him to think I'm crazy?"

Kevin looked at her like she *was* crazy.

Sam folded her arms across her chest. "I'm not crazy."

"I never said you were," Kevin replied.

Much too quickly and not convincingly enough for Sam's liking. Mentally, she prodded Jelly Brains. *Why don't you say something? Pop into his head and poke him some. Invade his privacy like you do mine.*

"It is not possible," came the reply. "Your companion's mind is closed to me."

"Probably because he's totally screwed up," Sam replied aloud.

"Who's screwed up?" demanded Kevin.

Sam shot him her ugliest look. "I was *not* talking to you."

Kevin wanted to ask her just who she was talking to but thought better of it. "I give up." He turned and walked over to where Nicolette was checking over Gig and Sequoia's injuries.

"How are they?"

"They're fine. Nothing but cuts and bruises."

"Easy for you to say," whined Gig. "What's going on anyway? Where the hell are we going now?"

Kevin looked up. The day was coming upon them. A line of jagged mountains stood maybe twenty miles ahead. "By the looks of it, I'd say we're headed that way."

# 39

The forest was cool, damp and dark. Kevin closed his eyes and rested his head on a bed of yellow-green mosslike substance. Spongy and softer than any mattress he'd ever slept upon. This stuff would be worth a fortune back home, he thought, as he drifted away.

He dreamed of Earth and New York City. The Earth had become a horrible, impersonal place, filled with mostly two kinds of people—horrible people—and the people they preyed on. Nature had long been defeated and lay huddled in distant, unseen corners and was best seen in books of the past.

The spirit of man had also been defeated. It seemed that to survive as a species, they'd had to turn into slaves to the greater society they now served.

Of course, all that had certainly changed now. The Mitoc had seen to that.

Nothing like a swarm of aliens sweeping down on your planet to shake things up a bit. Snatching up a few billion bodies for duty on Planet Death. There must have been chaos back on Earth. Chaos and confusion.

Good, thought Kevin, maybe it would give humanity and even nature itself an opportunity to fight back.

"You awake?"

Kevin opened his eyes, yawned and nodded.

"Are you scared?" It was Nicolette and she appeared pale and weak.

"Sure," answered Kevin, though he wasn't so sure that he was. But he thought it would make her feel better to think he was too. The truth was, he was too fatalistic to be scared.

"Do you think we'll be safe in the cavern?" Nicolette nervously picked at her nails.

"As safe as we can be," Kevin reassured her. Dodder had finally explained that there was a cavern secreted away at the foot of the mountain range, with a cold water lake that could easily supply their needs.

Dodder had been exploring the local region for weeks since being stranded on the planet. The lone survivor of her expeditionary force, she'd been keeping on the move, exploring and evading the Booties in a constant game of cat and mouse; a constant state of alert, with her freedom and life the ultimate cost for failure.

Nicolette squeezed Kevin's hand. "I'm glad you're here."

Kevin jerked reflexively. He couldn't remember anyone having said those words to him before—if they had, it had been a very, very long time ago. As a result, he had no idea what to say in return. His eyes gave him away.

"It's okay," said Nicolette. "You don't have to say anything." She tapped the tip of his nose with her index finger. "And don't be embarrassed, or" she added more sternly, "so modest. You're a hero."

"Ha!"

Kevin spun around in time to see Sam striding into the clearing, weapon ready at her side. She'd gone out reconnoitering ahead and had returned to find Nicolette cozying up to Kevin, several sluggards sleeping, Dodder dismantling the boat—their only form of transportation besides their aching feet—and absolutely no one standing guard, and said so. "If I can come strolling into camp without anyone so much as blinking, don't you think the Booties can?"

"Sorry," said Kevin, sheepishly. "Gig promised he'd keep a lookout." Kevin glanced at the base of a fat-trunked tree where Gig lay sprawled out on his stomach, fast asleep. So much for promises.

"And what the heck is Dodder doing taking our boat apart?" She'd dropped her pack and marched over to where Dodder was working without even waiting to hear Kevin's answer. "We need this thing."

"Not according to Dodder," replied Kevin, who had followed her. "She says it will be impossible to get through the forest. Too dense. Besides," he added, "she's disassembling the engine and components to help your friend Alice Ermine."

Sam gawked at him like he represented the world's biggest idiot, plus one. "Who the hell is Alice Ermine?"

"Your alien friend."

Sam turned to the uncovered cart. Its sides were streaked with dirt and debris. The whole thing look pretty shaky, like it might collapse any minute. "You mean Jelly Brains?"

"Her name is Alice Ermine," said Kevin.

Sam's eyebrows jumped. "It told you this? I thought it couldn't communicate with you."

"It can't. But Dodder can. She told me."

"Why didn't you tell me?" Sam said aloud to the blob in the basket.

"You did not ask."

"And what kind of name is Alice Ermine?"

"It is the closest sound that matches your tongue."

"So," said Sam, peeping at the blob more closely, looking for clues as to its sex, "you're a girl?"

Kevin replied. "Not exactly. The issue actually confuses Alice. I tried talking to her about it. But among her species there are no separate sexes apparently or even a concept of sex."

"Interesting," Sam rubbed her chin. She was looking at Kevin. "Probably makes life a lot simpler."

Kevin stared her down. Unsaid words hung in the air like rain refusing to fall.

"I still don't see what all this has to do with your friend Dodder here wrecking a perfectly good hovercraft."

"Like I said," replied Kevin, "Dodder made it clear that the vehicle is too wide to get through the forest we face ahead."

Sam nodded. She'd gone ahead. She had seen those trees but kept her nod to a minimum, she didn't want to give the moron reason to gloat.

"So she's taking apart the engine assembly for two reasons. Number one," he lectured, raising one finger, "the vessel will be disabled. No chance of any of our enemies using it against us."

"Makes sense," Sam was forced to admit. "And number two?"

Kevin smiled and pointed to the Bootie-sized, concave-bottomed chair ripped from the craft. It was lying on the ground and Dodder was squirming around behind it. "Alice gets locomotion."

Sam looked more than a little skeptical. "What are you going to do? Fasten wheels to it?" She laughed. Not with him, at him. "Great. Now we'll have to push *Alice* and her chair through the forest instead of the cart." Sam applauded halfheartedly. "Congratulations, you've succeeded in making the task twice as difficult."

As she laughed, the large, clumsy looking chair rose from the ground and hovered a couple of feet in the air with barely a hum.

Sam's jaw dropped.

Dodder did a little dance. "Good, yes?"

"Good, yes," answered Kevin. He slapped Dodder across the back. "What do you think, Sam? Dodder's hooked up the boat's hover engine to the chair. Genius, huh? Alice can ride in style."

"You knew about this?" Sam yelled at the cart.

"Of course," answered Alice. "I know everything. Now, help me out of this laundry basket. Let's test this new device and see how well it accommodates my weight."

Sam and Kevin lifted Alice while Dodder held the chair steady. Alice was surprisingly light for her size.

Sam had to admit the whole thing was rather elegant. Alice settled into the chair like a clam in its shell. Now all they'd have to do was sort of guide Alice along.

Alice bumped Sam in the knees. Sam backed up. The chair came up and bumped her again. She struggled not to get annoyed but when the chair bumped her in the shins for the third time, she snapped. "Somebody want to control this stupid thing? I'm getting bone bruises here!"

Kevin and Dodder burst out laughing.

"What's so funny?" She snatched the chair, or tried to. "What the—" The chair scooted out of arm's reach. She lunged one way and the chair side-stepped in another direction. "All right," she demanded, face red and cheeks puffed, "what's going on here?" Her fists were clenched.

"I really do think you should stop teasing poor Sam," said Nicolette.

Sam shot deadly bolts at the girl. One thing she most definitely did not want was for Nicolette to be thinking of her as "Poor Sam."

"Okay, okay." Kevin could see he'd been pushing Sam to her limit.

"So what's the story?" asked Sam, the red receding from her face. The chair had stopped running away and she examined it more closely. "You and Dodder rig some sort of remote control to this thing?" The small white motor had been fastened to the bottom of the chair but Sam couldn't make heads or tails out of the alien technology.

"Not exactly," explained Kevin. "Alice is controlling the chair."

"Excuse me?"

He tapped the side of his head. "Thought control. It's really not that big a deal."

Sam nodded. She knew such things were possible, even on Earth. "Nice," she replied. "You could have told me," she added, her hand thumping the back of the chair.

Alice thumped her back.

"Oh, great," moaned Sam, rubbing her stricken hip, "Jelly Brains cannot only read my mind, she's now mobile and can strike back."

"Something you should keep in mind, Sam," Alice said, giving Sam a friendly nudge.

"Okay, enough fun and games," said Sam, turning serious. "Are we done here?" She was looking at the disemboweled watercraft.

Kevin and Dodder conferred a moment then Kevin said they were.

"Then I suggest we get out of here and get moving to that cavern hideaway Dodder's promised us." Sam snatched up her pack and began marching without even bothering to look over her shoulder to see if anyone was following her. She figured if they had any sense, they would.

# 40

As the craggy purple mountains loomed closer, Kevin felt even further from home. However, he'd grown closer to this small group of humans and aliens he was traveling with than he had ever been with any humans back on Earth. His exchanges and interactions with people had always been superficial, random, based on necessity or chance alone. With his parents and siblings, even with his wife; sadly, even with his daughter, he had simply never fit in.

He had befriended a stray dog once in the park. A yellow lab. He'd gotten along well with her. She'd stayed with him for about a month and then one afternoon she was gone and he'd never seen her again.

He sometimes wondered whatever happened to her. Where was she now? Was she alive?

Were his wife and daughter alive? Were they lying out there on the battlefield now? Rotting under the alien sun, their flesh being picked to the bone by some Bootie version of a vulture?

Kevin stopped in his tracks. What was he thinking? Where was he going?

There was nothing for him ahead. There was nothing for any of them. And he didn't fit in.

And he needed to find his wife and child. He needed to give them a proper burial if they were dead, a hug if they were alive. And since he couldn't take them back to Earth, he'd have to provide for them here. Dead or alive.

"Hey, moron!"

Kevin looked up to see Sam glaring at him from beneath the canopy of the dense forest. He hadn't even realized he wasn't moving. "Sorry." He looked back towards the direction they'd come.

"What are you doing? Move your butt before you get left behind." Sam took a step in Kevin's direction and motioned for him to get moving.

He shook his head. "No, you go ahead. I've got things to do. Bye, Sam." He turned on his heel.

"Hey, wait!" Sam shouted, running after him. She grabbed Kevin's arm at the elbow and he jerked to a stop.

"Let me go, Sam," he said evenly.

She rapped the top of his head, hard. "Have you gone batty? Is the heat getting to you?" She studied his eyes. "Have you got some sort of space sickness?"

Kevin shook his head and struggled to free himself. "No, Sam. But I have something I need to do."

"What?" she said, obviously annoyed and confused.

Kevin stood silent a moment before answering. "I'm going back."

"Back?" Sam looked over Kevin's shoulder. "Back where?"

Kevin shrugged.

"There is no going back, Kevin. We're stuck here." Sam sighed. "Unless the Mitoc decide to ship those of us who've survived back to Earth, or the Booties decide to deport us as undesirables."

"No." Kevin shook his head. "Back to where we were dropped. To look for Sarah and Quinn."

"Oh, Kevin. You don't even know if they're there. You have no way of even knowing if they ever *were* there."

He looked at her, unwaveringly, as she continued. "We don't know what ship they were on—we never saw them on our ship, did we?"

Kevin admitted they hadn't.

"And we don't know what ship they were on or even where the Mitoc sent them. They could be a billion miles from here. Fighting some other enemy we never heard of, on some other planet for all we know. I'll bet even the Mitoc don't know where any two particular individuals are. It's not like they're going to keep a manifest of the millions of us they've scooped up. Why would they? What do they care? Face it," said Sam, "we're just a bunch of meat to them." She grabbed Kevin by the arms, her eyes boring into his. "Your ex and your daughter could be anywhere." Or nowhere, she thought.

"Or they could be lying out there on the battlefield right now, Sam. Think about it," argued Kevin. "They could be hurt, helpless. They need me."

Sam resisted rolling her eyes. She saw Kevin's pain. "Kevin," she said, squeezing his wrists, "if they are out there," she hesitated, hating what she had to say next, "they're dead. There is nothing you can do." She let her words sink in. "But there are people here," she pointed down the trail the others had disappeared down, "who need you. Who are counting on you."

Kevin slowly shook his head once more.

"Would you quit that!" Sam snapped. "You are the most annoying, most exasperating man I have ever met. There are times Kevin that I just want to—"

Kevin help up his hand. "Shhh!"

"Don't you shush me, Kevin Kent, you bobble-headed moron." Sam's temper was coming to a boil. "I've got half a mind to—"

Kevin threw his hand over her mouth. "Quiet, Sam!" he hissed. "Listen."

Sam roughly pushed Kevin's hand away and spat. "What did you do that for? That was disgusting." She wiped her lips with the back of her hand. "Don't ever do that again, moron."

"Listen," Kevin whispered harshly, his jaw set. Kevin strained his ears, nervously opening and closing his hands.

"I don't hear anything." And then she did. There were screams, and the sound of shots being fired. Alice sent her a mental picture. "Come on!" she hollered.

But Kevin was already moving.

# 41

Kevin slid precipitously down a steep, leaf-and-twig littered gully, banging his knee into a boulder the size of his head at the bottom. He tumbled head over heels, then head over heels again before coming dizzily to his feet.

He jumped out of the way and Sam landed beside him. Together, they raced up the gully. Ahead of them, a small battle waged. But it wasn't humans against Booties or any other aliens for that matter.

This was humans against humans.

Sam drew her gun and opened fire.

"Careful," cautioned Kevin, "we don't know who's who yet!"

"I know those three thugs attacking Dodder aren't the good guys."

"Good point."

Sam paused, narrowed her eyes, aimed and fired. Two of the three went down.

Dodder was still struggling though, for despite her greater strength, she was being hampered by a thick net that her attackers had thrown over her.

Kevin engaged Dodder's last attacker hand-to-hand then freed her from the netting. Once loose, Dodder went into overdrive, hurtling humans right and left.

The attackers seemed to become more and more confused and often struck blindly and stumbled over themselves. Several more went down in the continuing melee. Even Gig was doing his part, though his shots went dangerously wild at times, and Kevin had been nearly seared twice by the inept marksman.

Kevin brushed the sweat from his eyes and gulped for air.

"Stop!" he shouted. "Look, they're retreating!"

Sam cut down two more before relenting. "Why stop now?" she said. "These guys are like roaches. If we don't kill them, they'll just keep coming back." Her face was flush. "And there could be more of them. They could be going for reinforcements."

"I'm afraid Sam's right," panted Nicolette, dropping her weapon to the ground out of fatigue and disgust.

"But did you see the way they were acting in the end?" said Kevin. "It's like they didn't know what they were doing."

"That was Alice's doing," replied Sam. She explained how it had taken several minutes and all of Alice's mental powers, but she'd managed to penetrate their attackers' minds and confuse them.

"Thanks, Alice," Kevin said, once Sam had explained. He looked at the chair spinning idly in space. "Did she hear me, you think?"

"I heard you," replied Sam. "And so Alice heard you through me."

"Good enough," replied Kevin.

Though Sam was still not liking the idea of the alien wandering at liberty through the corridors of her mind, she had to admit it had come in handy in this situation.

"Can we please get out of here now?" whined Gig. "Before they come back?"

"Who are *they* anyway?" asked Kevin. "And why were they attacking you?"

"Yeah," said Sam, scratching her thigh with the muzzle of her gun, "after all, we're all human. We should be sticking together."

"You don't understand," said Nicolette. "These weren't just any humans."

"Yeah?" Sam said.

"This was Jason and his gang. "There are even more of them now."

Kevin nodded soberly. No wonder. Jason had a mean streak the size of a comet's tail.

"If I ever see that scum again—" Sam snarled, imagining all

the ways she'd kill him.

"You just might get your chance, Sam," answered Kevin, his voice flat.

"Oh?"

"Look around." He swept his arm across the air.

Sam looked. "What am I supposed to see?"

Kevin's smile was not a happy one. "It's not what you see. It's what you don't see."

"Stop playing games, moron." Sam stepped threateningly in Kevin's direction. "I'm in no mood."

"Where's Sequoia?"

Sam paused midstep. The muscles in her face twitched, her eyes scanned the group.

Nicolette gasped. "Sequoia!" She cupped her hands to her mouth and shouted again and again.

"Forget it," said Sam. "Alice says she can't sense Sequoia's presence. "She's long gone, out of range."

"Jason's kidnapped her," said Kevin, saying aloud the words no one wanted to hear.

Nicolette screamed.

Xian ran to console her before Sam did something more drastic, like slap her upside the head, which was precisely what she wanted to do.

"Let's get out of here before they come back," urged Gig.

"I don't think they'll be coming back," Kevin replied.

"Why not?" asked Xian. "How can you be sure? They outnumber us twenty to one, I'd say."

"Sure," said Kevin, "but we've got Alice and Dodder on our side. I'd say that gives us the edge." Slight though it might be.

Sam shook her head. "I wouldn't count on it. Alice is worn out. Spacing out dozens of humans at one time has taken its toll on her. Frankly, I'm not sure she could do it again, at least not immediately or anytime soon."

"Besides," said Gig, "what if Jason or one of the others figures out that it was old Alice here messing with their minds? What's to stop them from shooting a hole in her from a distance? If they do, that's the end of Alice and her powers over them."

Alice flashed that while she did not appreciate the image, she agreed with the assessment.

"All right," said Kevin. "This is what we'll do." He turned. "Dodder, how far do you estimate to this cavern of yours?"

Dodder thought a moment. "Maybe three of your miles."

"Okay then." There was a writing implement and a pad in his pack. "Can you draw me a map?

"What do you need a map for?" demanded Sam. "Dodder knows the way. Let's get moving. I'm getting tired of standing around doing nothing while Jason hatches his plans."

Dodder took the pad and writing tool that seemed to work by superficially burning lines into the paper, if paper it was.

"So I can find the cavern, of course," Kevin said matter-of-factly.

"Aren't you coming with us, Kevin?" Nicolette sounded anxious. She moved away from Xian and laid a hand on Kevin's chest.

Kevin took Nicolette's hands. "I have to find Sequoia. Rescue her."

It was a touching scene, so touching that Sam felt like puking and said so. "You're going to rescue Sequoia?" Her voice was filled with incredulity and doubt. "You won't last two hours in these woods. And who's going to rescue you when that happens, moron?"

"I've managed alright so far," Kevin said with a grin. "In fact, I seem to remember rescuing *you* not so very long ago, Sam."

Sam's face reddened. "Sheer luck. Besides, we'd have gotten away even if you hadn't shown up when you did." None of the others backed her up. She didn't blame them. She didn't believe it herself. "Fine," she snapped, "have it your way. Get yourself killed."

Kevin took the completed map from Dodder. "Be careful." His finger traced the path Dodder had drawn to their destination. "I'll meet you all at the cavern as soon as I've freed Sequoia. They can't have gotten far."

Nicolette asked him again to stay but said she understood that he had to go. "It's very noble of you." She kissed him on the cheek.

Sam frowned.

Kevin appeared confused and embarrassed. He'd never been called noble before. He cleared his throat. "You all had better get moving, too. And cover your tracks as best you can, in case Jason has any of his thugs circling back to follow you." He palmed his weapon. "I'll stop them if I see them."

"Enough sentiment," grumbled Sam. "Let's move out before even the trees are reduced to tears."

# 42

Kevin was not much of a tracker. It wasn't like there was much call for the skill in NYC. Leastwise, not that he was aware of.

Fortunately for him, Jason and his ragtag battalion weren't much good at hiding their tracks.

By nightfall, he was confident that he was not only following the right trail, but that he would soon catch up to them. And when night settled in and he noticed the signs of light spilling through the trees, he knew he had.

A person alone could travel much faster than an army, even a small one. They wouldn't be expecting him or anyone else—at least not yet. Hopefully, this would work in his favor. Once he rescued Sequoia, with a little luck, he and the girl would be long gone before the Jason army even knew what had happened.

Kevin had seen enough movies to know that Jason might have posted sentries. He crouched low and crept to maybe one hundred yards from the camp, located in a depression beside a lake. Artificial light suffused the bowl. Kevin carefully scanned the trees encircling him, watching for any signs of movement.

But all was still.

Spooky still.

The only sounds he heard were those that came bubbling up from the camp. One tent larger than the others sat at the water's edge. Kevin crept closer. The tent flaps parted and Jason appeared. There was no mistake. Kevin wasn't good at names but he was great at faces, especially ones as malicious and malevolent in appearance as Jason's. He spoke to two heavily armed men who nodded, then took off in a slender canoe.

Jason withdrew to his tent and the flaps pulled together behind him.

Kevin was sure this was where he would find Sequoia. He saw no sign of her elsewhere. Besides, thought Kevin grimly, Jason obviously meant to have Sequoia all to himself. He'd been thwarted once before and wouldn't likely stand for being thwarted again. He'd keep her close at hand.

If he was in there with Sequoia now, Kevin realized he was going to have to move quickly. And he'd likely have to face Jason in all his fury.

Kevin stripped off his pack and covered it with some loose branches and leaves. Armed with only his pistol and a four-inch knife, he made his way to the edge of the camp without being discovered.

The tent sat near the water's edge to his left and he slowly circled that way, fearful that every footfall would rouse the enemy. Kevin put his ear to the side of the tent and listened. He could make out a couple of voices—human voices. That would be Jason and his people. Be he also heard some of the Bootie tongue, though he did not know what was being said. Nor did he recognize Sequoia's voice among the speakers. He didn't hear any female voices at all.

Lying on his stomach, Kevin ever so slowly prised up the bottom edge of the tent. He was rewarded with the ever so spectacular view of shuffling feet, scattered boxes and dusty and battered furniture legs.

Kevin could clearly hear Jason speaking to a man about what had occurred earlier in the encounter with Kevin and Sam's group.

"I'm telling you," hissed Jason, "it was crazy. It's like something or somebody put a curse on us."

Kevin lifted the tent fabric higher. It rustled lightly and he held his breath. Jason was throwing his arms around.

"Like somebody cast a spell on us."

"And who among that pitiful group could possibly have done that?" said the eerily familiar voice.

"How would I know? Ask them."

The two Booties began yammering and they sounded angry. "What did they say?" asked Jason. He sounded edgy. He'd never been comfortable with those *things*, as he called them. If they weren't human, they didn't count and didn't much matter. Though he'd been forced to make an uneasy truce with them for the sake of his own survival. If there was one thing Jason was, it was a pragmatist. A survivor.

"They said they'll have a force here in the morning and will do what you and your men have failed to do."

Jason cursed, an impressive, breathless stream of invectives, and stomped out of the tent.

Kevin heard chuckling within. Curiosity got the better of him. He was certain he'd heard that chuckle before. But where? He raised the tent a couple more inches hoping to get a better look. A tiny brown shape came rushing towards him, chittering excitedly. Before Kevin could let go of the fabric or react in any way to save himself, the shape struck him in the face. Kevin cried out despite himself.

Realizing he was in trouble, Kevin scrambled to his feet and whipped out his gun to thwart off whatever was attacking him. It was hard to make the thing out in the dark, but it felt like a hairy giant spider was climbing his pant leg.

As the thing reached his thigh, Kevin put the barrel of his weapon against its side, his finger flexed against the trigger and he hesitated. "Huxley!" Kevin's pistol fell to the ground and Huxley leapt onto his chest, clutching his shirt with his sharp claws.

"Gee, Fred, ain't this a touching moment? I'm really touched, ain't you?"

Kevin looked up to see Jason glaring at him. Huxley nuzzled against his neck.

The other man with Jason nodded, the sadistic grin on his face matching the one on Jason's own. At a word from Jason, the man grabbed hold of Kevin and pushed him into the center of the camp.

The entire camp had been alerted and all were scurrying about like ants whose hill had been tromped on by a boot. They grabbed their weapons and scanned the dark trees, expecting an enemy that Kevin knew would not come, and could have told them, as he was led into the heart of the camp.

"Where are your friends?" demanded Jason, as if reading his thoughts. "Out there?" He snatched an automatic weapon from one of his minions and sprayed the dense woods indiscriminately with gunfire. He grinned. "I hope not, for your sake." His grin widened into an ugly gash. "I hope *so* for mine."

Jason pushed himself into Kevin's face, so close Kevin felt his hot breath crawling over his skin like a deadly jungle disease. Huxley, clinging to Kevin's shoulder, growled viciously. Jason slapped the creature away with a backhanded strike that sent him tumbling to the ground, where he landed with a dull thud.

Kevin yelled in protest. Jason's fist drilled into his stomach, stopping him mid-sentence. Kevin keeled over, gasping, his hands reaching for Huxley.

"Bring him inside," Jason ordered.

Kevin was grabbed by a couple of goons, one of whom was a nasty looking woman with a row of black widow spider tattoos crawling up her right arm. They tossed him roughly through the tent flap. Kevin landed on his hands and knees, spitting dust. He struggled to get upright and fight back, but strong hands held him down at the shoulders and neck.

He twisted his head and looked up fiercely. "Henry!"

That was the familiar voice he'd heard. The two Booties in the tent eyed him quietly for a moment, then addressed Henry.

Henry nodded. "You're lucky, Kevin," he said with a gleam in his eye, his voice slicker than a snake oil salesman's. "They like you."

"Oh, goodie."

"In fact, they've taken a special interest in you."

"Yeah? I know all about the interest they have in me and the rest of us. The others told me all about it. What I don't get, Henry, is what your game is. Why cooperate with them? We're human." Kevin looked pointedly at the Booties. "They're the enemy."

Henry rose from his chair and paced. "The enemy, Kevin? Are they really? After all, we humans landed on their world and instantly set to slaughtering them." He loomed over Kevin and motioned for his captors to release him. "So who's really the enemy here, Kevin? The Booties...or us?"

Kevin stood unsteadily and dusted himself off, saying nothing.

"I dare say if a force of alien invaders landed on Earth and proceeded to exterminate us that we would do our best to retaliate."

Kevin remained silent. There was an unpleasant truth to what Henry was saying.

"No, Kevin. Man is the enemy here. Or," he said, holding up one finger, "more precisely, the Mitoc are the enemy here. And Man is merely one of their tools."

"And what about you?" Kevin said finally. "Aren't you, Jason, and the others simply tools of the Booties?"

Henry shrugged, sat and motioned for Kevin to do the same.

Kevin hesitated, then took the empty seat beside Henry. "I am a facilitator. The Booties are interested in learning about us."

"Exploiting us, you mean."

Henry nodded. "If you mean learning what they can by studying such humans as you and I and the others who appear immune to the Mitoc's bioengineering, then yes. But I would not characterize it as exploitation."

"Locking us up? Studying us like lab rats? Slicing up our brains so they can try to figure out what makes us tick or not tick?"

Henry shook his head like a professor expressing deep disappointment in his star pupil. "A certain amount of," he seemed to search for words, "scientific investigation is necessary for the cause," he conceded. "But I assure you, Kevin, the Booties' intentions toward you in particular are benevolent. You're different even among the different."

Kevin turned his gaze from Henry to the staunch Booties. "And you can tell those two that my intention is to rescue my friend and get out of here." His hands gripped the chair tightly. There had to be some way out of here. But how? There were too many of them. Besides, he hadn't found Sequoia yet. "Where's the girl?"

Henry exchanged words with the larger Bootie, then rose. "To show our good intentions and as a display of friendship, "Thekar," he pointed his chin at the steroid swilling Bootie, "says you may see the girl. In fact," Henry said with a rub of his hands, "they have an additional surprise for you as well."

"I hate surprises," Kevin muttered.

"Oh, but you'll like this one," smiled Henry.

Henry turned to Jason. "Fetch the girl."

Jason opened his mouth to speak but apparently thought better of it. Probably for the best, figured Kevin. Jason was incapable of true thought. Jason turned on his heel. He stopped at the entrance though and glared angrily at the Booties and said, "You promised me the girl."

"We'll discuss that later, Jason." Henry stared him down.

Jason returned minutes later with Sequoia in tow. She looked frightened and downtrodden.

Kevin leapt to his feet. "Sequoia!" They embraced and he looked her over. The poor girl was dirty, exhausted and scared, but otherwise none the worse for wear. "Have they hurt you?" His eyes went from Sequoia to Jason.

Sequoia shook her head. "No. But I'm not sure what they mean to do with me. Us." She looked worriedly at Jason, who smiled back malevolently.

The smaller of the two Booties held a beeping palm-sized device to his face, listened, then spoke.

"Ah," said Henry, rubbing his hands together with delight. "That other little surprise I promised you is about to arrive."

The Booties exited the tent. Whatever Henry was up to, it was well choreographed, thought Kevin.

"Shall we?" Henry gestured for Kevin to lead the way.

Grabbing Sequoia's hand, Kevin left the tent followed by Henry and Jason. Huxley clung to the inside of his trouser leg. "So what's the big surprise?" said Kevin, frowning. "It's not my birthday, is it? I don't see any cake."

"Shut up," snapped Jason.

Kevin ignored him. He sensed that Jason was almost as powerless as he was in the present situation, and found that oddly satisfying. But Jason was no less dangerous for all that, he reminded himself. And possibly more so. An angry Jason was a dangerous Jason.

A mad and frustrated Jason was like a nest of enraged yellow jackets—and could prove deadlier.

A crowd of Jason's men had gathered by the shore and the sound of electric buzzing grew louder. The two Booties waited patiently, ankle deep in the muck.

Sequoia was shaking, more from fear than the cold, Kevin suspected, for she held onto his hands with a grip that practically brought him to his knees. A ball of light grew larger and soon the outline of a long, flat barge became apparent. And it was bustling with troops. Bootie troops.

Kevin drew in a breath to steady himself, realizing that escape had just become doubly hard.

The barge came to a stop several yards out and Booties began leaping out and splashing their way to the shore. A smaller, spindly Bootie dressed in white struggled through the mud, his face hidden behind a cowl. His feet stuck in the mud and the Bootie to his rear gave him a callous shove.

# 43

"Hey," the little one complained, "no need to manhandle me, you lousy reject from a horror movie."

Kevin flinched. That was English he was hearing! "Lance?"

The face lifted and the cowl fell away. "Kevin, dude!" Lance ran to Kevin, beaming like a five-year-old with ice cream. "How are you doing, man?"

Kevin looked pointedly around the camp. "I've had better days."

"I know what you mean," said Lance, his head bobbing up and down. "I know what you mean."

"How about you?" asked Kevin. "Are you okay? Where have you been?"

"Oh, man," sighed Lance, trying to shake off the mud and water clinging to his trousers. "Hey, Sequoia, how are you, girl?" He turned back to Kevin even as she opened her mouth to reply. "Where haven't I been. Since being captured by this jerk and his Bootie buddies," he shot a finger at Henry, "I've had my butt hauled all over this marble. Whole shooting place is unstable, what with all the battling and mayhem. The cities aren't safe. So the Booties just keep moving. I think they're planning to evacuate the planet—those that haven't already."

The Bootie soldiers distributed themselves throughout the camp while Jason's men watched with uneasy suspicion and obvious distaste. An escort of Booties and humans led Kevin, Sequoia and Lance onto the barge and to a small berth with a portal that only Huxley could even hope to squeeze through.

"Get some sleep," said Henry. "We'll discuss your future in the morning."

"Yeah, pleasant dreams," snorted Jason, giving Sequoia a look that sent her cowering in the corner. "I'll be thinking about you. You, too," he said, turning his icy glare on Kevin.

They heard Henry locking the heavy door behind him.

"What's going to happen to us?" said Sequoia.

Kevin wanted to tell her not to worry, that everything would be all right. But he couldn't. How could he when he didn't know himself? Huxley bumped his nose against Kevin's finger and he idly petted his head and listened to him coo.

"So where's the rest of the old gang?" asked Lance as he slid to the ground and rested his back against the hard wall.

Kevin explained all that had happened since that fateful night when Henry Hemming had set them up. Sequoia filled in the gaps.

"So Dodder was that spooky creature I was hearing? And she saved your life? Cool," Lance said. "I wondered how you had managed to disappear after Henry's Bootie buddies got their paws on me." Lance was silent a moment. "She good looking?"

"Who?" Kevin arched up on his tiptoes and peered out the tiny window towards the moons above.

"Dodder."

Kevin made a face. "Yes, I guess so." He scratched his arm. "In an exotic, alien, what-on-earth-are-you-thinking sort of way," he said, his voice rising in disbelief. He winked at Sequoia.

"Okay, okay." Lance threw up his hands. "Just asking. Can't a guy ask?"

Sequoia giggled.

"What's so funny?" asked Kevin, though he considered her giggling a good sign. He'd been concerned about her mental well-being every bit as much as her physical well-being.

"Nothing. I think Lance is adorable."

"Oh?" Lance slid a little closer to her.

She moved an equal and opposite distance away. "I said adorable," she frowned, "I don't know—like a stray dog. You know he smells, he's probably got fleas, and probably bites and will destroy the furniture. And pee in the house. Still, adorable.

But," she added, "that doesn't mean I want to take him home."

Kevin's laugh filled the small room. Lance shook his head furiously. "A guy can't get no respect. I wish I had one of my axes with me." He wriggled his fingers. "Me and Mr. Gibson could write one heck of a song right about now."

He strummed an invisible guitar and sang. "Trapped, rejected. On the verge of total destruction. And my friends keep putting me down." He sang the impromptu words while his blue eyes fixed accusingly on Sequoia and Kevin.

"Don't you think you're exaggerating?" said Sequoia.

"Yeah, we're not dead yet," replied Kevin. There had to be some way out of this.

"May as well be," Lance said softly, "we're good as..."

"Don't be such a pessimist, Lance," Sequoia insisted. "Go ahead." She gestured towards his invisible guitar. "Play us another tune. Something upbeat. Fun."

Lance looked at his hands, then back at Sequoia, obviously trying to figure out if she was making fun of him.

"Wait a minute," interrupted Kevin, who'd been deep in thought. "What do you mean we're as good as dead? Are you talking about the threat of Jason killing us?"

Lance shook his head. "Nah."

"The Booties cutting us up to see what makes us tick?"

Lance shook his head even stronger. "No, no. I'm talking about the whole shebang going up." His hands spread out in opposite directions.

Kevin and Sequoia were looking at him strangely.

"You know, ka-BOOM!"

"What's he talking about?" Sequoia demanded.

Kevin shrugged helplessly. He found it hard enough understanding the way Lance's mind worked under the best of conditions, and under confinement with no obvious means of escape, and duress, he found himself completely baffled.

Lance balanced himself on his knees. "You mean you really don't know?"

They shook their heads in unison.

Lance chewed his lower lip.

"Out with it, Lance," Kevin ordered.

"They're going to blow it up."

"The boat?" said Sequoia, glancing nervously at the decking.

"No," replied Lance, "the whole shebang. This planet, Splurj —if you want to call it that, though it isn't really one, a planet, I mean. These Bootie things built it for their masters. It's going to go. Go nova," Lance said rather dramatically. "And when she goes…" Lance spread his arms. "The way I hear it, it's going to take out a big piece of this system."

Sequoia gasped and clutched her knees. "Why would they do such a thing? We'll be killed. All the Booties will be killed."

"Mind you, it's Henry that's told me all this. He's the one that can talk to the Booties. I've barely picked up a word or two. He speaks like a freaking native."

"Please, Lance," said Kevin, "get to the point."

Lance frowned. "The point is that the Booties and some other aliens called Flems have been going at it with the Mitoc for a billion years. Each trying to take the other one out—blot each other out of existence, you know what I mean? Anyway, this world is actually a giant exotic bomb that the Flems had the Booties help them build.

"I guess they knew that if they built it, the Mitoc would come. And come they did. Supposedly, there are Mitoc ships hovering nearby. And by nearby, I mean within a few hundred million miles of here."

Sequoia gaped. "Maybe they could come get us? Take us home?"

Lance shook his head. "Not bloody likely. Besides, the point is that when this bomb blows it's going to take out everything within about half a billion miles of here. And I do mean everything."

Lance scratched the back of his neck. "To hear old Henry tell it, everything within five hundred million miles of here is going to be reduced to subatomic soup. He says the fighting here's been going on so long, that's why this area is such a void, with so few stars, generally speaking." He cackled. "These freaks have been obliterating whole chunks of universe like it was nothing. Snack cheese."

Kevin remained silent, attempting to absorb Lance's words, take them all in. It wasn't easy. "How much time do we have?"

Lance shrugged. "Who knows? Soon though, from what I gather—the next couple of days maybe."

"Couple of days!" Sequoia gasped.

Lance continued. "Whoever is in charge of this war against the Mitoc isn't telling. All the Booties know is that their time is just about up."

"A fat lot of good that does us," complained Sequoia.

"They did say that when the time comes, there would be no doubt."

"What's that supposed to mean?" Kevin asked.

Lance squirreled up his face. "I don't know. Some kind of alien machinery cranking up or something—apparently it's gonna unleash a bunch of ginormous tremors or something."

"But you have no idea when all this is supposed to happen?" Sam pressed.

Lance shrugged. "Soon is all I know. I mean, those goons I got away from sure seemed to be in a hurry—like it was life or death, know what I mean?"

Kevin did.

"Hey," Lance said suddenly, "I think we're moving!"

"Worse," answered Kevin, peering out the window. "We're sinking."

Lance joined Kevin at the window, smashing Kevin's nose against the glass. "You sure?"

"Either that or the Booties are preparing to submerge." He turned to Lance, rubbing his nose. "Does this tub look like a submarine to you?"

Lance gulped. It didn't. "We'll drown like rats."

Sequoia raced to the door and banged with her fists. "Let us out! Let us out!"

Kevin and Lance joined her. Several minutes of pounding

did nothing but raises bruises on their fists. Kevin and Lance slammed their combined weight against the door but it barely flinched.

"What are they doing out there?" cried Sequoia. "They went to all this trouble to capture us—why would they leave us to die now? I mean, they wouldn't, would they?"

"I don't know," Kevin was forced to admit. They heard an awful commotion going on outside. Sounds of anger and confusion rose from outside.

The boat suddenly listed to the left. A few minutes more and Kevin expected the water to come rushing in the window. But he was wrong.

Water began creeping in under the door. Soon they stood ankle deep and struggled to remain upright in the bobbing vessel. Huxley dug his nails into Kevin and chattered nervously.

The boat was now listing so badly that the sole window was nearly above them. The sound and thud of a shockwave was quickly accompanied by a violent lurching of the troubled craft.

"What the hell was that?" Lance trembled.

"An explosion," replied Kevin.

"Explosion?" said Lance. "Are you saying somebody is trying to blow us up?"

"It could be that the Booties are under attack," replied Kevin, struggling to stay on his feet. That would make as much sense as anything. "Or maybe the engine blew or something." Or something was right. It could be sea monsters for all he knew.

Sequoia clung to Kevin. He told her not to worry. What good would worry do? Maybe he could get Huxley out the window—at least one of them would make it out of here alive.

The door rattled and blew open, followed by a rushing wall of water that sent the three of them sprawling into the far corner and, Kevin feared, soon to their deaths.

Kevin wrapped his arms around Sequoia's waist and pulled her to him. Wiping water and hair from her face, he looked toward the gaping doorway. "Sam!"

"Oh, brother," snapped Sam, with down-turned lips, her eyes

taking in the sight of Kevin and Sequoia locked in an intimate embrace. "You just can't keep your hands off the ladies, can you?" She strode into the wrecked cabin and pulled Lance out of the knee-deep water by the scruff of his neck.

"Ouch!" he complained, though he didn't resist.

Sam turned to Kevin. "Come on, moron. You don't prefer to stay here and drown, do you?" She headed through the open door, pulling Lance along. "Though I don't know why I shouldn't let you," she muttered.

"Where are we going?" demanded Lance.

"You'll see," answered Sam, dragging him mercilessly around the corner.

On deck, they could see clearly how oddly tilted the boat was. The boat shook every several seconds like a snoring leviathan, or more likely, thought Kevin, a dying leviathan.

"What about the Booties?" asked Lance as they caught sight of several of the enemy clinging to the highest points of the troubled vessel.

Sam stopped and smiled. "Turns out Booties can't swim. Sink like—" she paused, then said with satisfaction, "sink like this boat is going to sink."

"Really?" said Lance, sounding only somewhat heartened. "I'm not so sure I can make it to shore myself."

"Are you sure they can't swim?" Sequoia's voice trembled.

"Yeah. Who knows? Maybe it's something in their bone structure." Sam led her small group to the stern, bobbing unnaturally in the air. She pointed to a rope knotted to a cleat.

"Now what?"

"Take a look," said Sam, pointing.

Kevin went to the rail and peered over the side. There in the glassy shadows, bouncing down below was a canoe, if not the one he'd seen earlier, then it's twin. "A boat." Kevin felt like hugging Sam but the look on her face dissuaded him.

Sequoia cried in surprise.

"Go ahead," said Kevin, giving Sequoia a hand.

The surviving Booties hurtled angry shouts as they realized

what was happening. The humans were escaping and they were trapped on a sinking vessel.

"Looks like they're up the creek without a life preserver." Lance waved and grinned until they started shooting and it was only the unpredictable movement of the sinking boat that kept the Booties from finding their mark.

"Hurry," urged Kevin, hoisting Lance over the side with Huxley in one hand.

Sam returned fire and brought down two Booties.

"Your turn, Sam," Kevin ordered. "Give me your weapon."

"No way, moron. Go!" The boat dropped a foot and Sam stumbled.

Kevin snatched the gun from her hand just as one of the Bootie's shots hit the deck between their feet, sending a shower of splinters into the air. "Goodbye, Sam." Kevin grabbed Sam by the waist and hoisted her over the siderail. Sam shouted, cursed and kicked her feet. "If I were you, I'd grab the rope," said Kevin. "It's a long way down."

Still cursing, Sam shot daggers at Kevin, and angrily grabbed the rope. She slid quickly down—much too quickly—burning her hands and thighs on the way. Her feet hit the canoe with a thump that sent them all tumbling.

Straightening, Sam looked up and shouted Kevin's name. Half the boat was underwater now and what was left above water hung at a sixty-degree angle. Three Booties remained and they were armed. They also had the advantage of being on higher ground than Kevin.

With no other weapon, Sam could only watch helplessly from below. A massive bubble of air surged to the surface. The line holding the canoe to the craft's side snapped. The canoe bounced away from the larger boat, now sinking dangerously fast. The Booties had given up fighting Kevin and were now fighting for their lives.

Sam feared that if Kevin didn't do something soon he'd be sucked under with the boat. A second explosion was followed by a fireball that filled the night sky with a yellow-blue blaze that practically blinded her. She could barely make out Kevin's dark shape clutching the shattered rail. "Jump!" Sam shouted. "Jump!"

# 44

Kevin couldn't say whether he'd jumped or if the sinking barge had knocked him overboard. Either way, he found himself flying headfirst over the upended rail and racing towards the black roiling water below.

His only thought now was wondering how deep the water was and whether or not he'd plunge through several feet of water followed quickly by several feet of thick rock breaking his neck.

As these thoughts swirled through his mind, he hit the surface, went under, and came up again, disoriented and confused. Rough hands grabbed his arms and yanked. Sam, Sequoia and Lance pulled him upward.

Several shots came from the direction of the camp, but whistled harmlessly overhead. They were out of range of any real threat. But that wouldn't stop Jason and Henry and their small army from seeking them out.

Armed with the canoe's lone paddle, Sam steered them to the closest point of land, a small finger-like spit thrusting out into the river and surrounded by tall reeds. They fell over the side and sloshed through the shallows to the shore.

Lance dropped to the ground in exhaustion, then rolled over on his back. "Now what?" he gasped.

"We can't stay here, that's for sure," said Kevin, wringing the cold water from his clothing as best he could. Huxley shook himself. A shower of water erupted over them.

"Knock it off, monkey!" Sam complained.

Kevin shivered. "They'll be after us." He looked pointedly at the dark forest.

Sequoia followed his gaze. "Do you think so? I mean, don't you think that they will at least wait until morning?"

"Maybe," Kevin said, though his voice lacked certainty.

"Maybe not," added Sam. "Come on, let's move." She rose.

"Not me," said Lance. "I'm exhausted." He threw his arms and legs out spread-eagle. "I need a rest." He closed his eyes.

Kevin called Huxley. The creature was picking pea-sized fruit from a nearby thorny bush. Sequoia pleaded with Lance to come but he refused.

Sam followed an opening in the trees and headed inland.

"Last chance," called Kevin. "Once we plunge into these woods you'll never find us."

"I'm tired," Lance said firmly. "I'm staying."

"Okay," said Kevin, "have it your way." He started, then stopped. Sequoia clung to his shoulder. "Oh, and say hi to Henry and Jason for me." Kevin followed Sam's footsteps.

"Yeah, and don't worry, Lance, I'll be sure to come visit your brain in the pickle jar whenever I get the chance!" bellowed Sam.

Kevin smiled as his ears picked up the sound of mad thrashing and the rushed footsteps of what could only be Lance racing to catch up from behind, muttering oaths of protest with each step.

Kevin slowed until Lance caught them.

"You're cruel, Kevin," Lance said. "You look all sweet and innocent, but you've got a real mean streak in you."

"Come on," grinned Kevin, choosing to ignore the insult, "before Sam leaves both of us behind."

But Sam wasn't far ahead.

"Just curious, Sam," Kevin said, "do you know where you're going?"

"I got here, I can get back," said Sam testily. "Unlike some people."

"What are you doing here anyway?" Kevin said, swatting away a flying insect that persistently went for his nose.

"I figured somebody was going to have to come to Sequoia's aid. You didn't seriously think you could rescue her, did you?"

She shot him a look. "Or that it was even remotely likely?"

Kevin remained silent, pacing along beside her.

"I've been following you since you left. Some rescuer. You didn't even know you were being followed the whole time."

Kevin reddened, grateful for the hiding darkness. "I wasn't looking behind me," he said in his own defense. "I was more concerned with where I was going and who or what might be up ahead."

"And he did rescue me," Sequoia added, patting Kevin's arm.

Sam bristled at the way Sequoia touched Kevin and looked at them both like they were crazy. "Jason and the Booties had you both!"

"Yeah," said Lance. "And we were about to drown."

"Actually," confessed Sam, "that was my fault."

"Your fault?" Kevin said.

Sam explained how she had sabotaged the boat in an effort to create a diversion and help their escape.

"What if it hadn't worked?" Kevin said. "What if you hadn't been able to get to us? What if the boat tipped the other way? What if the door was impassable? We could have drowned!"

"That was a chance I was willing to take," Sam said a little too glibly. "We have to get to the others," she said, suddenly switching gears. "They'll be at the cavern by now."

"What's the point?" asked Sequoia, sounding broken. Kevin knew the feeling. "I mean, what if what Lance says is true? We'll all be dead soon anyway."

Sam forged ahead. "Let's worry about that when we reach the others."

Kevin agreed. "Besides, we don't know how much of a lead we have over Jason and the others."

Sequoia clung close to Kevin. "I'd rather be blown to pieces than fall into his hands again. He frightens me."

"Don't worry," Kevin took her hand. "You're safe with me."

Sam laughed. "Sure, until this rock goes ka-boom. Don't think Kevin's going to be much good to you then." She'd heard Lance's story of the end of the world. And though the guy was a complete idiot, she wouldn't put it past the Booties to set a match to the whole place. Booties, Mitocs, they were all a bunch of freaking idiots—only difference between them and Lance was that they were idiots on a universal scale.

"Must you, Sam?" complained Kevin.

"This really sucks," Lance groused, twisting his foot yet again on uneven ground impossible to see in the dark. "I'm tired, hungry, chased by thugs...and for what?" He angrily swatted at one of the increasingly bothersome insects circling his face. "All to get blown to bits at the end. It's not fair."

"Nothing's fair," replied Sam. "Get used to it."

"I agree," Kevin said. "Besides, there's nothing we can do now. We're stuck here till the end."

"Yeah," said Lance, wincing in pain. "It just sucks, that's all. If only we could get to the ship."

Sam spun around, grabbed Lance by the collar and lifted him off his feet until he dangled by his toes. "What ship?" she hissed, her eyes hard as concrete.

"Hey!" yelped Lance, fear dancing in his eyes. "Kevin, how about a little help here?" He tugged at his collar. "I can't breathe."

Kevin whispered for both of them to keep their voices down. Huxley tightened his arms around Kevin's neck, nearly closing off his own windpipe. They had stopped in a small clearing and he felt exposed under the moonlight, like a nocturnal insect caught in the beam of a flashlight.

"What ship?" growled Sam once again, her voice hard as an iron bar.

"The ship that the Booties are chasing after," said Lance, nervously watching Sam's face. "Didn't you know?"

Sam and the others shook their heads.

"Tell us about the ship, Lance." Sam sounded like she was trying to keep her voice calm, steady, soothing—trying not to do what she obviously really wanted to do most—strangle Lance until the truth oozed out.

"Make her let me go first," whined Lance. He struggled uselessly to pull her hands from his tattered shirt.

223

"Sam," Kevin said evenly, "let Lance go."

Sam reluctantly released her grip on Lance. He scrambled to get out her reach, rubbing his neck.

"Now," said Kevin, "tell us about the ship."

And so Lance did. "It's a Mitoc ship. Disabled, but not destroyed. That's never happened before."

"And why do they want the ship?" said Sequoia. "So they can disassemble it, study it, like they want to do with us?"

Kevin shook his head. "No, they want to use it to escape, don't they, Lance? Before their world blows up."

Lance nodded. "Yeah, that's right. They plan to fly it right out of here."

"If they can get it working," Kevin said.

"They can." Lance shrugged. "At least they say they can."

"Why do they need this ship?" asked Sam. "Don't they have ships of their own?"

"I guess not. Not here, at least."

"Do you think we could fly it?" Sequoia asked Kevin.

"I don't know. I don't see how. The Mitoc ships are impossibly large. You saw them. And who knows what makes them work."

"Not this one," stated Lance. "I mean, I don't know how complicated it is, but it's not that big. The Booties said this is a smaller, more specialized craft. Big enough for all the Booties in the camp, plus Jason's gang. That's why they are so determined to find it. But it is not some kind of leviathan like we dropped in on."

"I can't believe they told you all this," said Sam, sounding skeptical. "Who's to say they weren't lying?"

"Why not tell him?" countered Kevin. "They plan on leaving us all to die anyway, so what's the harm?"

"Can't argue with you there," said Sam.

Kevin nodded, deep in thought. This meant that there was a chance. Slim, but visible. Like a hairline crack in an otherwise ugly future.

Sam pushed her nose in Lance's face. "Where's the ship, Lance?"

Lance stuttered. "There." He titled his neck and pointed to a tall, black craggy peak, visible above the treeline, in a meandering range of mountains in the far distance.

Kevin's eyebrows shot up. That range of mountains was precisely where they'd been heading from the beginning. That's where Dodder was leading them. And, with a little luck, that was where Dodder and the others would be waiting for them, safely hidden in the cavern Dodder had discovered.

A slight tremor shook the ground beneath his feet. Did it signal the beginning of the end?

If they hurried, they could catch up with Dodder and the rest of the group. And beat Jason, Henry and their whole stinking army of Booties and humans up the mountain. To the ship.

"Let's go," Kevin ordered.

# 45

An enormous streak of light suddenly appeared in the night sky, illuminating their faces. Kevin looked up. It was as if some Greek god had clumsily spilled ten thousand gallons of phosphorescent paint that now fell bleeding down from the heavens.

"Wow, way cool," exclaimed Lance.

"Not cool," said Kevin, grimly. "My guess is that it's the Booties' doing and they're looking for us."

They dove into the woods leaving the dizzying display at their backs.

"I don't like this at all," complained Sam. "In the middle of an alien forest being chased by Jason and his gang *and* the Booties. And not so much as a popgun or a pea shooter between us."

Kevin couldn't argue with her there. He'd left his pack somewhere in the forest near the Booties' camp and his only weapon had been snatched from him. He'd lost Sam's rifle when he'd plunged into the river.

Worse yet was the uncomfortable feeling he had and could not shake ever since Lance explained to them that they were on some kind of manufactured planet—aliens playing at being gods. A hunk of metal and rock designed to house a few disposable creatures and a galaxy's worth of explosives. The mother of all bombs. And now it was about to blow.

He didn't like it. Knowing it was artificial made it all seem less real somehow. The ground less solid. Every time his feet hit the ground he feared that ground would cave beneath him and he'd sink up to his hips into some inescapable artificial unreality.

He had always had enough trouble with his brain. This

new knowledge was making coping all the harder. Kevin's ears pricked up to the sound of distant howling. Kevin recognized that howling. It was the cry of the Booties and they couldn't be far behind. If dinosaurs could have yodeled, he imagined this was what they would have sounded like.

As if sensing his tension, Huxley bounded nervously from shoulder to shoulder. Kevin and Sam looked at one another. Like Kevin, she recognized the tune. She picked up the pace.

"Just get us to the cavern," Kevin muttered. He had no real way of knowing if Sam knew where she was going. But she moved unerringly, without hesitation, at least, threading her way through the thick dark maze of trees and shrubs, ever closer to the mountains. A small stream, no more than a rivulet, now separated them from the steep rocky sides of a mile-high obsidian tower.

The sound of their adversary was unmistakable now. Even Lance and Sequoia noticed it. "They're coming," trembled Sequoia. She started to run.

Kevin held her back. He pointed. More sounds and bouncing beams from flashlights moved closer from the left.

"They've outflanked us," Sam whispered.

"We're doomed," said Lance.

"Shut up and keep your voices and your heads down," Kevin ordered. "They may know our general position but let's not tell them exactly where we are, okay?"

The others silently nodded.

Kevin wondered how the Booties had managed to find them so quickly but didn't have time to ponder the matter. They had to move now before they were trapped. He scanned the surroundings, three sides forest, one side mountains, and enemies roaming in every direction. "Come on," he said, heading for the rough scrabbled side of the mountain, following the path cut by the stream. "And be quiet about it."

Angry shouts coming from all sides of the forest left no doubt that they'd been discovered as Kevin led them upward. Sam brought up the rear with Lance and Sequoia sandwiched between herself and Kevin. A shot from the left shattered the boulder beside Kevin's hand as he urged the others forward.

The channel was deeper here and Kevin followed it. The sharp fissure in the rock would protect them from being hit—at least temporarily.

"I thought they wanted us alive," moaned Lance.

"Maybe these guys didn't get the memo," quipped Sam, shoving Lance forward. "Keep moving."

Lance nodded and scrambled up the rough groove.

Kevin's heart pounded in his chest as he pushed ahead through the shadows. Sharp jagged rock cut his arms and legs. His body sagged from overexertion, compounded by confusion and the growing fear that he'd let his friends down—led them into a blind and potentially fatal alley.

They'd have to turn around, go back down. Look for another route of escape. Try to find Dodder and the others before their enemies found them.

Even as Kevin shouted for everyone to turn around and go back, he felt himself being roughly and mercilessly pulled, squeezed and folded into what was certain doom.

"Kevin?" cried Sequoia, reaching the spot where he had disappeared. "Kevin!"

Huxley scampered in mad circles around Kevin's footprints.

"Where's Kevin?" cried Sam. The sound of running feet coming closer and excited shouts seemed to come from all sides.

Sequoia swung in confusion. "I-I don't know. He's just gone. One minute he was there and now he's just gone." She looked like she was going to start crying again.

Sam wanted to slap her but refrained. "Pull yourself together," Sam snapped. "He can't have simply disappeared."

Could he? Who knew what the rules were on this crazy world. She was still trying to figure them out. "Think," said Sam. "You must have seen something." The weird cries of the ever advancing Booties sent shivers up her arms. She shook the girl. "Think."

"I don't know," moaned Sequoia. "I thought I felt something, like the earth vibrating. Did anybody else feel that?"

Sam snapped. "What? I didn't feel any—"

"Wait!" cried Lance. "Look!"

Sam followed the line of Lance's trembling finger. A long, dark shadow, blacker than all the rest, uneven and running up the cliff face like a scar caught her attention. "What is it, Lance?" It hardly seemed worth interrupting strangling Sequoia over a shadow.

"It's Huxley," Lance explained. "He went in there."

Sam hesitated only a moment then pushed Lance forward. "Move!" If he bounced back, she'd soon know if it was merely a shadow.

If he didn't, well, who knew what it was, what it meant or where it went. But they'd know soon enough. Besides, the one thing she did know was that it was not here. And here was one place she did not want to be.

"You're next," she said, giving Sequoia an unexpected and not so gentle push.

# 46

"Dodder!" Kevin, recovering from his initial disorientation, hugged his monolithic friend.

Dodder smothered Kevin in return and then set him down. "Sequoia?" asked Dodder.

"Outside," replied Kevin, still somewhat shaken, as Huxley appeared out of nowhere between his feet, then scurried up his leg. Kevin winced. He was definitely going to have to clip Huxley's nails one of these days.

Kevin peered into the black crevice from which he'd emerged. "I'll have to go back and get her and the others." He shivered at the thought. He wasn't a fan of tight spaces.

"No need to, bro," sang Lance, popping into the dimly lit cavern. "Lance is in the house." He was practically bowled over as first Sequoia and then Sam quickly followed behind. "Hey, watch out!"

"Quick, we've got to hurry!" cried Sam. "They aren't far behind!"

Dodder looked at Kevin.

"It's Jason and his gang," Kevin explained. "Plus Henry and another hundred or so Booties. They've been chasing us and are apparently right on our tail." Kevin glanced about the shadowy cavern. "We really should get moving, Dodder. Which way?"

"No need," answered Dodder, grinning as her powerful hands gripped the slab of rock lodged beside the slender opening. She gritted her teeth and shoved.

When he realized what she was up to, Kevin joined her. Sam, too. The huge slab hung suspended for a moment, defying gravity, then crashed against the opening with a force that set off a small avalanche of rock that completely blocked the entrance.

Kevin coughed up dust. There was no way the Booties could get to them now. Not without tools or blasting equipment. And Kevin doubted they had either.

Of course, he also realized, as the dust settled, that it meant there was no going back for them either. Despite the inherent coolness of the cavern, he was sweating. Were they trapped? Had they sealed themselves in their own tomb? Sealed their own fate? "Where are the others?"

"Small room there," replied Dodder. She pointed and led the way to where Gig, Xian and Nicolette had encamped. A small glowing light illuminated the circular chamber. The chamber was so low at the entrance that Kevin had to bend over nearly double to get inside.

"Kevin! Thank goodness!" Nicolette's face brightened at the sight of Kevin and the others. "Are you alright? What was all that commotion?" She tenderly squeezed his wrist.

"I'm fine," answered Kevin. "We all are." At least for the moment. Looking back, Kevin would remember little. Running, chase, shots, pulled into a crevice and being mashed, squeezed, thinking he's going to die, then popping out on the other side in a dimly lit cavern.

"Told you I could get us here," quipped Sam.

Kevin made an unflattering comment regarding the tight squeeze, both literal and figurative. Tight spaces gave him the willies. And he still hadn't let go of how Sam had almost drowned not only him but Sequoia, Huxley and Lance, too.

"You? How do you think I felt about it?!" said Gig.

Kevin noticed the guy had dropped a few pounds since landing on Splurj. Nothing like being dropped ill-prepared on an alien planet to do battle and then running and battling for your own life for endless sleepless days to trim the fat. Maybe he'd write a diet book, but then again, who to sell it to?

"Sequoia!" Nicolette squealed on seeing her friend. They embraced and traded stories. Nicolette then approached Kevin, now resting on the floor of the cavern, and kissed his rough, unshaven cheek. "Thank you."

Kevin shrugged and his face reddened, though he hoped no one could notice in the dim light. "Don't thank me, thank Sam," he replied. "Without her, Sequoia and I would probably still be trapped back there—prisoners of Henry, Jason and the Booties." Huxley riffled through Kevin's pockets, no doubt looking for scraps of food.

Nicolette took a step towards Sam. "Thank you, Sam." She extended her hand.

"Oh, brother," groaned Sam. "What are we all thanking each other for?" she said, ignoring Nicolette's extended hand. "We're stuck inside a mountain for heaven's sake. Dodder," she demanded, "which way is out?"

Dodder shifted her big feet. "Not sure." Her eyes took a keen interest in her toes.

"Not sure?" Sam's voice rose and echoed off the hard walls. "You blocked us in and you're not sure of the way out?"

"Not sure of any other way out," Dodder mumbled. "I only know one exit." She pointed lamely.

And that was the one they'd just sealed up. "Even if we could clear it, we'd be facing nothing but trouble," said Kevin.

"But still," argued Sam, "Dodder should never have—"

Kevin cut her off. "That's enough, Sam. Dodder did the right thing. The only thing she could do to save us. At least for the moment. And the moment is all we have. We have to survive each moment, one after the next, if we're to have any hope at all."

"I agree," said Xian, with a nod. "Better to be in here than out there." He jabbed his thumb at the pile of rubble sealing their fate.

Sam fumed then stopped, suddenly realizing there was no one poking around in her brain. "Where's Alice?"

"He reconnoiters," answered Dodder.

"Yeah," added Gig. "He said he wanted to explore some. He said he was getting some kind of vibes." Gig wiggled his fingers on each side of his head.

"Vibes?" Sam sounded skeptical.

Gig shrugged. "What can I say? He's another alien nut job. Don't ask me to explain what he was talking about, you figure it out. Personally," Gig said, "I'd rather he stopped walking around in my head at all. You know what I mean?" Gig tapped his skull.

Sam knew.

Kevin picked up the glowing lantern. "We may as well get started." They fell in line behind Dodder, following her to the frigid hidden lake she had described to Kevin. Here they drank their fill and topped off their water bottles.

Dodder urged them on. Kevin stayed close behind, now waving a flashlight Nicolette had given him. Dodder apparently needed no such contrivances for she slinked through the darkness without a stumble, whereas, even with the flashlight, the others were stumbling and bumping into the rocks and each other. A low rumble shook the ground and they all froze, expecting the end. But the end never came and they continued on.

Kevin guessed it was all of fifty degrees in the sprawling cavern, and damp. The excessive humidity soaked through his skin, drowning his bones. Huxley clung to him as much for warmth as for comfort.

And it was deadly quiet in the caves, like a tomb, he thought with a shiver—which is what it would become if they didn't find another way out before they ran out of food.

Kevin, too, wondered what had become of Alice and whether Alice would be able to find them now that they themselves were moving, and lost in the bowels of this elaborate cave system.

He said as much to Dodder. Dodder told him not to worry. So he decided not to—not much at least.

Besides, they had more pressing things to worry about, like getting out of here alive, like not falling into any yawning unseen pits of death, things like that. Things that he feared could happen with every step.

The soft rustling of pebbles skittering down a rocky incline echoed in the dark distance and for the first time Kevin wondered if they were truly alone. Were there other denizens of this deep? Would they be hostile? Probably. So far, pretty much everything else on this world had been.

The ground beneath Kevin's right foot gave away. He yelped as he slid helplessly downward, landing on a small ledge some ten feet below where he had last stood.

"Kevin, are you okay?" Nicolette called nervously, shining the lantern over the cliff edge, scanning slowly side to side.

"Yeah." Kevin hugged the sloped wall of the narrow ledge. "Lost my footing." He cursed himself for letting his mind wander, for not paying enough attention. "Can you get me out of here?" He couldn't afford such mistakes. This could have been the end of him.

By way of a reply, Kevin howled as a rope snapped him in the face. "Hey, watch it!" He rubbed his stinging nose and ducked as the rope swung past his face once again.

"Grab hold, moron," commanded Sam.

Kevin didn't wait to be told twice. He felt himself being lifted effortlessly to the ledge top where anxious hands pulled him safely to them.

Dodder let go of the rope and Sam coiled it about her waist. "Let's be more careful," she said, "all of us." She started forward, then stopped dead in her tracks. She sniffed the damp air. "Anybody else smell pancakes?"

Lance looked at her funny. "I'm smelling something, but it smells like a big load of crazy."

Sam huffed.

"What is it, Sam?"

"I think it's Alice."

"In Wonderland?" Lance said with a barking laugh that came to a sudden stop when Sam's fist landed in his abdomen. "Ooof!"

"Keep it up, wiseguy," warned Sam, "and you'll be in Wonderland."

With Sam and Dodder leading the way, the tired group wound upward through the dimly lit cave. Gig complained at each step. Xian's unflagging encouragement was the one thing that seemed to keep him going. The two men seemed to share a bond that neither Sam nor Kevin could fathom.

They were all more than tired. They were tired and scared. And though many of them grumbled at following Sam based on her purported sniffing of buttermilk pancakes with Vermont maple syrup—hardly the stuff to pin one's hopes and life on—they grudgingly tromped on.

Because they really had no better ideas or options. Following was pretty much their only choice. Besides, following was the one thing they did best.

That was what had got them stuck on this hostile world in the first place.

Uncountable hours later, a small dim shaft of light appeared high overhead.

Sam stopped. "There." She pointed.

Dodder nodded and continued her steady pace.

They found Alice hovering in the custom chair in front of a six-foot oval opening in the rock. Fresh, cool air sent shivers up Kevin's arms.

"Hallelujah" Lance said, dropping to his knees at the entrance.

"Alice," cried Sam. "You found a way out!"

"More than that," announced Kevin, gripping the edge of the opening and peering out into the starry night sky. "Alice found the ship."

"Are you sure?" Nicolette pushed up against Kevin's side and studied the distant darkness.

"It's got to be," replied Kevin. "It fits. Look." He took her finger and guided it to a slender silver object that pulsed rhythmically near the summit of a peak connected to their own by a perilous looking natural stone bridge.

"But can we fly it?" wondered Sequoia, squeezing in beside them. She wrapped her arms around her chest for warmth.

"Alice can," said Sam.

All eyes turned.

"Alice confirms. This is his ship."

An uproar of excited chattering filled the air. Gig stuck his head outside. Fat, wet drops of snow, or something very much like it, struck his hands and face. "It's bitterly cold out there." And a strong wind was pushing up from below. Snow danced in all directions. One large flake landed on his nose and he struck it away. "We go out there, we'll freeze to death," he predicted, glumly. "We'll never reach the ship." He shoved past the others and rubbed his limbs for warmth.

"Sure, we will," said Nicolette, with a smile of encouragement, which she reinforced by patting Gig on his cold damp arm.

He frowned. "Even if we could somehow manage to climb down this mountain, cross that shaky looking rock bridge, and hike up the other side, we'll freeze to death before we're halfway to the ship."

Or get picked off by the Bootie-human army that might be lurking out there, thought Kevin. Thoughts he wisely kept to himself. They had no choice, after all, but to try, and he said so. They all knew he was right. There had been two more tremors in the past hour. And if Lance was right, they signaled that the end was near.

Kevin sighed as he gazed outward, contemplating the cold stormy darkness. It seemed he had very little real choice in this world he'd found himself in.

Xian cleared his throat. "What if the ship is damaged?"

"We'll repair her," shot Sam.

"What if it's out of fuel?"

Sam squeezed her eyes shut. "Alice tells me that will not be a problem."

"But where will we go even if we do manage to get it off the ground?" persisted Xian.

Gig was nodding vigorously. "Yeah. That's a good question. Is that ship going to get us back to New York?"

"It's going to get us someplace that isn't scheduled to blow us all up, scattering our subatomic remnants all over this region of the universe." Sam cocked her brow at Gig and Xian like a warning sign. "That work for you, boys?"

Xian gulped and nodded while Gig's shoulders slumped forward. Sam took their responses for a yes. "Let's get going then. No point waiting when this place could blow up under our feet any moment." She stepped out into the near darkness. It was so bitterly cold that she could barely breathe. It felt like her lungs had turned to ice.

Gig and Xian looked uncomfortably at each other and then the ground.

"Not so fast," said Kevin, pulling Sam back.

"What is it now?" she complained, crossing her arms over her chest.

Kevin wasn't sure if she was doing it to try and keep warm or to try to keep herself from taking a poke at him. "I don't think we should go pushing out without thinking this through."

"Such as?"

"Discussing our options and what we'll do if something goes wrong."

"I thought that was pretty clear. If something goes wrong, we die."

"I agree with Kevin," said Dodder.

"You would," Sam muttered.

"This may be our last hope."

"Fine," conceded Sam. "Talk."

"Maybe we should wait until morning to cross," suggested Nicolette. "Wouldn't it be easier in the daylight?"

"We could be dead by then," replied Xian, probably figuring that if he didn't say it, Sam would, pessimist that she was.

"Jason, Henry and the Booties could have taken control of the ship by then," added Sequoia. Leaving them no chance of escape.

"She's got a point," said Gig. "Any chance I can catch a ride down the cliff with Alice?" He eyed her levitating chair jealously.

"Forget it," Sam said quickly. "It would never support your weight, anyway."

"Just asking," Gig said, sounding like a wounded sea cow and skulking away. Xian slinked after him, whispering.

"It does look quite treacherous," noted Sequoia, studying the steep drop on this side and the equally precipitous climb up the other more distant peak.

"We can do it," Kevin asserted. "It won't be easy, but if we all stick together, we can do it." He told everyone to gather up everything they had and lay it in a pile. He took inventory. Four weapons between them. One for every two persons. Plenty of water, a fair amount of food, if you didn't mind going around hungry all the time, assorted gear that may or may not come in handy in the next day or so, two coils of stout rope, and six knives.

"Wait a minute," Nicolette said, kicking the pile with her toe. "Wasn't Gig bragging about how he'd taken a second weapon from one of the dead Booties?" She turned to Kevin. "I don't see it here."

"Gig." Sam drew the word out, half warning, half exasperation. But the word suddenly stopped and was replaced by the unearthly howl bellowing from her lips, so horrible a sound that she didn't even recognize her own banshee-like voice.

Sam fell forward, gasping, struggling to retain consciousness. Her head throbbed and her eyes cried volumes. It felt like someone was repeatedly and savagely driving a four-tined fork in and out of her eyeballs.

"Sam!" Kevin reached for her, uncertain what was wrong and even less certain what he could do to help.

With effort, Sam regained control of her voice and shook her head. "Alice," she managed to gasp, before collapsing on her face. Dodder gently lifted her head.

"Kevin!" Nicolette grabbed his arm. "It's Gig. He's got the lev chair!"

Kevin forced himself to leave Sam in Dodder's hands. There were none better. Dodder would aid Sam even if her own life was forfeit.

He ran to the opening and discovered Alice lying inert on the ground. He had no way of knowing if the alien was all right or even alive. Alice didn't have access to his mind. He could only hope she was okay. Without her, the spaceship would be useless to them. They'd be doomed. Stranded on this alien-made world.

Looking up, Kevin spotted Gig running out the mouth of the cave pushing the chair. "Leave me alone!" he cried. "I'm getting out of here. I need this chair!"

"No, Gig!" shouted Kevin. "You can't. Remember what Sam said—the chair will never support you!" He raced after Gig, already a dozen yard ahead of him.

"Hurry, Kevin!" Nicolette shouted.

"Sam's lying!" shouted Gig.

"Listen, Gig," said Lance. "Sam's a lot of things, and I mean *a lot of things*—" He glanced nervously at Sam, no doubt fearing she'd rise and smite him. "But she's not a liar."

"I don't believe you. I don't believe any of you!" huffed Gig. "You're all liars. This planet is a lie. And I'm sick of all of it!"

"Gig, no!" Kevin's teeth rattled as he ran up the slope. Gig strapped himself into the lev chair and pushed off.

Kevin surged forward.

A black shape knocked him sideways and he ricocheted off the jagged rock.

"Oh, no, you don't!" shrieked Xian. "This was my idea. I'm going too!" Pushing past Kevin, Xian threw himself on top of Gig, who howled in outrage.

Kevin climbed to his knees and looked up. One minute Gig and Xian were hovering in the air over the edge of the ledge, the next moment they were gone.

Kevin scrambled to his feet and rushed to the edge.

"It's too late," Nicolette said softly. She had reached the edge before Kevin and stood peering downward at the carnage far below.

Kevin followed her gaze, nodded, draped his arm over her shoulder. He led her slowly back inside, away from the wreckage and out of the cold. The frigid snow tried to follow them but surrendered after only a few steps.

# 47

Kevin and Nicolette rejoined the remaining members of their little troop gathered in a half-circle around Sam. Her face was ashen and her eyes remained shut, her body still. "Is she going to be alright?" asked Kevin.

"Yes." Sequoia patted a damp cloth over Sam's forehead. "It must have been the shock. She and Alice were very close."

"Speaking of Alice," said Kevin, "is he dead?" He glanced at the massive alien blob lying inert on the cold floor of the cave near the entrance—tossed there like a sack of potatoes by Gig.

And a fat lot of good it had done him.

"I don't know," answered Sequoia. "I think I sense something from him." She gently rubbed Sam's head. "But I can't be certain. It might be my imagination, wishful thinking." She looked meaningfully at the unmoving alien shape on the cave floor. "Sam was the one with the strongest link to Alice. We'll just have to wait and see."

Kevin nodded and lifted Sam's hand. It felt warm. That was a good sign, wasn't it?

Dodder asked about the lev chair.

"Over the side," replied Kevin, "with Gig and Xian."

Sequoia gasped. "They escaped?"

"If you can call plummeting to death down the face of a cliff an escape."

Sequoia trembled, then turned. "Sam's stirring."

"What about the lev chair?" Dodder asked again. " Can it be saved?"

Kevin shrugged. "I don't know. It's so dark. Smashed, I suppose." If Alice was alive, he wondered how they'd ever manage to get her down one mountain and then up another. And if she wasn't alive?

"I will check." Dodder headed to the cliff's edge, returning moments later. "The chair is wedged on an outcrop approximately one hundred feet below."

"And Gig and Xian?"

"They landed much further down. They will not have survived."

Kevin nodded grimly. Dodder's sense of vision was far keener than any human's. If that was what she saw, he didn't doubt her.

"With a rope, I can retrieve the chair," Dodder stated.

"Is there any point?" Kevin asked.

"Get the chair, moron."

Kevin turned. "Sam!"

Sam sat up and rubbed her temples with her fists. She rolled her eyes at Kevin. "Where's Alice?"

"Here." Kevin assisted Sam to her feet. She rose unsteadily and let him lead her to where Alice was lying motionless on the cold, rocky floor. "Is she okay?" Kevin asked.

Sam squeezed her eyes shut and concentrated. "I can't be sure."

Sequoia had laid her jacket over the giant creature and Sam pushed one sleeve aside. She dropped to her knees and placed her hand atop Alice.

Kevin felt a tap on his shoulder and turned. Dodder stood with a coil of rope over each shoulder. "Come," she said. "I will retrieve the chair."

"Okay." He wasn't going to repeat what he'd said earlier. Besides, helping Dodder get the chair—futile or not—would give him and the others something to do.

Dodder quickly tied the two coils together and gave them a tug. They held and she nodded her satisfaction.

Kevin and Nicolette knotted one end to a trunk-thick stalagmite closest to the cave's narrow mouth and Dodder dropped nimbly over the side.

Kevin stood at the edge and watched anxiously as Dodder

secured the other end of the rope to the lev chair.

Dodder waved to Kevin and he waved back. "Step back, Dodder!" he called. "We'll lift her."

He and Nicolette tugged on the rope to no avail. Despite the cold, sweat rose on Kevin's brow and he frowned, dropping the rope.

"It's stuck!" Kevin hollered down to Dodder, already pulling away at a large wedge of rock, using nothing more than her brute strength. She put her shoulder behind the chair and rammed it as hard as she could.

"Careful!" cautioned Kevin. The last thing he wanted to see was Dodder flying backwards off the ledge. But the jarring impact sent the chair popping into the air and then just as quickly falling. The rope pulled taut and the chair came to a stop a few feet below Dodder who was now hanging on with one hand.

"Be careful!" repeated Kevin. He really did not want to lose anyone else.

Dodder grinned and regained her foothold.

Kevin, Nicolette and now Sequoia, who had joined them, pulled the chair up. Kevin then gave Dodder a hand, not that she needed one.

Kevin and Dodder gave the chair a once over. Kevin had no idea what he was looking at or for but made a good show of it.

"What do you think, Dodder?" Kevin wasn't sure what to think. The chair looked pretty banged up. Would it still function, or had Gig and Xian managed to wreck it completely?

Dodder pulled open the makeshift engine cover and examined the interior, humming and hawing, her lips twitching.

The sharp crack of an electric discharge followed by a flash of light sent her backwards. She landed on her rear end and cursed, wiping her blackened hands.

Kevin took all this for a bad sign, but when Dodder stood up she was smiling. Her eyes twinkled in Kevin's direction a moment, then she turned and replaced the engine cover and motioned for Kevin to take a seat.

Having just seen the way the chair had bucked and how easily the burst of untamed energy had tossed the mighty Dodder like she was a mere dandelion, Kevin was disinclined to do so. "I don't think so, Dodder," he said, emphatically shaking his head and backing away.

With some prodding and looks from the girls that gave no quarter, Kevin found himself sitting rather uncomfortably in the lev chair. He gripped the edge of the seat with white knuckles while Dodder switched on the power.

For a moment, nothing happened. Kevin shot Dodder a look of 'I told you so' and was about to climb down in triumph when the chair suddenly took off like a rocket. A rocket with no place to go but up. And up was the very solid, very close cavern roof.

The chair went straight to the ceiling but miraculously didn't strike it—because Kevin's head striking it first with an awful crunch had kept that from happening. Lucky chair. Unlucky Kevin.

Huxley screeched.

The chair and Kevin fell back to earth just as quickly as they had gone up. Kevin howled in pain as Nicolette and Sequoia unstrapped and succored him.

Dodder swiveled the lev chair around with one beefy hand and chewed her lip. "Needs minor adjustment," she declared.

"Minor adjustment!" shouted Kevin, only making his head hurt all the more. "That chair tried to kill me!" He pointed at the thing as if it were some wild and dangerous animal.

"I will fix," Dodder said calmly.

Lance laughed.

"What are you laughing at?" scowled Kevin.

"Hey, sorry, bro. But, I mean, better you than me." He turned away but Kevin could still hear his soft chuckling echoing off the rock walls like a dozen hooting Lances. Kevin supposed he should be grateful that he'd been able to provide his poor downtrodden troupe with some comic relief.

Dodder went back to work on the lev chair while Kevin

went to check on Sam and Alice. Though he first had to suffer Nicolette's ministrations. Not that he suffered all that much. He found her concern for his wellbeing touching. Maybe it was that caring and a need to express that caring that had led her to become a teacher. She cleaned his scalp wound with a small red towel soaked in water and insisted he not remove the makeshift bandage until the bleeding stopped completely.

He felt a little silly with a towel draped atop his skull, but complied. "How's Alice?" Kevin inquired, leaning over the creature. The corner of the towel fell into his eye and he pushed it aside.

"She's coming around," said Sam. "She hit the ground pretty hard. Gig is an idiot."

"*Was* an idiot," Kevin corrected.

Sam nodded solemnly. "Right. I'd almost forgotten." She looked toward the mouth of the cave. "Are you sure?"

"Dodder says so." Kevin touched Alice. Was it his imagination or did she seem a bit warmer now? "Funny thing is, the slope isn't that bad. I mean, it's going to be a whole lot of slip-sliding down, but the descent is doable. If he and Xian hadn't tried to use the lev chair—"

Sam rose. "They chose their own fate. They'll get no sympathy from me." She wiped her hands on her thighs.

"Don't you think that's kind of harsh, Sam?" Nicolette asked.

"Not even a little bit," Sam answered, pushing past the two of them.

Lance agreed with Sam.

"Is the chair ready, Dodder?" Sam asked.

Dodder gave Sam the thumbs up.

"Then let's get moving," she said. "I'm not a fan of caves."

Kevin agreed. He was not a big fan of caves or any sort of confined space.

Together, Kevin and Sam loaded Alice onto the lev chair and strapped her in securely.

"Ready, Alice?" Sam asked.

Alice said she was.

The small troop gathered up their meager belongings, bundled up as best they could against the cold, and approached the precipice. It was still dark outside. It was also still snowing, blowing hard and brutally cold, but no one complained aloud.

Maybe they were too tired or too past complaining or simply happy to get out of the confines of the cave and moving forward. Even if it was to their doom.

# 48

Kevin went first, followed by Nicolette, Sequoia, Sam and Alice, Lance and Dodder taking up the rearguard position.

Sam wasn't taking any chances. She stuck close to Alice and the lev chair. Dodder was sticking close to the rock wall, which proved good for all of them, because more than once they might have slipped and tumbled to their deaths on the rocks below had Dodder's strength and steady hands and feet not anchored them.

They'd had the foresight—or the stupidity—to tie themselves together by the waist before beginning their descent.

In retrospect, Kevin realized it had been foolhardy, incredibly stupid for, if one of them had precipitously fallen, they would all have had to follow.

But in the end, they made it safely down to the small plateau that was their goal, with little more than a few minor cuts and abrasions between them.

Xian and Gig's corpses had beaten them there, of course, and they lay some yards away, a couple of life-sized broken marionettes, sprawled on a cold, stark and broken landscape.

"I'm not sure this was such a good idea," grumbled Lance, with an accompanying shiver. "It's bloody cold."

"Have you got a better idea?" shot Sam. Though she couldn't deny he was right. It was bloody cold, despite their heavy exertion. She made a point of looking up the mountain face they'd just descended. "You want to go back?"

"I'm just saying it's cold," replied Lance, defensively, though dawn was breaking over the alien horizon, barely visible between the jagged mountain peaks. The nitid snow seemed almost alive. Maybe it was.

The distant alien sun produced no appreciable warmth. Kevin's fingers were numb and he was pretty sure his nose had fallen off sometime during the climb, because he couldn't feel it at all. Huxley clung to him in silence, his breath coming out in tiny puffs.

They stopped after a time and ate what scraps of food remained, then achingly resumed their march. For the first time, Kevin noticed how loose his pants had become, how much weight he had lost being taken by the Mitoc on this crazy journey. Alice had assured them that there were resources aboard the ship—sophisticated alien devices that could be tuned to produce all the food and water they might need. He hoped Alice was right.

The natural rock bridge was far narrower than they'd expected, no more than three feet across at its widest points. A wave of vertigo washed through Kevin.

"They could at least put up some handrails," groused Lance.

"Something tells me they don't get too many tourists along here," Sam said. She didn't sound too keen about crossing herself.

"Just don't look down," Kevin counseled, though he couldn't stop looking at his feet. It was hard not to with the uneven path being so narrow. And it was a long way down, thousands of feet. One misstep would mean certain death.

And it wasn't helping that the wind was blowing like the devil was beating his archangel wings in an effort to dislodge them all.

"I'm scared," said Nicolette, grabbing onto Kevin's arm.

"Me, too," Sequoia said softly.

Sam scowled at them. "It's a little late in the game to start getting scared now."

Kevin leaned into the wind, keeping his head down. Sam and Dodder struggled with Alice and the lev chair, which was being constantly buffeted by the stiff winds.

Kevin heard a scream and twisted. A gust of wind had caught

Sequoia off guard. She lost her balance, crashing into Lance and Nicolette. Sequoia and Lance landed in a tangled heap that probably saved them both. But Nicolette went sliding feet first over the edge and let out a yelp.

Kevin lunged for her and barely managed to grab hold of her shirt. He felt the fabric stretching, tearing and giving way in his fingers. He grabbed her arm with both hands and held on.

"Kevin," gasped Nicolette, twisting in the air.

"Hold on," he grunted, realizing what a stupid thing he'd just uttered. Did he really think she might let go?

Sam appeared. She reached down and grabbed Nicolette's other arm. Together they pulled the girl to the relative safety of the rock bridge.

Nicolette sprawled shaking atop the rocky surface. Kevin draped his arm around her shoulders. Sam turned away, rolled her eyes, and went to assist Dodder.

"You okay?" asked Kevin.

Nicolette nodded. "My heart's racing." She forced a laugh. "Otherwise, I'm fine."

"Can you stand?" She said yes and Kevin helped her to her feet. "Okay," Kevin said loudly, "everybody, let's be more careful." He looked ahead. "Ten minutes," he predicted, "and we'll be across to the other side."

"Or the bottom of the bloody ravine," countered Lance. He spat. "I wish I was anywhere but here at the moment. Even a gig in a country-and-western band, replete with rhinestone-studded shirt and matching underwear, would be preferable to this miserable world."

"Suck it up," said Sam, in her usual tone, once again refusing to lend sympathy.

Though it was light enough to now see—light enough to see they were in one lousy predicament—thick wet clouds had rolled in to fill in the gaps in the mountains.

"How's Alice doing, Sam?" As much as he hated it, all their hopes of escape depended on the creature. If she died or wasn't healthy, all their efforts would have been for nothing. All the fighting, all the lives lost. And for what? To end up stranded, cold and hungry, atop some unnamed alien peak?

There might not even be a ship up there when they got to the top. The Booties and their human allies might have beaten them to it.

Kevin wondered how they intended to fly the craft. Did they have an Alice of their own?

"She's hanging in," answered Sam, who was uncharacteristically showing signs of stress and fatigue herself. "Don't worry. She'll be ready when the time comes."

"If her ship's even up there," said Kevin, squinting upwards to no avail and watching the dark clouds knock each other about as he cautiously hiked the anfractuous path.

"It's up there," replied Sam.

Kevin shot her a look. "I wish I had your confidence."

"It isn't confidence. Alice says she can sense it up there. It's in her makeup. In her blood, I guess. The Mitoc may have built that ship, but Alice is the one who can fly it."

"Good," said Kevin. "Tell Alice I said that's good."

Sam grinned. "She knows." She took a deep breath without breaking step. "We'll be safe soon."

Kevin nodded, turned and stared into the distance.

Sam stopped and rested her hand on his shoulder. "You know, Kevin, your ex-wife and your daughter probably aren't even on this world. The odds are that those lousy Mitoc dumped them on some other world thousands of lightyears from here."

She paused, cursing herself, as she realized her words were probably only making things worse. She'd never been good with words. Words were for saying what she felt, making her point, getting what she wanted. She'd never used them much for sharing, caring.

She gently pulled Kevin around and looked him in the eye. "There's nothing you can do, Kevin, except your best. You can't save everyone. But you've been helping all of us. Because of you, we're all still alive." She squeezed his hand. "We have a chance."

Kevin shook his head, as if shaking away ghosts. "I don't

know. I haven't done anything."

Sam laughed. "Are you kidding? Don't be modest, moron. You've done plenty. You've done more than anyone. Just ask the others." Sam smothered him in a bear hug. "You've done your best," she said, quickly pulling away.

"What if my best isn't good enough?" Kevin said softly.

Sam smiled. "It's good enough for me," she replied, kissing him softly on the lips. "Now," she cleared her throat, afraid she might be getting all soft and misty, "come on," she said sternly. "We don't want to get left behind and separated from the others, do we?"

Dodder was already tackling the next mountain, atop which sat their goal. Lance and the girls stuck to Dodder's heels.

Kevin shook his head.

"Then let's go," said Sam, giving him a playful shove. "They're counting on us, moron."

They climbed and kept climbing. Dodder was in the lead. Sam and Kevin nudged Alice along. Nicolette and Sequoia had their hands full trying to keep Lance moving in the right direction— sometimes it was hard to keep him moving at all.

An explosion of rock threw sharp fragments, dust and ice into their faces. The blast had caught them by surprise. Kevin squeezed his eyes shut. "What was that?" he coughed.

"We've got company." Sam pointed over Kevin's shoulder. Through a break in the misty clouds, Kevin spotted a small force of Booties and humans marching toward the summit. They were far to the right of Kevin's own small party. He judged their way to be more circuitous and precipitous than their own chosen path, but their rivals were also a good quarter of a mile or so above them. There was every chance that Jason, Henry, and the Booties would reach the summit and Alice's ship before they did.

"What are they trying to do, kill us?" shrieked Lance.

"You only just figure that out?" said Sam.

"But I thought they wanted us alive?"

"I'd say all bets are off now."

"It certainly seems that way," Nicolette said, shaking bits of rock from her hair.

Sequoia asked, "Don't you think they need us anymore?"

Sam shook her head.

"I think it's too late and they know it," Kevin replied. "They are beyond caring about us."

"They only want to save their own miserable hides," mumbled Lance.

Kevin said nothing. He really couldn't blame them for that.

"But what about Alice?" asked Sequoia, apparent to everyone that she was clutching at straws. "Surely they wouldn't take a chance of any harm coming to her?"

"Sequoia's right," chimed in Nicolette, with hope in her eyes. "They need Alice to fly the ship. Right, Kevin?"

Despite her unspoken plea for assurance, Kevin said, "I wouldn't bet on it, Nicolette." Lance had explained to him how the leader of the Bootie expedition had been the officer in charge the first time they'd climbed this summit and captured Alice. Kevin was sure the Bootie had something up his alien sleeve. Otherwise, why go to all this trouble if you couldn't fly the ship out of here once you'd secured it?

Kevin voiced his thoughts.

"So maybe Alice here gave up some secrets," said Lance, eyes narrowed.

"Not intentionally," replied Sam, her voice menacing. "Alice wouldn't do that."

"Okay, okay." Lance threw his hands in the air. "Just saying."

"Well, stop saying."

"Enough," interjected Kevin. "Let's get moving before the fog clears and they take another shot at us."

No one had to be told a second time. The small, tired band resumed their climb with renewed vigor and determination.

"Do you ever wonder what things are like back on Earth?" asked Nicolette, huffing, her breath heaving in the thin air.

"Some," said Kevin, helping Nicolette around a sharp thin trail of loose black stones.

"Not me," answered Lance. "What's the point?"

"I wonder what they're doing back on Earth," said Kevin, "right now?"

"Who knows?" said Lance. "The whole world of our existence has gone wacky. I mean, for all we know, a millions years have passed on Earth and the whole shebang is being run by robots."

"Earth pretty much was run by robots, anyway," quipped Sequoia. "A dull world run by dull drones whose only god and goal was power and money."

"Amen," replied Lance.

Kevin couldn't disagree and said so. He thought he'd have felt differently but realized now that there wasn't a lot that he missed about Earth.

"What about you, Sam?" asked Nicolette.

Sam had been uncharacteristically silent. "You want to know what I think?" she said, harshly. "I think the whole world has probably exploded in chaos."

"That's a bit strong, don't you think?" Nicolette said.

"Nope. Think about it. Aliens swoop down. And not just on New York City, mind you, probably all over Earth—London, Moscow, Berlin. Like a plague from outer space. They scoop up millions of people indiscriminately and fly off with them into the great unknown." She spat. "Adios, Earth. And good riddance."

Sam paused for effect, shook her head. "I'm telling you, I'm not sure whose predicament was worse—those that were taken or those who were left behind." Sam described a world of chaos, fear and fighting. And she described it vividly.

No one argued with her.

The last hundred yards to the summit were rough and cold. The precipitous slope was bleak and boulder strewn. They picked their way carefully between the sharp rocks. The only sounds were the clatter of loose stone, their hard breathing, and the constant complaining of the wind.

Dodder and Sam reached the small penultimate escarpment first and were assisting Alice over the side when Kevin called for them to halt.

"What's the problem?" asked Sam. "You should hear Alice. She's as excited as a sixteen-year-old school girl getting her first car. She wants to get back to her ship. Don't slow us down now."

"I'd like nothing better," said Kevin, climbing up alongside her. "But we've come this far," he lowered his voice to a whisper, "why don't we all try to make it the rest of the way in one piece."

"What's that supposed to mean?"

"It means the Booties may be waiting for us up there," answered Dodder, her hands tightly gripping the back of the lev chair.

"Exactly," said Kevin. "And they just might shoot whoever pops up first."

Sam scowled.

"Do you really think they're up there?" Nicolette shivered, hugging a man-sized brown rock close to Kevin for fear of the heights.

Kevin shrugged. "There's only one way to know for sure." His face was set. "Be right back." He launched himself forward.

"No you don't!" Sam grabbed his sleeve. "I'll go. That big head of yours is bound to get you killed."

"Forget it, Sam," Kevin replied with a grin. "You know what they say—morons before beauty."

Sam's hand fell from his sleeve and he pulled quickly away. Sam's jaw still lay where it had dropped. Had he really just said that? Had he just called her beautiful?

Kevin climbed several yards, then paused and glanced down. "If anything goes wrong, you and Dodder have to get the others to safety. I'm counting on you, Sam." He smiled and waved goodbye.

Sam bit her lip and nodded. She was not going to cry.

Kevin turned his gaze forward. The small escarpment was relatively flat and devoid of life. No barrage of death came from above. He forced himself to take a deep breath. He motioned to the others.

"If there's a coffee shop up there, bring me back a cup of hot chocolate!" shouted Lance, cupping his hands around his mouth to be heard.

"Be quiet!" demanded Sam. "You want to get him killed? Another outburst like that from anybody," she said, whipping around, "and I'll rip your tongue out. I don't care who you are."

Silently, their bodies pressed into the crevice between two massive boulders, they waited.

# 49

Kevin carefully picked his way up the uneven terrain, a rocky obstacle course of cold black boulders that looked like some giant had dropped them there by the handfuls some millions of years ago. He still found it hard to believe a bunch of aliens had created all this.

The cold, dense fog hovered in the air like death. The last ten feet or so were practically a straight up climb. Despite the cold, his upper lip was coated with a line of perspiration. And despite his volunteering for this mission and all his bravado, he wished he was pretty much anywhere else but here right now.

Kevin's right hand groped the sloped surface blindly. He kept his fingers close to the ground in case he was being watched.

He waited a moment, counting slowly to thirty. Silence surrounded him. He wondered if it had been wise to come up weaponless, but it was too late now to change things. He finished counting and, since nothing happened, he placed his left hand on the surface and pulled himself up to ground level. The small plateau greeting him was as barren and unwelcoming as the pictures Kevin had seen of Earth's moon.

He dusted himself off and took a look around. Alice's Mitoc reconnaissance ship lay nearby. The ship was a lot larger than he'd been expecting. It was big and boxy and a dull brown. He hadn't been expecting that either. He thought all spaceships were sleek and shiny.

The clunky brown ship may have been as graceful as a ballerina out in deep space, but here on the ground it didn't look like it could ever be made to lift off the ground, and seemed improbable that it ever had.

He moved closer. There was nothing resembling a window or even a door. Kevin pulled his tattered collar up around his neck. The cold up here was numbing, the air thin. Weird that there was no sign of their human and Bootie nemeses. He'd half-expected to find his old pals, Henry and Jason, standing there waiting for him, smirks on their faces, weapons in their hands.

He crossed the damp snowy ground and reached out a tentative hand. The ship was oddly warm. Perhaps that was a good sign. He hoped it was.

Once more, he wondered how they'd make egress but there was no point speculating. He'd know soon enough. All he had to do was get Alice up here.

He trudged back to the edge of the cliff and motioned for the others to come up. He never noticed that his were not the only footprints disturbing the landscape. Even if he had, he might have judged them to be nothing more than the prints left by the Booties who'd captured Alice in the first place. Kevin was no tracker and may not have noticed if a Diplodicus had been there before him.

He waved his party on again, impatient now to get inside the spacecraft. He wanted to get out of here while the getting was good.

Before the enemy arrived.

# 50

"I've got her," said Kevin, feeling the muscles in his back straining as he pulled Alice and the lev chair up over the lip of the summit. The chair kept Alice off the ground but just barely. According to Dodder, the chair's engine was losing power rapidly, even more precipitously since Gig and Xian had crashed it.

Fortunately, they didn't have far to go now. They could carry Alice on foot the last few steps if they needed to.

"Nice spot for a picnic," quipped Sam, taking in the desolate surroundings.

"Yeah, crack open a bottle of red," Lance said, rubbing his hands together for warmth. "I could use a drink."

"We all could," Sequoia agreed. "So that's the ship, huh?" Her dull tired eyes took in the rather pedestrian looking vessel. She looked at Kevin, but it was Sam that answered.

"It'll fly," stated Sam, to the unasked question. "Alice is certain of it. The ship was only temporarily disabled by a Bootie device, but she's sure it hadn't been crippled beyond repair."

"Then let's get started," said Lance. "Freezing my ass off out here." He started towards the ship. "Hey, Alice, has this baby got HVAC? You know, heat and air? If so, soon as we get inside, how about cranking up the thermostat? Lance is cold!"

Sam dragged the lev chair toward the ship. Dodder scanned the shadowy mountain.

"Something wrong?" asked Kevin.

Dodder kept her powerful eyes on the rocks and cliff faces. "Something does not feel right."

"You think they're close?" Kevin strained his eyes but could see little through the mist. Huxley chittered nervously and Kevin shushed him, placing a hand gently over the creature's mouth.

Dodder shrugged quite humanly, a gesture he'd picked up from consorting with them.

"Don't worry about it, Dodder." Kevin clapped her on the shoulder. "We'll be on our way soon. Off this stinking alien-made rock."

"I hope so," said Sequoia, looking around nervously as the ground shook violently side to side for several seconds.

"Sounds like this whole place is about to fall apart," Nicolette said.

"Yeah, well, let's not all fall apart now," Sam shot back. "We're almost home free." Well, maybe home was an inoperative word, but the general meaning held.

"So where's the bleeding door?" called Lance.

"Alice says it's up top," Sam replied. "Come on. Help me hoist her up." Together they managed to lift Alice up over the side. Dodder and Kevin helped lift Sam, Nicolette and Sequoia. Kevin handed his little pet, Huxley, up to Sam.

Dodder was going to come up last, after assisting Kevin.

"Piece of cake," exclaimed Lance, pulling at a cross-shaped latch. "It's unlocked." Lance shimmied down the unsecured hatch first, followed by Alice and the girls. Much to Lance's disappointment, the interior was dark and cold. "Anybody see the light switch?" he asked, fumbling around in the dark. "Ouch!"

"Quit your complaining and be careful you don't break anything," ordered Sam. "There are no interior lights."

"What?"

"The craft doesn't need them and was not designed with them. Alice doesn't need them. She flies using some intergalactic orrery."

"Huh?"

"A model of the universe."

"Why didn't you say so?" Lance chewed his lip. "So no lights and no heat? Great accommodations, just great."

"Shut up and help me get Alice to her seat."

"And just how are we supposed to do that in the dark, smarty-pants?" Lance asked.

"Here, let me help," came a chilling voice, while simultaneously a beam of yellow light cut through the darkness like a sharp blade.

Sequoia screamed.

A dead Bootie slumped against the bulkhead. Sam recognized him as the officer-in-charge, though this Bootie didn't look so in charge now. Thick purplish fluid oozed from a gaping wound in the side of his skull. No doubt Jason had shot him. No doubt he would do the same to them, given the chance—except for Alice. Sam figured he needed the alien pilot more than anything.

"Jason," said Sam, her mind racing through her options. Unfortunately, nothing good came to mind.

"Why didn't Alice warn us this thing was here?" asked Lance, scared and confused. "I thought she was a big time mind reader." He wriggled his fingers next to his ears.

"Yeah, well," Sam fidgeted. "She is pretty weak."

"How weak?" asked Nicolette, trembling.

"By our standards?" Sam sighed. "I'd say barely conscious."

"Barely conscious?" Sequoia replied, feeling only somewhat steadier. "You've been talking to her all this time. She told you she could fly her ship!"

Sam cleared her throat and shuffled her feet. "Yeah, well," she said again, "about that." Sam looked from Jason to her friends. "I sort of made that up. I spoke for her, you know?"

"You lied?" Nicolette said with a gasp.

"You mean we fought our way up this mountain, risking our lives and you don't even know if the only person," Lance said for lack of a better word, "who can fly this thing is even alive or dead?"

"Alice is alive!" snapped Sam. "And what else would you have had us do? Sit around and wait to die?" As if to accentuate her words, the ship trembled as the mountain shook. Another ominous sign of their impending doom.

"Ladies, gentlemen," said Jason with a sickly smile, "enough." He pressed the cold hard muzzle of his weapon against Sam's cheek. "I'm sorry to hear about your friend, Alice," Jason said in a scary, harsh whisper. "But I really need her to fly this ship." He stabbed Sam's cheek with the muzzle.

Sam froze.

Huxley leapt from her shoulder and sank his teeth into Jason's bicep. Jason howled and swung at the tiny creature with his gun hand. The creature fell to the ground and lay still.

Jason shouted at the others to get Alice into the pilot's seat. "Where are Kevin and his bigfoot friend?"

"They're—"

"They didn't make it," cut in Sam, glaring at Lance. "They're dead."

"Really?" said Jason, clearly skeptical, his eyes moving to Lance.

Lance nodded. "Yeah, dead."

"If you're lying, I'll kill you."

Sam shrugged. He'd probably kill her and everyone else given the chance anyway.

"Why did you kill him?" said Nicolette, motioning to the dead Bootie. "I thought you and the Booties were working together."

Jason smiled that cruel smile of his once again. "My friend, Strovan, here," he answered, kicking the dead Bootie's foot, "had a plan. I told him I agreed. We decided two could travel faster than a hundred. We came on ahead. Besides, the path up here is treacherous. The others were happy to wait for us at the shelter we set up below. Even that fool friend of yours, Henry."

"He's no friend," said Nicolette.

"You got that right," quipped Lance.

Jason snorted. "Yeah, pretty slimy, isn't he? We told the others we'd come for them once we got the vessel. Dumbasses. They'll believe anything you tell them, if it's what they want to hear."

He waved his gun around. "Once Strovan got us to the ship, I realized I didn't really need him any longer. He'd become a complication I could do without."

"When the Booties find out what you've done—"

"They'll die too," was Jason's reply.

# 51

"You really think you can take on the Booties?" asked Sam. She glanced nervously up at the hatch. What was keeping Kevin and Dodder?

Jason sneered. "The Booties are nothing. Mere henchmen of the Flems. They're the real bosses. The Flems use the Booties the same way the Mitoc use us humans and a thousand other species spread across the universe." He spat. "Cannon fodder."

Jason checked on Alice and played his flashlight beam over the console. "The way I see it," he said, casting a fleering look, "I deliver a prize of one or two of you so-called defectives to the Flems and I'll be a hero."

"You'd really do that?" gasped Nicolette. "Let them dissect one of your own kind?"

"Of course, he would," said Sequoia. "But I'd think twice about that if I were you," she added. "These Flems you talk about might decide to slice apart your brain, too."

Jason stepped closer and ran his gun hand through Sequoia's hair. "Not a chance," he whispered sickly. "I'm not a defective like all of you. The Mitoc called and I came running." His sick laugh filled the closed space as he kicked the bulkhead. "Like a brainwashed puppy!" His voice rose in anger.

Sequoia decided the time was now or never. She'd take that chance and hoped the others would spring to action, too. If not, well, it wouldn't really make much difference then one way or the other.

Twisting towards Jason, Sequoia grabbed the hand gripping the flashlight. Before he could react, she slammed the tip of the light against the console. The plexiglass light shattered and they were thrust in darkness.

Jason cursed her and swung out.

A shot went off followed by staccato screams that sounded much like shots themselves. Sam shouted for everyone to get down. As she spoke, a violent tremor shook the vessel like it was no more than an empty paper sack.

Dodder dropped from above and quickly disarmed Jason, her catlike eyes having no trouble seeing in the dark.

Nicolette pulled her own light from her pack, circling the tight space with its beam. Everyone was okay. Jason was sprawled out on the floor in a half-sitting position, dazed and confused. Blood oozed from the corner of his mouth where he'd struck the console on his way down.

Sam couldn't help but smile. She figured it was the least he deserved. She heard more shouting outside and the report of weapon fire. A jolt of fear raced through her. "Where's Kevin?"

Dodder stuck his head out but then quickly pulled it back inside. "Pinned down. Behind rock." She looked grim. "Henry and other bad humans have arrived. Booties, too."

"I guess Henry was too smart to trust you, after all," Lance said with a smirk as he stared down at Jason.

"What are we going to do?" Sequoia wrung her hands.

"Tell Alice to hit the gas," replied Lance. "We've got to get out of here."

"Not without Kevin," replied Sam.

"I agree," said Nicolette. "We can't leave without Kevin."

"Are you all crazy?" Lance said. "They'll swarm all over us and take this ship. Then what have you gained?"

Jason climbed to his feet and started shouting through the open hatch. "It's me! It's me! Listen, they're practically weaponless. Attack!" He bellowed. "Attack!"

Tension suffused the air of the tight ship. Sam had no idea what condition Alice or her ship were in. But they were trapped in this ship and the man she realized she loved was trapped outside. Okay, she'd said it. She loved him. But what was she going to do about it? About any of it?

"Come on!" urged Jason.

Sam, climbing to the entry, turned and said, "Will somebody please shut him up."

"I will." Sequoia turned swiftly and socked Jason in the jaw. He spun around, then fell to the ground like a marionette whose strings had been cut.

"Gladly," said Sequoia after the fact, smiling broadly as she rubbed her freshly bruised knuckles.

Dodder set to trussing Jason up while Nicolette ministered to Huxley. "The little guy seems to be coming around," Nicolette said, gently rubbing his nose.

"Kevin!" called Sam. "Can you hear me?"

"Sam, be careful!" He lay with his back to a flat-sided boulder and didn't dare to move. They had him pinned down.

"Hang on, Kevin! We're coming for you!"

"No!" answered Kevin. "Listen to me, Sam. You have got to take the ship. Go! Get out of here!" The ground rumbled like a herd of brontosauri stampeding across an open plain.

"I can't," said Sam. "Not without you."

"You've got to" said Kevin. "You have no choice. You have to help the others, Sam. You must."

Sam fought back tears.

Dodder laid a hand on her shoulder. "Kevin's right. We must get the ship up before they seize it or cause it irreparable damage."

Sam glared at the alien. "Give me the gun." She held out her hand.

Dodder hesitated, then handed her Jason's weapon. Clutching the gun, Sam popped her head up, fired twice, and was pleased to see that two bodies went down, one of which was that weasel, Henry.

As the attackers suddenly found themselves the attacked, they panicked and ducked for cover. While they were preoccupied with saving their useless skins, Sam called to Kevin. "Catch!"

He stuck his head up and their eyes met for a brief instant.

Sam's eyes suddenly filled with the river of tears she could no longer hold back. She flung the weapon to Kevin. She prayed her strength and her aim were good enough.

The gun landed several feet from the rock. Kevin scrambled out and snatched. "Got it." His heart thumped in his chest. "GO!" he hollered. "Get out of here!"

Sam felt gentle hands pulling her down. Felt Alice's gentle touch in her mind. Alice was ready. Sam felt herself being pulled down against her will into the safety of the ship.

Nicolette threw her arms around Sam. "It's okay, Sam," Nicolette said. "There's nothing anyone can do now."

Sam felt the ground vibrate beneath her. The hatch fell shut and the cabin sank into darkness. And she felt that they were moving. Leaving this awful place.

And leaving Kevin.

She cried and nobody saw her tears.

# 52

A tremendous shockwave laid Kevin flat. Looking up, he watched Alice's ship lift and knew that he'd be dead soon. He climbed to his feet. The ship was an orange light moving against the sky, dimly visible through the clouds and swirling mist.

He was alone on the escarpment with Henry Hemming's corpse and a few others, human and Bootie, whom he didn't recognize. The sudden shockwave had sent the rest of his hunters scattering for cover. Either that or they'd been blown off the mountain. Good riddance either way.

But soon those that had survived would be back for him. At least Henry had managed to leave this lousy world, though his body had stayed behind. Kevin knew he'd soon be following in Henry's footsteps. If the others didn't return to finish him off, this world would soon come to an end anyway.

And him with it.

He only hoped Sarah and Quinn were someplace far away. They could be anywhere in the universe. And it was a big universe. Just how big he'd never realized until his unbelievable trip here to this nonsensical world.

Even now, Kevin figured he was only seeing the tip of the proverbial iceberg that was the universe. He sat down quietly beside Henry and waited. The gun Sam had thrown him hung loose in his fingertips. He was at peace with himself. After all, he may as well be, what other choice did he have?

He heard the distant sounds of scuffling and arguing far below and knew that at least some humans and Booties survived. Were they now fighting amongst themselves or deciding whether to come and finish him off? Didn't they know the world was about to end?

No matter. They all faced the same ending.

# 53

"Man, what was that?" Lance grabbed hold of Sequoia for support as the ship shot up from the mountaintop.

"Shockwave," Dodder replied. She was smiling. "As anticipated." She nodded several times. "Good."

"I don't know what you're looking so happy about," said Sam, clearly miserable. "We just left Kevin back there. He was your friend, too. They'll kill him, you know. Kevin would never have done that to you." She stood off in a corner by herself, rejecting Nicolette's efforts to console her.

Suddenly the ship was plummeting!

A wave of nausea slammed into Sam. She felt like she was going to throw up. Her stomach tried to climb up out of her gaping mouth. She grabbed desperately for something to hold onto. What was happening?

No one said a word. Everyone was either too sick or too frightened to react. Probably both.

Only Dodder remained resolutely at her post, standing beside Alice the pilot, and gently stroking her side. They made for an odd pair—a giant, hairy, alien cat and old Jelly Brains—and Sam could only wonder what was going on in their alien minds.

The ship plunged straight down toward the mountain. Just as Sam was sure they'd impact and braced herself for the end, the ship abruptly braked, then came to a full smooth stop.

The hatch popped open letting in a beam of diffuse yellow light and a waft of frigid air. Dodder beamed. Sam stared at the alien in amazement. "Hurry now," said Dodder. "Effects of shockwave will not keep our enemies at bay for long."

"You mean this was just some stupid stunt? You and Alice did that on purpose?"

"Go," repeated Dodder.

"Right." Sam snapped out of her stunned inaction and raced out the open hatch.

Kevin watched the ship fall from the sky like a bird that had suddenly lost the ability to fly. In worried panic and with no thought to his own safety, he went running towards it. He perceived footsteps running behind him and knew that his hunters had also heard the ship and were racing him to the prize.

Sam's head popped up from the hatch. She extended her arms. "Get in, moron!"

Kevin grabbed her hands and clambered aboard. The hatch snapped shut behind them like a frog swallowing a housefly.

Dodder yelled for everyone to hold on even as they were all kicked to the floor by a team of invisible mules.

"Where are we going?" Lance asked. "Can we even hope to get away without being blown out of the sky? Will there be ships or attack satellites shooting us down like wooden ducks in an arcade?"

"Must you?" Sam snarled in exasperation.

"It would be nice if we could at least see something," Lance said, apparently unwilling or unable to end his ceaseless complaining.

The cabin was tight and dark. Dodder suggested that they could rig some lighting and set about the task.

"I hope you can rig up some toilet facilities," growled Lance. "My kidneys are about to burst."

"What are we going to do now?" asked Nicolette.

"Yes, where will we go?" Sequoia added.

Kevin idly scratched the top of Huxley's head. Alice's ship wasn't designed for human comfort, let alone transport across the vast expanses of space. "I guess it's something we need to decide as a group."

"I vote we go home," Lance said immediately.

"You mean Earth?" Sequoia replied. "What for? There's nothing left for us there, I'll bet. It was a sick planet filled with sick people *before* the Mitoc showed up. Can you imagine what it must be like now? After all the distress, disruption, and chaos their coming must have caused?"

Nicolette agreed. "Dead seas, dead souls. And, yeah, chaos. I'll pass."

"Maybe so," muttered Lance. "But I can't think of any place else to go. Can you?"

"No," admitted Nicolette.

"What do you think, Kevin?" Sequoia asked.

Kevin said he didn't even know if the small ship could even carry them back to Earth, let alone sustain them along the way. And was Sequoia right? Was there anything on Earth worth going back for? The planet had very probably fallen into chaos and disorder once the Mitoc had raped it, taking millions off to fight their absurd war. And there was no reason to think they would not be back to do it again. Come back for a new harvest. In fact, that seemed to be their standard operating practice from what he'd learned. He turned to Sam. "Sam? What does Alice think? Can we make it back to Earth?"

"Alice says we can. But," she added, "we'll have to stop at some, hopefully, hospitable planets along the way. For provisions and to refit the ship. According to Alice, that's our only hope."

"If the Booties or the Flems or the Mitoc don't blast us with some infernal laser and turn us to cosmic dust first," Lance said.

"There's always that chance," replied Sam.

"I don't suppose Alice knows where my ex-wife and daughter are, does she? Or even if they're alive?"

"Sorry, no."

"So what are we going to do, people?" Lance wanted to know.

Sam placed a gentle hand on Kevin's arm. "I'm with you, whatever you decide, Kevin."

"Me?"

"You're in charge, aren't you?"

"Me? Oh, no." But the others agreed and looked at him with eyes of hope and expectation that surprised and scared him every bit as much as it warmed his heart.

"Oh, brother," moaned Lance, coming to wish he'd never mentioned the possibility of returning to Earth. "We're going back to Earth, aren't we? A dead planet. Sorry I ever mentioned it." He singled out his fellow shipmates, one by one. "Full of dead souls and dead oceans, remember? Chaos. Complete and utter chaos."

His hands swept through the tiny space. "Confusion. Pandemonium. You know there's every chance that when we get back—if we get back—the Mitoc will snatch us up again and cart us off to some new battlefield of theirs," he finished with a scowl and plunked his butt down on the hard metallic floor. "To face some new monsters."

"You're right, Lance," Kevin said softly. "Absolutely right. There's every chance of that. Everything you said and more." And worse, he left unsaid. "Still, it would be nice to go home, don't you think?" He pictured Sarah and Quinn waiting for him in their apartment. One big happy family. "But who am I kidding? The past is gone. An artifact."

Lance frowned.

"Brace yourselves!" barked Dodder.

"Now what?" demanded Sequoia.

"Alice says we must enter a transdimensional plane."

"A what?" Nicolette asked.

"A passage through this universe and into another. It's only a matter of minutes until the world below us detonates. We must go in haste."

"Don't tell me," quipped Sam. "Annihilating everything for a bajillion miles?"

"And we do not want to be here in this sector of space when it does," Dodder confirmed.

"Yeah, because we'll be atomic soup," Lance quipped.

"Kevin," Dodder asked, "what course do I tell Alice to plot? You must decide."

"How about Route 66?" Lance joked. "Better yet, how's about the good old US of A in nineteen sixty-six? This thing happen to have a time machine switch?"

"Quiet," hissed Sam.

"Alice," said Kevin, folding his hands behind his back, "take us home."

"Seriously?" said Lance.

"*Your* home, Alice," Kevin said. It was the least he could do for her for saving all their lives.

"Alice's home?" Lance furrowed his brow.

"Kevin, like Dodder, Alice's home is no more," reminded Sam.

"Right." He'd forgotten. "What does everybody say? To the stars then?"

"To the stars?" Sequoia creased her brow.

"Sure," Kevin replied. "Nothing to go home to. Why not see what else is out there?"

Everyone but Lance agreed.

"Lance?" Kevin asked.

Lance frowned. "I swear, I don't know what's crazier, following the Mitoc into battle or following you to my certain doom. Fine, to the stars it is. What's the worst that could happen?"

"Just off the top of my head," Sam began, "I can think of a million things." She stuck up her thumb. "First, there's—"

"With all due respect," Lance snapped, hiding behind Sequoia, "shut your trap."

"Oh, yeah?" Sam took a step towards him. "Why don't I shut your—"

Kevin put his arm out and stopped her. "Thanks, Sam."

"For?"

"For not punching me in the face or calling me a moron when I kissed you."

"Kissed me? You never—"

And he did.

Nicolette blinked.

And then he saw stars. In fact, they all did. Millions and millions of them. Alice had successfully steered them through the transdimensional plane. The little voice in Kevin's head said not to worry, just enjoy the show.

Lance sidled up next to Sequoia. "Looks like we're gonna be roomies for a very long time."

She yanked his arm behind his back and savagely twisted.

"Yeow!"

"Looking forward to it," she said as Lance dropped to his knees, tears streaming from his eyes.

"May as well sit back and enjoy the ride." Sam settled on the hard floor.

Kevin joined her.

"How long to the next rest stop?" groaned Lance, wincing as he massaged his sore arm.

"Get some rest, everyone," Dodder suggested. "This may take some time but I know just the place."

Kevin took Sam's hand. Maybe this was all the product of his crazy—defective—mind. Maybe this was all a dream. Maybe this was one of Sam's crazy conspiracy theories and they were all part of some sick experiment.

Whatever. He squeezed Sam's hand. He'd go with the flow.

He had nothing to lose.

## Other Books
## by
## Glenn Eric

*Welcome To My World* - Ed Turner, P.I. Novel #1
*Hold That Ghost* - Ed Turner, P.I. Novel #2
*Aliens vs Voodoo* - Ed Turner, P.I. Novel #3

## Written as J.R. Ripley

*Five Minutes* - Todd Jones Comic Thriller #1
*Five More Minutes* - Todd Jones Comic Thriller #2
*Nailed It* - Todd Jones Comic Thriller #3